Early Praise

"When *Sunglasses At Night* is the main character's favorite song, you just know you're in for a fun and quirky '80s-centric novel!"

— Corey Hart, '80s Icon

"Steven Manchester's *Lawn Darts & Lemonade* is so much fun, filled with laughter, tears, and Big Hair."

— Taylor Dane, '80s Recording Artist,
Love Will Lead You Back

"*Lawn Darts & Lemonade* is the perfect stroll down memory lane, bringing us right back to the glorious '80s."

— Ed Asner, Actor, *Lou Grant*

"*Lawn Darts & Lemonade* is beautifully and tenderly observed with extraordinary attention to detail. A few pages in and I was pining for my Atari."

— Nik Kershaw, '80s UK Recording Artist,
Wouldn't It Be Good

"I read *Lawn Darts & Lemonade* and really enjoyed it. There is a raw honesty and purity of passion in this coming-of-age novel. Manchester has incredible skill as a novelist."

— Thomas G. Waites, Actor, *The Warriors*

"Steve Manchester's *Lawn Darts & Lemonade* charts youth where fights start accidentally, then last only two minutes. A time when Mom smoked in the house and our future was determined by the shake of a Magic 8 Ball. A poignant and funny reminder of a more innocent time."

— Mick Conroy, *Modern English*

"Every decade has its nostalgia, but Manchester's '80s is unusually exact, warm, funny, and true."

— William Atherton, Actor, *Ghostbusters, Die Hard*

"*Lawn Darts & Lemonade* is a good read, really up to scratch."

— Colin Hay, Lead Singer, *Men at Work*

"Bestselling author Steven Manchester takes readers on an incredible journey into the perilous world of growing up in the pre-teen stage of life set in the '80s. This book is a great read, with Steve Manchester at the top of his' game!"

— Warrington Gillette, Actor, *Friday the 13th (Jason)*

"As a reader, I'm a big fan of Steve Manchester's work."

— Mike Reno, Lead Singer, *Loverboy*

"*Lawn Darts & Lemonade* is a fun coming-of-age story that brings us all back to those memories deep in our minds—times that we never thought we'd survive but did."

— Bob Stanley, MLB Pitcher, *1984 Boston Red Sox*

"In *Lawn Darts & Lemonade*, Steve Manchester takes us back in time for a walk down memory lane. What's cool is that he skips all the bad neighborhoods."

— Robbie Dupree, '80s Recording Artist, *Hot Rod Hearts*

"I enjoyed *Lawn Darts & Lemonade* and loved returning back to 1984."

— Tony Dow, Actor, *Leave It to Beaver*

"I just finished reading Steven Manchester's brilliant book, *Lawn Darts & Lemonade*. It brought to mind the simpler times in the '80s when life seemed far less complicated than it seems now. A time when kids still went out to play and video games were just beginning to make the world less social. It serves up a slice of Americana. It takes us along on the journey through the joy and heartbreak that is part of growing up and standing on the precipice of manhood. Any of us who grew up in any decade from the '40s to the '80s can relate to this story and these characters. It had me laughing and crying. What a great walk down memory lane."

— Benny Mardones, '80s Singer, *Into the Night*

"If you don't laugh reading *Lawn Darts & Lemonade*, then you should go get your head checked."

– Lenny Clarke, Actor/Comedian, *Rescue Me*

"As with all of Steven's bestselling books, life's lessons permeate throughout them. But with *Lawn Darts & Lemonade*, the reader is destined to encounter the greatest lesson of all…that life can easily be missed if you're distracted by the past or the future—that it's best to stay in the present. *Lawn Darts & Lemonade: Tackling the '80s* is a must read!"

– M.L. Carr, NBA Player, *1984 Boston Celtics*

"*Lawn Darts & Lemonade* is a really good read. Trust me, you'll be hooked."

– Pat MacDonald, Lead Singer of Timbuk 3, *The Future's So Bright*

"Steven Manchester's *Lawn Darts & Lemonade* takes us back to a simpler time, when the Atari gaming system was considered cutting-edge technology. Kids still played outside, and they even pedaled newspapers to be able to buy penny candy at the corner store. Manchester's stroll down memory lane will have you laughing hysterically one minute and humming the music that premiered on MTV the next."

– Steven Greenberg, '80s Composer/ Producer, *Funkytown*

"*Lawn Darts & Lemonade* totally represents its decade! Steven Manchester found a tasteful way to incorporate a plethora of '80s references and even nailed a few abstract ones that really hit home with me. I was completely reliving each moment with the characters. This coming-of-age story is an entertaining read, indeed!"

– *'80s Station (Las Vegas)*

"Steven Manchester's *Surviving the '80s* series really could be the next *A Christmas Story*! Steve expertly weaves the importance of family and confronting one's fears with the music, games, shows, and so much more that defined the 1980s. The writing is crisp and fast moving; the characters are unforgettable. Highly recommended!"

– Patricia Perry, Author, *The Realm of Dark and Light Trilogy*

"If you had siblings growing up, you will see yourself somewhere in *Lawn Darts & Lemonade*. If you had no siblings, enjoy the experiences Steve Manchester recalls and shares. In either case, prepare to laugh, cringe a bit, and at times fight back a tear or two; better yet, let them flow. *Lawn Darts & Lemonade* is a timeless story, floating on a cloud of reality we all share. Mr. Manchester is that type of author who opens his heart and soul, allowing us to relive part of our past. His powerful, down-to-earth openness also allows us to understand we are all one. Steve is a bestselling author, in part because he touches us with the soul we all share. *Lawn Darts & Lemonade* is a wonderful read and one you will not soon forget."

– Barry M. McKee, Professor Emeritus

"I loved *Lawn Darts and Lemonade*. It's my favorite installment in the series thus far. Steve Manchester captures summer in New England during the 1980s to the finest detail. This quirky family is like the Walton's of the '80s —and I want to learn so much more about them!"
— Linda Murphy, Lifestyle Editor, *Fall River Herald News*

"I thoroughly enjoyed *Lawn Darts & Lemonade*, so it is no surprise that I wholeheartedly recommend Steve Manchester's follow-up, *Lawn Darts & Lemonade*. This coming-of-age tale is dripping with '80s nostalgia while taking you on a timeless and emotional journey, creating heartfelt moments of laughter and even some tears."
— Old School Tim, '80s writer, contributor, and aficionado from Twitter's @ *OldSchool80s & more*

"Reading *Lawn Darts & Lemonade* is a much-needed trip back in time to our beloved decade. I never stop smiling when reading Steve Manchester's technique of taking his readers back to such a glorious time in our lives. Thank you for giving us another memorable chapter in the lives of these colorful characters!"
— Steve Spears, Creator and Co-Host, *Stuck in the '80s* podcast

"Steven Manchester hits the mark once again! *Lawn Darts & Lemonade* returns to the '80s, bringing back long-forgotten memories to anybody who grew up in the most awesome decade. Upon taking this trip to the '80s—given in splendid detail—you may not want to come back. This book is most excellent for all!"

– Paul Stroessner, Editor, *Return to the '80s*

Praise for Prequel, *Bread Bags & Bullies*

"If you loved the ever popular *A Christmas Story*, be prepared for another classic. *Bread Bags & Bullies,* is a must read! Funny, poignant, and heartwarming—Steven Manchester is a master storyteller."
— Jamie Farr, Actor, *M.A.S.H.*

"In *Bread Bags & Bullies,* the writing is so vivid, the pace and rhythm so quick, that I truly felt I was watching it on screen."
— Joan van Ark, Actress, *Knots Landing*

"*Bread Bags & Bullies* rocks!"
— Billy Squier, '80s Rock Icon, *Stroke Me*

"*Bread Bags & Bullies* is a detailed, eye-opening experience of the Big Hair decade. Enjoyable, whether you were there or not—or just can't quite remember it."
— Barry Williams, Actor, *The Brady Bunch*

"Steve Manchester's *Bread Bags & Bullies* is a fantastic blast from the past, evoking all the fun and nostalgia of the '80s—even my big hair!"
— Audrey Landers, Actress, *Dallas*

"An extraordinary recall of 1980s pop culture, *Bread Bags & Bullies* will make you laugh out loud as you revisit the pains and pleasures of growing up. The book made me want to pick up the phone, call my brother in Nebraska, and reminisce about our own snow-day adventures."
— Douglas Barr, Actor, *The Fall Guy*

"In *Bread Bags & Bullies*, Steven Manchester captures the '80s to the smallest detail. With each page turned, memories flood back. Using the lightest of touch, he tells his story with tongue firmly planted in cheek. *Bread Bags & Bullies* is a delight!"

– Nick van Eede, Lead Singer of Cutting
Crew, *Died in Your Arms*

"Travel back in time to the wonderful '80s. *Bread Bags & Bullies* is an incredibly fun read!"

– Rebecca Holden, Actress, *Knight Rider,*
The Love Boat, Three's Company

"*Bread Bags & Bullies* is so—like, totally—'84, it makes me want to get out my leg warmers and glow sticks, backcomb my hair, and romp around the room to *Footloose*. And then I remember, I don't *have* any hair."

– Thomas Dolby, '80s Recording Artist,
She Blinded Me with Science

"*Bread Bags & Bullies* is not only fun, but educational in its own way. What an entertaining read!"

– Marla Gibbs, Actress, *The Jeffersons*

"You can like this book if you want to. You can leave your friends behind. Because if your friends don't like this book…well, they're no friends of mine."

– Ivan Doroschuk, Lead Singer of Men
Without Hats, *Safety Dance*

LAWN DARTS
& LEMONADE

Tackling the '80s

by

Steven Manchester

Enjoy memory lane!

Luna Bella Press

Print ISBN-13: 978-1-7377899-0-1
E-book ISBN-13: 978-1-7377899-1-8

Visit our website at www.LunaBellaPress.com

Book Design by Barbara Aronica-Buck
Cover Art by Brian Fox & Keith Conforti

First Luna Bella Press Printing: March 2022

Printed in The United States of America

For Ma, my foundation

ACKNOWLEDGMENTS

First and forever, Jesus Christ—my Lord and Savior. With Him, all things are possible.

Paula, my beautiful wife, for loving me and being the amazing woman she is.

Evan, Jacob, Isabella, Carissa, Laura, and River—for inspiring me.

Dad, Mom, Billy, Julie, Caroline, Caleb, Randy, Kathy, Philip, the Baker girls, Darlene, Jeremy, Baker, Aurora, Jen, Jason, Jack, Lucas, the DeSousas—my beloved family.

My talented and generous BETA Team: Dan & Sue Aguiar, George Austin, Darlene Ballard, Stephanie Borden Brown, Heather DiMartino, Jason & Jen Fazzina, Binnie Fogg, Brian Fox, Bella Manchester, Evan Manchester, Jacob Manchester, Paula Manchester, Randy Manchester, Russ McCarthy, Linda Murphy, Sue Nedar, Todd Parent, Jeff & Julia Schoonover, Claude Tetreault, Hen Zannini.

Westport High School's Class of 1986.

Lou Aronica, my mentor and friend.

My life has been richly blessed for having known each one of you.

"It's fun to visit the past, but make sure you don't stay there too long. If you linger, you'll miss the present—moments in your life that you won't want to miss. So, stay in the present, okay?"

– Ma

AUTHOR'S NOTE

Dear Reader,

In twenty-five years of writing fiction, I've never written a sequel—until now. At my core, I am a storyteller, and there are times when a story requires a bit more real estate than a single novel. *Lawn Darts & Lemonade* is one of those stories.

With many more lessons to learn—and fears to overcome—Wally, Herbie, and Cockroach step into the unforgettable summer of 1984.

Within each comical passage and every heartfelt scene, *Lawn Darts & Lemonade* is a tribute to my greatest heroes—my mother and father—who believed it was their job to raise me and my siblings. Thankfully, they took their job very seriously and worked hard at it.

My siblings and I are eternally grateful to them both.

Enjoy the stroll down memory lane,

Steve Manchester

It's the summer of 1984, a season of dodging lawn darts and chugging lemonade—or at least the discolored tap water Ma tried to disguise as lemonade.

Growing up is never easy, no matter what era you do it in. For generations, teenagers have suffered peer pressure, bullying, fear of rejection, and a sadistic obstacle course of one unexpected challenge after the next. Three brothers, Wally, Herbie, and Cockroach, learn that the past can be filled with questions—even shame and regret—while the future might be shrouded in worry and fear. But staying in the moment, now that's where the sweet spot is.

CHAPTER 1

PRESENT DAY

SITTING REDNECK SHIVA

"To be loved this much by so many people…" I paused to compose myself. "…now that's what I call a successful life." I'd been reduced to an eight-year-old again, feeling lost—even orphaned. Losing my dad was wreaking havoc on my inner child, making me feel panicked. Failing miserably at concealing this, I raised my glass and was immediately joined by my mom, my wife and children, my siblings, nieces, and nephews: the family my mother and father had created.

I pictured my dad's smiling face. "I did this," Pop used to say, referring to our family. As a dad myself, I now understood the incredible pride that the old man carried with him. *Family is the whole shebang,* he'd say. *Everything else is a distant second.*

Glasses clinked, with everyone drinking to the memory of a man who'd earned their eternal love and respect.

Mourning Pop's death, our family sat for redneck shiva at my and Donna's house, grieving for him as hard as any human beings could grieve another.

To the twang of country music playing in the background, we ate takeout food—Chinese and Italian—served to supplement Donna's bottomless pan of mourning pasta and washed it down with Pop's favorite beer. Even the sheet cake was dedicated to the old man. *Have a Nice Weekend* was written in blue scroll across the center; it was our father's quirky reference to death.

My boys, Dylan and Alex, were seated in the dining room beside their cousins. It was important that they hear the stories of their grandfather, learning all they could about the man who'd raised their parents. It was equally important to see their parents cry—to understand that grieving was a shameless process that was absolutely healthy and natural. *They need to know that it's all okay.*

"Your dad really loved you kids," Ma told me and my four siblings, wiping her nose with a tissue. "He adored each and every one of you." She took a few deep breaths. "He may not have said it often, but…"

"He didn't have to," Alphonse, the successful businessman, chimed in.

"He showed it," Wally finished; he'd just flown in from some racetrack in the south to lament with the family.

I nodded. "For as long as I can remember," I added.

"Us, too," Louann said, speaking for her and Lynn.

To help Ma through the difficult process, we'd packed up some of Pop's things and brought them to my house, the new family hub.

Louann and Lynn—our younger sisters by nearly two decades, both moms extraordinaire—began going through the old man's things: three shoeboxes, a half-dozen manila envelopes, and two full plastic crates. Framed photos, record albums, old greeting cards, and once-important documents were amongst the lot. The things our father had stored away told us as much about his heart as any words—spoken or written—ever could have. There were several silver dollars and two-dollar bills he'd saved for his grandchildren in an old Claussen pickle jar; two stacks of photos bound by dry-rotted elastic bands, a pocket watch, jackknife, and his grandfather's dented harmonica. There was a worn leather Bible, a handful of plastic trophies that read *#1 Dad,* and a ream of Crayola masterpieces that each one of his five children had once created for him. The list went on, each seemingly worthless item telling a story all its own. *Priceless,* I thought, *every piece of it.*

But divvying up his things paled in comparison to the many stories we shared about him.

The family sat together for hours, drinking bad beer, listening to terrible music, and riding the roller coaster of grief.

"I remember eating lunch with Pop at the Woolworth's lunch counter," Wally said, kicking off our story exchange. "An iced-cold Coke…sausage and gravy with eggs."

"What about those K-Mart chopped ham sandwiches?" Alphonse asked, his eyes twinkling from the memory. While Wally and I remained wide and sturdy into adulthood, Alphonse maintained his scarecrow physique, wrapped in olive-toned skin. His slender nose and darker eyes inspired more than a few family members to tease our mother about his real father's true paternity.

We laughed.

"Yeah, when the blue light hit, lunch was a real steal," I added.

"What?" Louann and Lynn asked. With light hair, brown eyes, and our father's mischievous smile, our younger sisters looked exactly like sisters.

"The sandwich was nothing more than a wafer-thin slice of ham on a potato roll, covered in mustard," Alphonse explained, "and Pop loved them."

"Of course he did," Lynn said.

There was more laughter, followed by tears.

"Remember how prepared he was for any storms that might come along?" Louann said.

I nodded. *He sure was.*

"And for buying Ma the most intimate gifts," Wally teased, "like a microwave oven or air conditioner."

Ma was taking a sip of tea when she nearly coughed it up.

"I still remember the day Pop picked up a hitchhiker in a bad snowstorm…" I began.

"And saved the man's life, right?" Wally said.

I nodded.

"Sure, but scaring me to death in the meantime," Ma said.

"Pop was always helping people," Lynn said.

"Every chance he could," Louann confirmed.

"Especially me," Alphonse said. "He used to take me to the E.R. a few times a year."

Everyone laughed.

"He loved the food at Oriental Pearl," Wally said, "and Higson's Fish and Chips on Friday nights."

"Coney Island hot dogs, stuffed quahogs, and…" Lynn began to list.

Ma shook her head. "He was a real health nut, wasn't he?"

"I loved going quahogging with him," I added, still able to picture him as a young man. Pop had dark hair and brown eyes. He also had tattooed biceps, two sparrows in flight, holding a banner that read *Mom and Dad* on his left arm; on the right arm, he had a large red rose with my mother's name in a banner. All five of his children—the family roll call—were listed below *Emma.*

"Better you than us," Wally said, gesturing toward himself and Alphonse. "We hated working the river."

Our younger brother quickly nodded in agreement. "I couldn't stand my feet getting sliced up in that mud."

It was worth every cut, I thought. At a time when I had to take three steps to every one of my father's, I remember considering him a giant of a man—and it wasn't only his physical size which awed me.

"And he definitely had his favorite TV shows," Wally said, changing the subject.

"McHale's Navy," Ma said.

"Hogan's Heroes," Alphonse said.

"Cheers," Louann said.

"And Hee Haw," Lynn announced, like she'd just offered the winning answer to some strange game show.

Everyone looked at her.

She shrugged. "He used to make me and Louann watch the reruns."

There was laughter again.

"Don't forget about 'All in the Family,'" Ma added.

"Didn't you used to call him Archie Bunker, Ma?" I teased her.

Her eyes glassed over with tears. "Only when he deserved it," she said, her voice now gravelly, "which was more often than not."

After taking a sip of beer, Louann raised her shiny gold can. "And boy, did he love his beer," she said.

"Miller High Life," Lynn blurted, as though she was trying to win another point.

We all nodded, each lifting our can of the sludge and taking a sip.

During another round of pasta, the memories continued. "I remember

Dad teaching me how to drive," Louann said, a tear racing down her cheek.

"Yeah, those were the best times," Lynn said, "except for the country music."

I remember well, I thought. *Top down and music up.* Smiling, I got up and changed record albums, putting on Ernest Tubb.

The move was met by some playful groans, making me chuckle.

"He was a wonderful dad," Ma said, "and you were all very lucky to have him."

I stood and placed both my hands on my mother's shoulders. "True, but he's not the only reason we were so lucky," I said, choking on my words.

Picking up on my cue, Wally said, "I can still picture the clubhouse you made us out of a refrigerator box when we were small."

"I remember Ma reading to us every night," Louann said, jumping in, "never missing one. It's why I've always loved to read."

"And I can still remember you forcing us out of the house," Alphonse said, "no matter how cold it was outside."

"We would have been kicked out of that apartment, if I hadn't," Ma said, quick to defend herself.

"Thanks for letting us freeze, Ma," Wally said, giving her a hug. We all laughed.

"I remember going shopping on Pleasant Street with you, Memere, and Aunt Phyllis," I said.

While my brothers' eyes filled with tears, our mother was already wiping her cheeks. "Yup, they're all together now, playing pitch in heaven."

"And eating one of Grampa's famous clam boils," Alphonse said.

"I'm sure of it," she said, grabbing for the tissue box.

Returning back to her and Louann's era, Lynn said, "I remember the long Sunday drives, when Dad used to take us to go get ice cream."

Louann grinned at the memory. "He drove all backroads, so it took us forever to get there. We drove miles and miles to get to the Ice Cream Barn."

"That's what we used to do on Sundays," Ma said, her glazed eyes lost in her own memories. "I still love long drives with the windows open."

"Me, too," Wally said, referring to his stock car.

Everyone laughed.

"Until you end up crashing," Alphonse teased.

I nodded. "Once the Mangler, always the Mangler," I said.

"The Ice Cream Barn," Louann repeated, swept away in the memory, "the entire building looked like a big milk can."

Lynn nodded. "They made the best ice cream around, piled high on sugar cones."

"They sure did, though it was hardly worth suffering the motion sickness from sitting in the back seat for hours," Louann said, before turning to our mother. "You were a real ice cream connoisseur, Ma."

The older woman nodded proudly.

"Rum Raisin, Pistachio, Maple Walnut," Lynn began to list, "she loved them all."

"Still do," Ma said.

"That's when you taught us Parcheesi and Tripoly, and played with us for hours," Louann said, her face contorted from emotion. "I don't know too many moms who did that."

Lynn jumped in. "We had Nintendo marathons, playing Super Mario Brothers all through the night with Ma," she said.

"She got so addicted that she forgot to feed us, right Ma?" Louann added, teasing our mother.

Ma opened her mouth to defend herself but wasn't quick enough.

"She'd just sit there," Louann explained, "eating her Swedish fish and playing for hours."

Ma surrendered with a laugh. "I wasn't that bad, was I?"

"No, you were worse," Lynn said.

"Then she'd make it up to us by driving all around the city to deliver Girl Scout cookies," Louann said.

"That was way after our time," Wally said, "we were just lucky to have the Atari 2600."

"Yeah, and the only thing Ma did with that was take it away from us when we were punished," Alphonse added.

"Which happened a lot," I said.

Ma laughed. "If you didn't act like such animals all the time, then..."

"You mean angels, right?" Wally said.

"You were that, too..." She snickered. "...when you were sleeping."

Everyone laughed.

There was more drink and more food, followed by heavy bouts of crying and laughter. The entire process bordered on insanity. One thing was for sure, though—no one was going to keep the pain bottled up. As Pop would say, "Pain is poison and you gotta get it all out, or it'll eat you from the inside out."

After all these years, we were still following his advice—together.

Donna placed more food on the dining room table before giving me a kiss.

"I love you," she whispered.

"I love you too," I replied at normal volume. In all the years we'd been together, I'd never felt more grateful to my wife. Her support was unrelenting.

How did I get so lucky to marry my childhood sweetheart? I wondered. Our road, however, was not one I wanted to travel again. After multiple heart wrenching breakups and thrilling reunions, a litany of failed relationships on both sides, we finally met up again our senior year of college and never looked back. *Thankfully, we each got our oats sowed and out of our systems.* I gave her arm a squeeze. *Old love is deep love.*

"How did it go at the funeral home?" Wally asked Ma, pulling me back to the table. My older brother had flown in after we'd made Pop's arrangements.

Ma gestured toward me and Alphonse. "Guys?"

"The undertaker was a little creepy, I can tell you that," I said.

Alphonse nodded. "I think he played the child catcher in that movie, 'Chitty Chitty Bang Bang,' right Herbie?"

Both my brothers laughed over one of my greatest childhood fears. "Ahhh, the dreaded child catcher," Wally said.

I chuckled. "Stop," I said, "I've just recently gotten past the nightmares."

Donna was still laughing when she headed back into the kitchen.

"Everything's all set," I told Wally, "exactly what Pop wanted."

He nodded, gratefully. "Good, thanks."

As we continued to ride the insane merry-go-round of tears and laughter, the topics of conversation seemed as random as they were healing.

"I'm not surprised that your father left so quickly after Uncle Skinny passed," Ma said, shaking her head. Our crazy uncle had died three months earlier.

Wally reported, "I remember Pop telling me, 'I'm the last one left. I just lost my best friend.'"

Silence ushered in another round of tears.

As soon as my emotions allowed for it, I jumped in with some comic relief. "This might seem inappropriate right now, but I think Pop would love for me to share it."

Everyone nodded, a few of them sliding to the edge of their chairs.

"I remember the day Uncle Skinny passed on."

After all those years of being a bachelor, Uncle Skinny had finally decided he was tired of living alone. One day, completely out of the blue, he showed up with a new girlfriend named Rhonda. She was weird, really weird—perfect for Uncle Skinny. The courtship lasted a few weeks before they exchanged vows at the town hall. The entire family was in shock—everyone except Pop. Nothing that Uncle Skinny did ever seemed to surprise him. Pop usually just shook his head and laughed, saying, "That Skinny's something else."

I continued on with the story. "So, on the day Uncle Skinny passed, I'll never forget Aunt Rhonda and her mechanical cat. What a terrifying pair!"

I now had everyone's attention.

"As you know, by some strange coincidence, Uncle Skinny and Aunt Rhonda were living at the same retirement home. While Uncle Skinny had been on his last leg, literally, his wife was living out her final days suffering from Alzheimer's." I could feel my mind drifting off, returning to the vivid details of that bizarre day.

• • •

As soon as I got the call that my Uncle Skinny had just passed away, I hurried to meet my father at the retirement home. Pop and I exchanged a hug and some tears in the parking lot before heading inside. We were escorted to my uncle's room where his rigid hands lay one on top of the other across his chest. Any coloring he'd worn during life had already drained from his face; his skin was stark white, bordering on gray.

Touching his hand, I thanked him for all he'd ever done for me. I then offered several prayers before taking a seat near the bed. Pop had just claimed the chair beside me, when a nurse wheeled Aunt Rhonda into the room. Her mechanical cat, Mr. Kitty, was propped up in her lap.

For a few awkward moments, Aunt Rhonda said nothing. And then she began to speak to my uncle, babbling on in some gibberish that I assumed made sense to her. I didn't think much of it until she began asking him questions and pausing for a reply. "Did you finish your lunch, Skinny?" she asked him. I looked at Pop, but quickly turned away when I saw he was grinning. Instead of my uncle responding, Mr. Kitty began to purr loudly. Aunt Rhonda grabbed the stuffed cat by the scruff of its neck and lifted it until they were eye level. "You shoosh now, Mr. Kitty. I'm not talking to you." The cat purred more. "Enough with you!" she screamed at a high-pitched squeal. I couldn't believe my eyes or ears. In response to being screamed at, the cat began to hiss and shriek. It was like a switch had been thrown. Aunt Rhonda took a few deep breaths before soothing the cat by stroking its fake head and whispering something into its twitching ear.

I studied the mechanical animal for a bit. Mr. Kitty's eyes blinked; its tail wagged. *This is horrifying*, I thought. *I'm never going to sleep tonight.*

I looked at Pop again. His grin was wider than before. I turned away from him for fear that I may burst out laughing. *We're in the middle of The Twilight Zone right now.*

Once the cat had quieted down, my aunt pushed on my uncle's arm. "So did you eat or not, Skinny?" she asked. Having already been in heaven for several hours, my uncle remained silent. Mr. Kitty, however, did not. And we kicked off the bizarre cycle again— my delusional aunt screaming at the cat, the cat shrieking back, and my uncle refusing to answer any further questions.

Pop nudged my arm. "Promise me that you'll bat me in the head and put me out of my misery before I end up here."

I looked at my aunt and then back to Pop.

"Rhonda doesn't even know we're here," he said, like he'd learned how to whisper in a helicopter.

"So, I guess you didn't eat then, huh, Skinny?" Aunt Rhonda repeated.

As Mr. Kitty answered, I stood to leave. "I promise, Pop," I told him.

With a grateful nod, he followed me out of the room.

• • •

"Oh, Pop," Lynn said, stifling a laugh.

"He was such a character," Louann said, "that's for sure."

"Money or no money," Wally said, "Pop died a wealthy man."

"Not to mention his treasure trove of classic one-liners," Alphonse said.

Wally nodded in agreement. "You can't shine shit," he said, doing his best imitation of our father's voice.

"That's as smart as feeding more coins into a broken vending machine," Lynn said.

We all laughed.

"It's no use," Louann said, grinning, "...it's like filling your mouth with Saltines and trying to whistle."

The hair on my forearms stood on end, pushed by goosebumps. My mind flooded with our father's famous zingers. "*Tru da years,*" Pop used to say, "*I've found that everybody's full of shit until they're not.*" Pop wasn't nearly as eloquent as our mother, but he was much more creative and definitely more original.

After taking a quick bathroom break, I returned to the table to hear more laughter. *What now?* I wondered. We'd already spent hours ping-ponging between joy and pain, laughter and tears.

"Ma, I remember how you traumatized us by making us watch that After School Special, *My Mom's Having A Baby*," Alphonse said.

"Oh God," I blurted, reclaiming my seat, "I remember that."

Everyone laughed.

"It might have been awkward at the time, guys," Ma said, "but it was important that you understood how babies are born."

Sure Ma, I thought, *it wasn't the stack of dirty magazines in the cellar or watching movies like "Fast Times at Ridgemont High," that gave us everything we needed to know.*

Everyone was still chuckling, when Donna jumped in. "My mom made me and my sister watch that same After School Special."

"But it was probably a little bit different with just girls in the room," I said. "Imagine having to watch it with your father?"

"Ewww," she said.

"Yup, Ma told us that if we had any questions," Wally explained, "she'd answer them at the end of the show."

"And to make matters worse, she stayed in the room with us," I told my grinning wife.

Ma laughed. "Well, you learned how babies are made, didn't you?' She grabbed Alex and hugged him.

"Sure, Ma," Alphonse said, "long before you tortured us with that show."

I reached over to rub my mother's back. "You just enjoyed tormenting us every chance you had."

Everyone laughed again.

"If anyone was tormented in those days, it was me," she said.

While my brothers and I nodded, every one of her grandchildren left the room, bored with this trip down memory lane.

Laughter faded into another wave of quiet sobs.

Day turned to night. Every light in the house was on, with Donna happily taking care of the small details while we worked our way through this peculiar grieving process.

I'm such a lucky man, I was thinking, when Alphonse began laughing for no apparent reason.

"As much as he bitched and moaned, Pop loved going to the Westport Fair every summer," he reminisced.

Everyone nodded in agreement.

"He brought me and Lynn every year," Louann said.

"Remember that year he wore his slippers to the fair?" Alphonse said.

Wally laughed. "Because he had a corn on his foot."

"Oh, your father was one of a kind," Ma said, shaking her head.

I cleared my throat to speak clearly, or at least tried to. "I remember I'd just walked through the midway, past all the food trucks, when I was cutting through the pavilion. Of course, Pop was sitting in the beer garden, enjoying a cold one and listening to some God-awful country band up on the stage. I didn't think anything of it until I noticed that he was sitting there in his torn corduroy slippers with white socks."

Everyone laughed.

"And he saw me too," I said, "and began calling me over to him."

"Oh, man," Alphonse said, laughing, "with all the kids from school walking around?"

I nodded.

"What did he want?" Wally asked.

I looked around the room to make sure my kids weren't anywhere within earshot. "I don't know," I admitted with a shrug. "I pretended like I'd never heard him and just kept walking."

Alphonse whistled. "Wow, that was a big risk."

After all these years, I still felt bad about it. "I was too young and stupid to risk the embarrassment," I confessed.

"Damn," Lynn said, "I can't imagine ever ignoring dad."

"That's because you never saw those corduroy slippers," Wally said, smiling.

Everyone laughed again.

"But what I would give to have that moment back again," I said, the tears starting to break again. "I'd...I'd..." I stuttered, trying to finish the sentence. "I'd run right to him."

A wave of sobs hit the shore again.

"Those were some amazing summers," Wally said.

"They sure were," Alphonse said.

I chuckled through the tears. "When Wally handed down his paper route, I was finally able to pay off my Columbia Record and Tape Club contract," I told everyone, "buying all four titles at full price. Then, as a glutton for punishment, I joined the RCA Record Club, entering into the same foolish deal with them."

My brothers laughed.

"You weren't the only one," Wally said.

"Not me," Cockroach said. "That was a terrible investment."

We laughed harder.

It was late—really late—when everyone prepared to leave for the night, knowing that we'd be reconvening for another round of laughter and tears. *Day one of redneck shiva has come to a close*, I thought, shaking my head, *but not before one final toast to Pop.*

I raised my can of Miller High Life. "Everything Pop built, his entire life, is sitting right here at this table. We are his legacy, and all that we say and do in this world will be a direct reflection on him." I locked eyes with each one of my father's yawning grandchildren, who'd since returned to the room. "So, protect the name you've been given, keep your word—always—and always remember where you came from." I nodded. "Your grandpa would want nothing more."

"That's the truth right there," Alphonse confirmed.

Smothering each other in kisses and hugs—all of us squeezing a little tighter and holding on a little longer—everyone finally went home for the night.

"Goodnight, John-Boy," I called out after Wally.

"Goodnight, Erin," he replied, without missing a beat or even turning around.

I was still laughing when I shut the front door.

• • •

The boys were already in their beds when I stepped into their room to tuck them in.

"Are you guys doing okay?" I asked.

They both nodded that they were, but their tired eyes told a different story.

I took a seat on Alex's bed. "When I was just around your age, I lost my grandfather too," I told them. "It was devastating. I remember thinking that he'd taken a piece of me with him." I sighed heavily. "What I didn't realize until I got older was that he'd left many pieces of himself behind...and that I was one of those pieces." I smiled at the truth of it.

My boys nodded, politely.

"I remember that my dad, your grandpa, took me and your uncles for Coney Island hot dogs. On the ride, he told us, 'Death is just a temporary separation, boys. I believe that as much as I believe anything else in this world. We'll all be together again someday. Don't you ever doubt it.'"

I paused, realizing that those simple words now meant more to me than ever—and that I still believed each one of them. "Your grandfather," I added, making eye contact with them both, "taught me that none of us is ever alone."

They smiled wide, as though they both needed to hear that very message.

I nodded confidently. "We were connected before we came into this world, and we'll be connected long after we leave it," I repeated, adding a smile. "We're family."

I could see true faith seep into my sons' sad eyes.

"Now get some sleep," I told them, standing to turn out the light. "We have a rough few day ahead of us, but we'll get through it together because…"

"…we're family," Dylan said, finishing my sentence.

"Exactly." I smiled. "We're family." I steeled myself to finish my message. "And no one or nothing can ever change that…not even death."

It was beyond late when I finally slid into bed. Even though I was exhausted—physically, emotionally, spiritually—I knew I wouldn't be getting a good night's sleep. *Not happening*, I thought, *at least not tonight.* Even still, it felt good to lay beside my wife and feel the warmth of her body. I slowly turned toward her, trying not to wake her.

"Are you okay, Herbie?" she whispered, her eyes still closed.

"I'm sad," I admitted, "but I'll be fine."

"Which is how your dad raised you, right?" She opened her beautiful eyes.

Tears filled mine. "Thanks for all your help today. I…"

"Please don't thank me, Herbie," she said, yawning. "We're in this together." She looked into my eyes. "You know you're not alone, right?"

"I do," I whispered, my eyes filling.

"I love him too, you know," she added.

"I know." I kissed her, thankful that she hadn't used the past tense when referring to Pop. "Go to sleep," I told her, "we have another long day tomorrow."

As Donna dozed off, I lay still, staring at the ceiling. I suddenly remembered Pop telling me that, "When I die, I want to be cremated." I also remembered thinking, *You ought to go up like a matchstick, Pop, with all that beer you've drunk.* Although the memory forced a grin, I decided, *I probably shouldn't share that with my brothers and sisters.*

While my wife settled into a light snore, I lay in the darkness, my mind flashing one image of my father after another. *For a man who wasn't very spiritual, his death's been the most spiritual experience I've ever known,* I thought, *ever.*

I nodded. *Thank you, Pop…for everything.*

I slowly rolled off the bed and onto my knees to pray. *Father, please bless Pop and bring him home safely to you. Shroud him in your angels. Let him know that he'll be remembered and honored for the rest of my life. More importantly, please let him feel the love that I have for him in my heart.* As tears rolled from both of my clenched eyes, I could feel the wetness racing down my cheeks. *Although he's gone from this place, he isn't far from me. I can feel that. Bless him, Father. Forgive him of his sins and bless his soul, that he may rest in your peace and grace for all eternity. In Jesus' name, I pray.*

After blessing myself, I slithered back into bed. "Please give me a sign, Pop," I whispered, interlocking my fingers behind my head, "so that I know you've made it home safely."

• • •

It felt like seconds had passed when my eyes flew open. *6:02* glowed in bright red letters on the alarm clock; it was the address of my childhood home, the very place where Pop had taught me and my brothers to stand up and become men.

Thank you for the sign, Pop, I thought, another tear breaking free.

As I sat up, I could still hear my brother's voice from the night before. *'Those were some amazing summers,'* Wally said.

'They sure were,' Alphonse agreed.

We had some fun back in the day, didn't we, Pop? I thought, chuckling. *Even when you were getting after us.*

Slipping out of bed, I quietly stepped into the darkness of the living room.

Easing into my worn recliner. I inhaled once, maybe twice, before my tired mind sprinted back to the glorious summer of 1984.

CHAPTER 2

MAY 1984

SPRINTING DOWN MEMORY LANE

Toward the end of eighth grade, Donna Torres told me, "I think we should see other people over the summer."

"What?" I screeched; I was completely devastated.

To say that I entered into a state of depression would have been an understatement. I made a mixed cassette tape with all the depressing ballads from the early 80s: *Keep on Loving You* by Reo Speedwagon, *Faithfully* by Journey, *Cherish* by Kool & The Gang, *Waiting for a Girl Like You* by Foreigner, *Stuck on You* by Lionel Richie—amongst many others, each one making me quietly sob into my stained A-Team pillowcase.

By the time the final bell rang, ending the school year and releasing us from another year of prison, Donna and I were back together—at least from my perspective.

"I want to see you as much as I can this summer," I told her.

"Me too," she said.

"I want to see only you this summer."

She nodded.

As I awaited a reply that never came, I could feel the remnants of a Sloppy Joe sandwich rise into my throat. *We'll be fine,* I thought, desperately hoping that she was done playing hot potato with my heart. *We have to be.*

It was the last day of school, Friday, May 25 1984. Winter had melted into spring and, although most days felt like they went on forever, spring was finally giving way to summer. The black rubber boots, lined with bread bags, had long been tossed into the closet, along with our green snorkel coats.

Wally sat in the back of the school bus with his new best friend, Owen Audet, the bully who'd gotten his nose shattered by my older brother. Since their epic fight, they'd become inseparable, the best of friends. *Respect amongst ogres is a funny thing*, I figured.

I remained in my territory, seated a half dozen rows toward the front—and under Mr. Gifford's squinted gaze. The kid across the aisle from me had the volume turned up so loud on his yellow Walkman that I began to sing along with Alice Cooper—under my breath. "School's out for summer!"

We'd just gotten into an awesome paper plane fight when one of the high schoolers sitting behind me tapped me on the shoulder. "I bet you're gonna kiss a few of your cousins out near the woodshed over the summer, huh?" he said, poking fun at my redneck heritage.

Up for the exchange of wits, I immediately turned in my seat to face the smirking punk. "Yup, but only my boy cousins," I replied in a fake drawl. "I reckon we all like playin' spin the bottle." I grinned.

"You and your brothers gonna do any cow tipping?"

He's already onto my brothers, I thought. *Bad move.* "Just the cute ones that've led us on," I spat back. Laughing to myself, I picked up the pace. "I'm also looking forward to playing the moonshine jug in our family's porch band. Wally plays the washboard, and 'Lil Cockroach is on the spoons." I cackled like a real hick. "And that's when we ain't collectin' roadkill for Ma's suppa pot."

The kid didn't know what to say.

"And speakin' of mamas, let's talk about yours."

"Oh, I wouldn't," the guy huffed, his face instantly burning red.

"I'm guessin' she also slept with her own kin, which is where you came from." While my adversary's nostrils flared from hyperventilation, I laughed more. "For someone who can dish it out," I said in my normal voice, "you sure have some thin skin, Magilla."

Everyone started to laugh, making the kid's face turn a brighter shade of red. His dancing eyes were clearly weighing his options.

"Relax, dude," I said, "I'm just messin' with ya."

The crowd of onlookers was clearly amused.

"No need for you to take a beating on top of it," I said, dropping the smile from my face. Instinctively, my eyes narrowed, as I prepared myself for combat.

Although the punk's mouth hung open, he said nothing. Shock had paralyzed him.

"That's what I thought," I said, silently claiming victory. *And I'm guessing this'll be the last time Tweedle Dum screws with me.*

For a moment, my eyes reached the back of the bus to see Wally's acne-filled face grinning proudly at me. He gave me a single nod. Since his victorious bus brawl, no one messed with him.

I returned his nod before turning back in my seat. *Thanks for the training, brother.* Although I'd never admit it to anyone—especially him—I enjoyed his unspoken protection. But even though I was still reaping the benefits of him whooping on Owen earlier in the year, I could see something new in my adversary's eyes. *He was afraid to fight me,* I thought, smiling. *Me, not Wally.*

As Bus 6 rolled closer to our house, the truth of Alice Cooper's words struck hard. *School's out for summer!* I thought. *No more pencil shavings. No more chalk dust. No more of the screeching that makes my skin crawl when Mr. Jeronimo jots down some stupid math formula on the green chalkboard.* I nodded to myself. *No more double lunches, which is a bummer.* Still, the idea of being free made my skin tingle. Books had been turned in and lockers cleaned out. *No more pretending to do homework,* I thought. We'd just finished our Iowa Tests on green answer cards with a number two pencil. *All of it done!*

My mind abandoned the past and locked onto the future. I was looking forward to staying up late and sleeping in. *Playing in the yard all day or hanging down the railroad tracks. Secret trips to the amusement park. Logging miles and miles on our bicycles. Yes,* I thought, trying not to giggle, *summer's finally here!*

I stepped off Bus 6 for the last time that year, unscathed. Turning my face to the sun, I took a few deep breaths. *Let the games begin!*

Without a word, Wally brushed past me and headed for the cellar.

We lived at 602 State Road in an apartment just above a real estate office, in a town that had no more than a half dozen apartments. I approached the weathered shingled two-decker and hustled up the stairs. Stepping into our kitchen, I saw Ma standing at her white stove, prepping one of Pop's favorite meals—Salisbury steak and mashed potatoes. A large wooden spoon and matching fork hung on some busy wallpaper of vegetables and roosters.

"Are you sorry that school's out for summer?" she asked me, smiling. The vertically challenged woman had soft walnut-colored eyes and an infectious smile that always made me do the same.

"I'm so bummed," I told her, grinning.

Taking a break from the stove, she began another task at the cluttered kitchen counter. "Where's your brother?" she asked, pouring a heaping scoop of Country Time lemonade mix—from ten pounds of yellow granulated powder in a bulky cardboard drum— into a Tupperware pitcher. It was another exciting sign that pointed directly toward summer. Although we drank Kool-Aid year-round, once we were out of school, Ma switched us over to lemonade—as if it were healthier.

"In the cellar," I told her.

"Why?"

"Who knows with that wasteoid?"

"I hope he's being quiet down there. They're working downstairs, you know," she said, referring to the realtor office on the first floor.

"We know, Ma. We know."

"Where's your report card?" she asked, ignoring the comment. Shuffling across the worn yellow linoleum toward me, she extended her open fingers. "How did you do?"

"I didn't stay back, Ma," I told her, handing over the flimsy paper that smelled of strong ink.

"I hope, for your sake, that you did much better than that, Herbie," she told me, unfolding the sheet.

"I finally made it out of Middle School," I told her, "and that's all that matters."

"Your report card's not bad," she said, scanning it over. "Not up to your potential, but not bad."

Shrugging, I poured myself a tumbler of the room temp lemonade.

She gestured toward the massive Country Time tub sitting on

the counter. "This had better last you animals the entire summer," she said.

As long as you're the only one making the lemonade, it might last two summers, I thought, starting for the plastic accordion door that separated our bedroom from the kitchen.

Our bedroom consisted of a single bed, a set of bunk beds and two mismatched bureaus. Against one wall was Cockroach's pad-locked toy box. A tiny black-and-white TV sat on a rickety fake-wooden stand, the Atari 2600 console and joysticks lying in front. A stained carpet had recently been replaced, while two duct-taped beanbag chairs had been discarded—helping to declutter the small room.

"You did okay," Ma confirmed, "you're lucky."

Smiling, I took a seat on my bunk.

"I need you to run to the store for me," she called out.

"That's Cockroach's job now, and he'll be home in a half hour," I reminded her. "Besides, I need to go get my paper route done."

Her silence announced that she wasn't arguing the point.

Mission avoided, I thought, just as Wally opened the kitchen door.

"So, let's see that report card," I heard Ma tell him.

Good luck with that, brother, I thought.

I looked up from my Atari joystick to find Cockroach standing in front of me, showing off several blue ribbons. He'd participated in his final elementary school field day and couldn't wipe the smile off his handsome face.

"What did you win those for?" I asked him, putting the controller down.

"The forty-yard dash and tug-of-war."

Relaxing on his bed, Wally snickered. "Tug-of-war, my ass."

"It's true, Wally," Cockroach said. "We smoked them."

"Yeah, okay."

I laughed. "Good job, Alphonse."

My little brother quickly searched my face to make sure it wasn't another set up. Realizing that I was being sincere, he smiled. "Thanks, Herbie."

"So, what do you want to do?" he asked.

"Get the hell out of this house," Wally said, before jumping off his bed and heading out of the room.

Cockroach looked at me. "What's his problem? It's the last day of school. Why isn't he happy?"

"When's the last time you saw Wally happy?" I asked.

He thought about it for a moment before shrugging.

"Let's head outside and figure it out," I told him.

Ma was poking out a cigarette when she caught us at the door. "I want you boys in when the streetlights come on," she told us, "and not a minute longer."

"Yeah, Ma, we know." But we also knew that we'd only abide by this rule for a week—maybe two, at best—before we were hanging out late into the night. It was summer, with no school to wake up for in the morning. Ma would hem and haw, but she'd eventually grow tired of us and surrender, pretending that we were still minding her rules. And as long as we were out of the apartment, there was less threat of us making too much noise and getting evicted.

For now, Ma was on a roll, trying to lay down the law. "I know I don't want you boys in this house all summer," she said, "I know that." She nodded. "I want you outside."

No worries, Ma, I thought, *you'll be lucky if you see us at all until September.*

While some friends were scheduled to head off to summer camp, we weren't. Our neighborhood was our camp—with no camp counselor, no uniforms, no schedule, and definitely no rules. We basically ran amok. In past years, Wally spent the warm months tackling me. I'd then tackle Cockroach for laughing. And our little brother stayed busy tackling a long list of childhood fears. *But this year will be different,* I thought. Wally, the pioneer, had recently started his first real job as a dishwasher at the Oriental Pearl restaurant. By default, this meant that I finally got his paper route, and that Cockroach took over the R&S Variety Store runs for Ma and her beloved cigarettes, Carlton 100s.

I stood on the outside stairs for a moment, taking everything in.

Our backyard was nearly a football field in length but only half the width. From the top, it pitched down and left. It was wide open, and my brothers and I knew every rut and divot. There was a moon crater—'the ankle breaker,' we called it—toward the left side, putting our unaware opponents at a serious and dangerous disadvantage when playing on our turf.

An old swing set stood at the bottom of the yard. I laughed at the sight of it; I could still picture my brothers and me tackling it like young baboons, the rusted poles lifting up out of the ground.

As I scanned right, I spotted Wally sitting on the picnic bench under the weeping willow tree in the front yard.

"Hey, do you want to play rundown before you go to work?" I asked, yelling at him across the yard.

He shook his head. "Not enough time," he said. "Maybe tomorrow."

"So, what do you want to do?" I asked.

"Chill," he yelled back. "That's what I want to do…I want to chill out before I have to slave away tonight."

I looked at Cockroach, who only shook his head.

Boinker, I thought. Although I understood that Wally had to work, I still didn't like it.

Cockroach and I were taking a drink from the garden hose attached to the side of the house, when I heard the most beautiful song of any childhood; although it was still somewhat faint—a ways off in the distance—it was a final confirmation that summer had indeed arrived.

Gus and his neighborhood ice cream truck had announced its daily arrival, playing a carnival-like song. It always freaked me out a little, reminding me of the long-nosed, creepy child catcher in the twisted movie, *Chitty Chitty Bang Bang.*

"Let's go!" I told my brother, dropping the green hose and sprinting for the house to scrounge enough change for a cold treat. "Do you have any extra money?" I asked Cockroach on the run.

"No such thing as extra money," he yelled back.

"You know what I mean…do…do you have money?" I was already gasping for air.

"What do you think?"

"Well, can I borrow a dollar until I get paid?" I asked, slowing my run. Begging for change was about as pathetic as I got. Somehow, I always seemed to swallow my pride at the first calliope notes of that damned ice cream truck.

There was a pause from my little brother, stopping me in my tracks.

"Fine," Cockroach said, "but I want it back as soon as you get paid."

"That's what I said, didn't I?"

"Just make sure." He shook his head. "I don't know why you still have to borrow money from me, Herbie," he muttered under his breath. "You're the one who's working now."

I considered going off on him, but wisely decided against it. *Otherwise, I may not score one of those Screwballs that I love.*

This awkward exchange was followed by the usual chase, with the ice cream truck stopping a half block down, making us run—which only seemed to add to the overall experience.

When we finally caught up to it, I studied the colorful, pictorial menu on the side of the white box truck—as if I didn't already know what I wanted. *Let's see…ice cream sandwiches, Bomb Pops, the red, white and blue popsicles, Fudgsicles, Creamsicles, strawberry crunch bars, chocolate crunch bar, Nutty Buddies, Push Pops, Screwballs with the gumball at the bottom.* I nodded. *That's the winner right there!* I thought, ordering one of them when it was my turn.

"Sorry, we're all out of those," Gus told me, adding an unapologetic shrug. "What about a malt cup, or a Chipwich, maybe?" The man had a terrible comb over that was always very distracting.

You've already run out of Screwballs? I thought. *How? Summer just started.* I shook my head. *I really wanted that gumball on the bottom.*

He waited for my second choice.

Of course they're out of stock, I thought. *Everybody loves those, because you get ice cream and gum, all in one shot.* "Give me a chocolate crunch bar," I finally ordered, slapping the borrowed change onto his metal counter.

He handed me the novelty bar.

"You gonna get more Screwballs?" I asked him, studying his hair.

He grinned. "I'm looking at one right now," he told me, before directing his attention to the customer behind me—Cockroach. "What'll it be, young man?" he asked over my shoulder.

While Wally had already headed home. Cockroach was still taking his sweet time to decide, causing those behind him in line to start yelling at him.

"Let's go, numb nuts," one kid called out. "I ain't got all day."

Cockroach looked back at him. "Of course you do, wing nut," he said.

For a kid who can't fight, Cockroach has a razor-sharp tongue, I thought.

Another kid yelled in his order to Gus. "I'll take a Screwball!"

"Second choice?" Gus asked, pointing to the *Out of Stock* sign he'd just scribbled on his menu.

"Unreal," the kid complained. "Every time."

He's right, I thought.

My little brother continued to weigh his options, while I stood off to the side, waiting for him. "You'd better hurry up and decide, Eeyore," I told him, "before Gus runs out of everything else."

The short, paunchy ice cream man leaned further out his window to cast me a harsh look, a few strands of long hair falling across his face. For a split second, he resembled a werewolf—*like maybe he eats children or something.*

Without chewing my chocolate crunch bar, I swallowed hard.

It was our first day of freedom. If it were even possible, my brothers and I were already getting bored.

"Let's head up into the willow tree and shoot the shit," Wally suggested.

At his age, it was a rare treat when Wally even bothered with us, so both Alphonse and I jumped at the chance.

Like a small squad of Special Ops soldiers, we advanced on the weeping willow tree in full attack node.

"I don't have much time," Wally reminded us, "so hustle up."

Wally was part black bear, able to scurry up a tree in no time, making me think, *I wonder when the last time was that he clipped his fingernails?* As usual, he got to the top, where he swayed back and forth, taunting me and Alphonse with insulting challenges that could have probably been heard the next town over. "Let's go, Strawberry Shortcake, you're next. But if you're too scared, then..."

Part of me really hated my older brother because he was better than me at everything. What was worse was that he didn't hate me in return. He didn't need to.

"Come on, Sally," he repeated.

Although the nickname could have been meant for either of us, I knew it was my cue to begin my ascent. *Anything to shut his big fat trap.*

I was a bit slower than Wally during my climb, more cautious and methodical. Each move was calculated and approached with a high degree of focus.

When I got just under Wally's dangling feet, our big brother began squawking again, challenging Cockroach with a relentless barrage of dares. "Come on Lollipop, you can do it."

Ugh, I thought, *lollipop.* That one word was a trigger for each of us, inspired by our salty father.

Our baby brother grabbed the first limb, pulled himself up, and then just sat there, perched like Toucan Sam.

"Is that it, Smurfette?" Wally yelled down.

I laughed. *It doesn't matter what stupid names Wally comes up with now*, I thought. *Cockroach is in the tree, and that's all that matters to him. He isn't going one limb higher, no matter how bad he's razzed.* I respected him for it.

Wally must have, too, because he quit the name-calling. "So, what are you guys up to tonight?" he asked.

"The usual for a Friday," Cockroach answered, "a movie rental, if Ma or Pop will take us to Silver Screen, or we'll just watch the Dukes of Hazard. Either way, we're in for a paper bag of Ma's famous fries."

Wally sighed heavily. "I already miss those," he said, surprising me.

"You don't like the dishwashing job?" I asked him.

"Of course I like it," he said. "The work's pretty beastly, but the money's choice."

"I can't wait until…" Cockroach began to say, when there was a loud screech; it sounded like a banshee unleashing her wrath.

I scanned the yard before realizing that the God-awful sound was coming from Ma, her entire head stuck out the second-floor window. "Alphonse!" she yelled. "Alphonse!" She sounded like she was in real trouble.

All three of us descended the tree branches, Planet-of-the-Apes style, a group of aggressive chimpanzees prepared to defend our territory.

"What, Ma?' Wally called up to her. "What's the matter?"

"I need Alphonse to run to the corner store for me. I'm almost out of cigarettes."

My brothers and I looked at each other in disbelief.

"Now, Alphonse!" Ma yelled, before slamming the window shut.

Wally shrugged. "Well, it is an emergency," he said.

We laughed, while Cockroach hustled off to the house to take Ma's order.

"I need to get ready for work," Wally said.

Ma did ask me to make a store run a while ago, I remembered, shrugging. *I've got my own work to get done.*

It seemed like it had taken forever, but I finally got my own paper route, which Wally was thrilled to pass down. As a paperboy, I could treat myself to the occasional lunch: a Chow Mein sandwich at Oriental Pearl for a buck and a half, washed down with a Mello Yellow from R&S Variety. It was heaven being able to pay my own way, making decisions I'd been unable to make when I was always broke. Even the clam cakes from McCrays tasted better when I paid for them—and ate them alone.

On my very first payday, I bought a new copy of "*Mad Magazine.*" *The days of finding those hidden pictures in Highlights are finally over*, I decided, feeling like I'd just taken my last step out of childhood. *Hallelujah!*

While Cockroach prepared to head out on his errand—undoubtedly planning to embezzle a few purchases on Ma's tab—I looked up at the sun as if I was part Native American. "I'd better head out and get my route done," I announced.

Cockroach met me back in the yard. I could see a look of desperation in his gaze. "How about I hurry back from R&S and then tag along with you today, Herbie?" he suggested. His tone was pleading, bordering on pathetic.

I shook my head. "Not a chance, Sweet Pea," I told him, feeling the same power Wally must have felt for all those months. *Someday, little brother*, I thought, *but not today.*

"Fine," he huffed. "I'll remember this the next time you ask me for something!"

"When do I ever..."

"Almost every day, Herbie," he said, talking over me. "You're always asking to borrow money, or one of my things, or..."

"Not today, Alphonse," I told him. "but soon." I shrugged. "I just need to get it done faster than usual today."

"Why?"

"Because it's movie night...remember, airhead?"

He thought about it for a moment before giving me a nod. "Okay then. Soon." I was jumping on my bicycle when Cockroach yelled, "Did Ma agree to let us rent a movie?"

"Not yet," I said, "but she will."

• • •

Pop had finally worked enough overtime to buy the family a brand-new VCR, a top-loading Betamax. I knew right away that life would never be the same.

We felt rich, having our own home entertainment center. It was similar to MTV, opening up a whole new world for us. I loved going to the video store and renting movies. For 99 cents per movie, we watched *Friday the 13th, Caddyshack, Stripes, Mad Max, National Lampoon's Vacation*—even *Star Wars*. Of course, this cut into some of our regularly scheduled programming. *But how many General Lee car jumps can a guy watch? How many fantasies can someone watch come true on some remote tropical island?*

"I really want to see *Porky's*," Cockroach whispered to me when I returned from delivering newspapers,

"Me too," I said, "but there's no way Ma will…"

"What if we just tell her that it's a movie about Porky Pig and Bugs Bunny?" he said.

"Are you out of your mind? She'd never buy that." I shook my head. "One look at the tape cover and she'll know it's not a cartoon." Our mother could be gullible, but she wasn't blind. "Don't be such an idiot."

Ma was kind enough to take us to the local video store.

Silver Screen Video was Westport's version of Blockbuster. It was a bit smaller, but we didn't care. They had the same sections to choose from: New Releases. Action. Drama. Comedy. They stocked the same films; they just carried fewer copies, so we needed to get there as early as possible on Fridays.

There was a black curtain in the rear of the store; the sign over it read, *Adult Section*. Although Wally and I were intrigued, Cockroach was actually twitching to slink behind that black velvet to see what the future had in store for him.

Ma was browsing the store when I approached her with a copy of *Fast Times at Ridgemont High*. "Can we rent it?" I asked her, putting on my innocent face.

Grabbing the boxed tape from me, she looked at the cover before turning it over and starting to read. "Any sex or nudity?" she asked.

I immediately shook my head. "I have a friend at school who just saw it, Ma, and he never mentioned sex or nudity." I smiled. "Trust me, he's the type of kid who wouldn't stop talking about it, if he'd seen anything."

"Fine," she said, handing it back to me, "you can rent it, but that's it for the weekend."

"Thanks Ma," I said, stopping my face from celebrating over my clever lie. There was no friend at school who'd seen the flick. For all I knew—and hoped—it was loaded with nudity. *But I never mentioned the friend's name, I thought, and if Ma walks into the living room while some actress is ripping off her bra, then I can still play stupid and get away with it.*

Mr. Deschenes sold microwaveable popcorn and extra-large candy bars, along with huge boxes of Good and Plenty and Bit O' Honey at the counter. We didn't dare ask Ma for anything more. *The movie's more than enough*, I thought.

As Mr. Deschenes rang us up, he looked at Ma when he got to the *Fast Times at Ridgemont High* rental. My brother and I held our collective breath, waiting for the man's warning. He bagged the movies without a word, punching Ma's card. "After nine rentals, you get the tenth one free," he reminded her.

We exhaled.

As we walked out of the store with a couple of movies in a plastic bag, it dawned on me. *Renting movies could be the best thing that's ever to happened to us. There's no way Ma and Pop would ever spend the time researching them.*

Our living room was decorated in flowered wallpaper and framed family photos. There was a brown couch and love seat, the fabric slightly softer than burlap. Both pieces of furniture were as worn as Pop's burgundy recliner. Atop a tan shag carpet sat a bulky walnut-paneled Hi-Fi stereo in one corner of the room, while a three-layered shelf—cluttered with Ma's knickknacks and Pop's beer steins—sat in the other. Steel radiators, painted silver, sat at the base of lead-painted windows and doors. And in the middle of it all was the family's floor model 25-inch Zenith TV.

Ma and Pop never stepped foot into the living room that night. Neither one of them could be bothered with "some stupid teenage movie." Instead, they played Gin Rummy at the kitchen table—the room engulfed in cigarette smoke, the kitchen table covered in empty golden beer cans. *I wonder who's worse behaved,* I thought, *us or them?*

It wasn't long before Cockroach lowered the volume on the old Zenith, so our parents couldn't hear how bad *Fast Times at Ridgemont High* actually was. Each scene was dirtier than the one before it: a young man and young woman disrobing, breasts shown before they begin to engage in sex; posters of naked women on Spicoli's bedroom wall; and Stacy discovering that she's pregnant after having sex with Ramone. There was also a fantasy scene, with one of the guys imagining a girl taking off her bikini top, showing off her boobs—before he starts masturbating. People kissed…more boobs were shown…a guy was thrusting. There was even talk about oral sex, followed by a carrot demonstration.

Damn, I thought, falling in love a few times. It almost felt like I was cheating on Donna, and I felt a bit guilty because of it.

Quickly learning how to use the Rewind button on the VCR, we were able to watch each wonderfully inappropriate scene several times, while taking turns keeping watch at the door. Cockroach's eyes were wide and his breathing shallow. At one point, I thought he was going to have a seizure. "Easy, dude," I told him. "Easy."

As I finally pushed Stop on the VCR, I grinned. *Told you, Ma,* I thought. *No sex or nudity. Clean as a whistle.*

"Be kind," Cockroach told me, "rewind."

After giving him a bad look, I rewound the tape and then hit the Eject button—making a small wish that it popped out intact. Similar to cassette players, there was always the risk that the evil machine would eat the tape. If that happened, we'd have to cut the tape and yank it out of the VCR, which instantly turned it into junk. For a rental, this obviously posed a real problem.

Thankfully, *Fast Times at Ridgemont High* survived the mechanical journey whole.

"Goodnight Ma, goodnight Pop," we called out, as we reached the plastic accordion door.

They both looked up from the kitchen table, peering at us through the thick cloud of smoke.

"Your mother cheats at cards," Pop joked, sipping his beer.

"That's not true," she said, looking toward us. "I think we all know better than that."

We laughed. "Goodnight."

Settled into our darkened bedroom, I called up to the top bunk. "Don't be nasty up there tonight, Alphonse," I told my deviant brother. "I know that movie was pretty wild, but if this bunkbed starts rocking like a stagecoach, then I'm gonna…"

"Take it cheesy, dude," Cockroach said, "and mind your own beeswax."

I scrambled off the bed and leapt to my feet to face him. "You ever say that again," I told him, as he shuffled to the back wall, "and I'll slap the ugly right off your face."

Flexing his dimples, he flashed me his Leif Garrett smile.

"Don't try me," I told him, holding my scowl.

His smile vanished.

Retiring to my own bunk, I fought off my own urges until I finally fell asleep.

• • •

Rubbing my bristled head, I studied the colorful, pictorial menu at the side of Gus's Ice Cream truck again. We'd gotten our summer haircuts—just shy of full buzz cuts—or we knew we'd have to listen to Pop call us "hippies" all summer. The old man could be relentless, and keeping the extra hair just wasn't worth it.

Like I don't already know what I want, I thought, listing off the options in my head. *Ice cream sandwich, Bomb Popsicles, Fudgsicles, Creamsicles, strawberry crunch bars, chocolate crunch bar, Nutty Buddy, Push Pop. Screwball...*

"Give me two Screwballs," I told the short, hunchbacked ice cream man.

"We're fresh out," Gus spat back at me. "Pick something else... and hurry up, I ain't got all day."

"Why even have them on the menu when you're always out of them?" I muttered under my breath, before returning to the metal menu.

"What's that?" the dwarf-like man snapped, the wind lifting his hair off the side of his head, making it dance like one of the flags that lined a used car lot.

"Nothing, just give me one of those..." I stopped.

Gus's face had instantly changed, his eyes turning to enraged slits, his nostrils flaring. While the calliope notes of a carnival song rang out into the dark night, he grabbed me by the wrist and began yanking me into his singing truck.

I pulled back, but barely reclaimed an inch of ground. *Gus is strong*, I thought, while being pulled deeper into the dark abyss, *unusually strong*.

Hair hanging down one shoulder, he continued to ratchet me in. *Not again*, I thought. *Please God, not again.*

Gus gave me one last tug before kicking the metal door shut behind us.

Although it was dark, I still made out the silhouette of something strange sitting in the corner. *What is a Fryolator doing in an ice cream truck?* I wondered, my heart pounding out of my chest. *It doesn't make any...*

The little man cracked me upside the head with something hard, and the world suddenly turned to slow motion. I then watched as Gus—a twisted smile now covering his bloated face—plunged my forearm straight into the bubbling Fryolator grease.

Oh, my God! The pain was excruciating, mind-numbing. As I struggled to stay conscious, I could smell something pungent. *Like fried pork, except...* I looked down into the steaming oil bath to see bright red skin bubbling—until a large patch slid off the bone and rose to the surface, where it curled and crisped brown. *That's not pork,* I thought. *It's my arm.*

The sounds were a nightmare all their own—a boy screaming for his life, a man laughing hysterically. I dry-heaved once, twice, before...

• • •

I awoke. Covered in a film of cold sweat, I sat erect, dry-heaving myself out of the horrific nightmare. Fighting off the urge to vomit, my breathing was shallow, my heart thumping as quick and loud as the chopper blades on a scene from Rambo.

What the hell? I thought. *This cannot be happening again!* I shook my head, like I was trying to shake off some tenacious demon. *It better not be.*

I had long gotten over Clarence and the recurring nightmare I'd suffered during our school's winter break. Getting older, I figured, *my fears should be more practical now.*

Sucking in some deep breaths, I jumped off the bunk bed and headed straight for the plastic accordion door. *I need a cup of lemonade and a few splashes of cold water on my face,* I told myself. *That ought to break me out of it.*

CHAPTER 3

JUNE 1984

RIDING A COMET

Every morning was Saturday morning now. Chomping on heaping bowls of milk-changing Cocoa Krispies, we'd just finished watching Elmer Fudd hunt "wabbits" and were about to hang out with Fat Albert and the gang, when Ma stepped into the living room.

"What do you guys think you're doing, eating in the living room?" she asked.

"But Ma," Cockroach said, beginning his defense, "you let us eat in here on Friday nights sometimes."

She nodded. "Right, and this isn't Friday night." She pointed her thumb toward the kitchen. "Go finish your breakfast in there. Your father and I can't afford to replace this carpet."

Groaning, we grabbed our bowls and did as instructed.

Ma's kitchen had a real lived-in country motif. The floor's linoleum was curling up and chipping at the corners. A few patches were missing—the high traffic areas where everyone walked or dragged kitchen chairs out from under the table—revealing the dark wood beneath it. There was an old refrigerator and some scarred pine cabinets filled with the odds and ends Ma had collected over the years. There was also a massive microwave oven sitting on the counter, looking completely out of place.

We finished fueling up our tanks for the day, while quietly preparing for our great escape.

"Let's just do it," Wally whispered. "What's the worst that can happen?"

Cockroach shrugged. "I'm in," he whispered.

I remained silent, making my older brother smile.

For the past several years, my Magic 8 Ball had been responsible for most of my major decisions. During one of my tantrums, I'd smashed it. Fortunately, I was able to replace the shiny plastic ball; it was one of my first purchases from the money I earned pedaling newspapers in the rain.

Grabbing my personal adviser, I stepped into the kitchen and shook the smooth ball three times. "Should we take off for the day and head over to Lincoln Park?" I quietly asked the sage.

My answer appeared on the small triangle floating in purple fluid—*Reply hazy, try again.*

I did exactly as instructed. "Should we sneak off to Lincoln Park for the day?" I whispered.

I shook it three more times—harder this time—and took another deep breath before looking into the tiny window.

Concentrate and ask again.

I closed my eyes. *Come on now*, I thought, *I need to know if we should take the risk.* I shook the swishing ball multiple times. *Should we?* I turned it at different angles. When I finally flipped it over, I smiled.

Yes.

"Done deal," I told my brothers, "the wizard has spoken."

Wally shook his head. "You are seriously messed up."

It was a Thursday. Wally had no work and I'd already talked Vic—my best friend who we'd nicknamed Fish Stick—into covering my paper route. Although Ma would be furious about us bicycling a few towns over, my brothers and I decided, *It's so much better to ask for forgiveness than for permission on this one.*

It seemed funny to me that all three of us were wearing cutoff blue jeans, fashioned from school pants worn threadbare the year before. With a pair of scissors, Ma magically turned our fall wardrobes into mismatched summer attire.

As we headed out for the day, Ma asked, "What's the plan for today, boys?"

"Going out to play," Wally said, careful with his words.

"Just make sure you're home before the streetlights come on," she reminded us.

"Of course, Ma," I said.

As soon as we hit the driveway, we jumped on our bikes—three steel ponies—and pedaled out of the yard like we were escaping from an asylum. Lincoln Park was miles away.

The sooner we get there, the sooner we can tackle those rides!

Past the roller-skating rink and bowling alley out front, we sprinted toward the ticket gate. Murals of smiling clowns holding balloons and lollipops beckoned us inside. There was a pink booth where we purchased a *Ride-All-Day* hand stamp for $5.50. Some kids tried to get one stamp and then transfer it onto their friends' hands. *I'm not sure anyone's ever gotten away with that one.* Either way, once we had our coveted hand stamps, the land of thrill seekers, big crowds, and long lines opened up to us.

"Man, $5.50 is expensive," Cockroach commented.

"Best money you'll spend all summer," Wally reminded him.

Three steps in and a slew of stimuli nudged us into a frenzy of squeals and high-fives. Flashing lights, carnival sounds, and joyous screams filled the park. From popcorn to vomit, the smells were overwhelming. A world of vivid colors—dark reds and yellows and blues—covered everything.

Wally ran off toward the rides. "Come on!" he yelled to us.

Alphonse and I took chase.

The Dodgems, or bumper cars—famous for its epic traffic jams—was our first stop. Electric poles rubbed against the steep grated ceiling, throwing off sparks and the smell of sulfur. Throughout the ride, the operator kept yelling, "Step on the pedal and turn the wheel. Step on the pedal and turn the wheel." With Pink Floyd playing in the background, Wally and I targeted Cockroach and chased him all around the slick oval. Every time we slammed into him—jolting his back and neck—we laughed uncontrollably. At one point, Wally switched his prey and hunted me down like an escaped fugitive, smashing me into all four walls. His laughter was contagious.

The Bubble Bounce was located right beside the Dodgems. This contraption was a square car with a fixed steering wheel in the center. It spun and twirled, claiming as many victims of sudden illness as any of the rides in the park. After the second time we rode it, Cockroach's face was pale white. "I think I'm gonna ralph," he announced.

Behind the Bubble Bounce, the Teacup Ride—with its eight-foot-tall daffodil light posts—was one of the park's tamer adventures. Although Wally and I were tempted to pass it by, we gave our little brother a break and gave it a spin.

"Enjoy this while you can, Alice," I yelled at my little brother over the wind, "because we didn't come here to spin around in tea-cups."

Taking a brief reprieve from the spinning rides, we made our way over to the Giant Slide. This waxed, yellow ribbon of grooves tickled the belly more than Pop racing the station wagon down President Ave in the city. A long, steel staircase ascended toward the heavens, and the heavy swags of shag carpet draped over a rail were carried to the top. For whatever reason, I always seemed to choose the rattiest swag of carpet to go down the huge yellow slide, just like the tattered, rectangular pieces of rug in the clubhouse down at the railroad tracks.

"Just grab the next one and keep moving," the ride operator told me, his greasy mullet swaying in the breeze.

Once we received the second operator's signal, we sat on the car-pet, pushed off with both hands, and shot to the bottom in a fraction of the time it took to walk the carpet up all the stairs. *It's like sledding Sampson's Potato Farm without the freezing wind and frostbitten feet,* I decided, *and it's well worth all the work to hump up to the top.*

Next was the Paratrooper Ride. With dangling legs, we sat beneath a lighted umbrella and watched the world swing in circles. Though the ride warned of only being intended for adults, it hardly warranted another wait in line.

"Let's take a break from the rides and play a few games to win something," Cockroach suggested.

Wally shook his head. "Too rich for my blood," he said.

"Me too," I added.

"What are you guys talking about?" our little brother said. "I'm the one who doesn't have a job, remember? How can I afford to play, but you guys…"

"If you want to play games," I said, interrupting him, "then you can do it alone."

"Yeah," Wally said, "we'll just come back and get you before we head home."

"Paupers," he said under his breath.

Wally and I laughed the comment away.

Still shaking his head, Cockroach marched on without further complaint.

As we worked our way through the park, hidden speakers spouting the moans and wails of ghouls and mutants lured us in. All three of us stood abreast in front of The Monster Ride.

"This place looks a little like Fish Stick's house," Wally said.

Cockroach and I laughed in agreement.

"But not as scary," Cockroach said, already done sulking.

"I wouldn't be surprised if we saw his mother inside, frying fish in her flowered housecoat," I added, stalling.

Those who dared to ride were greeted by gaudy, lurking statues of hideous creatures with horns, sharp teeth and insane eyes. Of course, to the older, more discerning eye, the giant plaster of paris knickknacks were absolutely absurd.

As usual, Wally led me and Cockroach toward the unknown. This time, our little brother wouldn't hear of it. "Not going to happen," he said, "at least not for me."

"Come on, Scaredy-Cat," I taunted.

It didn't matter. No matter how much teasing we heaped on, Cockroach wasn't budging. "I won't sleep for weeks," he admitted, claiming a seat on the closest green bench.

"No need to wig out," Wally told him. "Just stay there. We'll be right back."

"Oh, I'm not going anywhere," he promised.

I have no doubt, I thought.

While I concealed my own fears, Wally and I shared the car with two ghosts painted on the side.

From the moment we hit the double doors and entered pitch darkness, I considered shutting my eyes and never opening them until we hit sunlight again. But I didn't.

"Do you think we should get out and hide in some corner to scare people even more?" Wally asked.

"You're the one who's not right in the head," I told him.

"Well?"

"No!"

While hideous mannequins waited in the shadows, the car took jerky turns on a track that needed a good greasing. "Eeeek," someone kept squealing in the car before us. Wally laughed.

Through all the screaming, the smells of the midway wafted in, while several rays of sunlight streamed through the cracks in the old, wooden boards. Though these reminded me that my plight was sur-real and only temporary, it still didn't matter in the devil's den. At one point, I nearly reached for Wally's hand. Thank God I resisted.

As the car came crashing through another set of double doors and back into reality, I sat up straight. Through squinted eyes, Wally and I exchanged a conquering nod.

One and done, I thought, prepared to label the ride lame if Wally insisted on another go.

A .22 caliber shooting gallery with targets of speeding boats and spinning ducks had some guys showing off their feathers. The rifle barrels were so bent, though, that the plush animals on the wall were older than most in the park. *Only someone with crossed eyes has a chance at winning here,* I thought.

"It's a waste of money," Wally said, confirming my assessment.

At the Spill the Milk game, it cost fifty cents to toss three softballs into a milk can that couldn't have possibly fit them. Beside it, there was another game where gamblers could place bets on a board of numbers, while a wheel was spun to randomly pick the winner.

"Step right up and try your luck!" heckled another carnie.

Although Cockroach lagged behind a few steps, hoping Wally and I would succumb to his wishes, we never broke stride.

At the Tiger Stand, people threw baseballs at fake tigers, hoping to knock out a few teeth and win a striped kitten. I wasn't willing to spend a week of a paperboy's wages to win a giant stuffed animal. *If Donna was here, maybe,* I thought.

Cockroach grinned at me, like he was reading my mind.

A dozen steps later, we arrived at the Tilt-A-Whirl, one of my favorite rides in the entire park. With no line, we jumped into its rainbow-colored half shell. With a steel bar resting across our laps, we began to spin in circles, while each individual car traveled its own circular track. When the ride hit a certain slant, the momentum had our car whipping around in a rush of uncontrolled madness. Wally sat on one end, I sat on the other, and Cockroach claimed the middle. Depending on the angle, each of us felt the weight of our brothers pressing against us. "Yoohooo!" We all laughed until it hurt, riding it twice more.

"I'm gonna be sick," Cockroach muttered again.

As we passed behind the giant roller coaster, we found rows of smiling families sitting in the Picnic Pavilion, eating clam cakes and chowder. The smells of onions frying on a grill and buttered sweet corn had us stop long enough to wish we had the cash.

It was an arched-roofed building with open sides, rows of long tables, and a stage at its front. Though it hosted free outdoor shows of magicians, ventriloquists, and animal shows, it also had a beer stand that sent men—like Pop—staggering through the park, red-faced and slurring their words.

"We get enough of this at home," Alphonse mumbled.

I nodded.

"You guys sure you don't want to go find Uncle Skinny in there?" Wally asked.

Laughing, we trudged on.

Throughout the park, the choices for lunch were endless: candy apples, hot dogs, fried dough, spicy Portuguese sausage, cotton candy, French fries, salt-water taffy, hamburgers, ice cream dipped in chocolate and then dipped again in fresh peanuts, thick juicy slices of watermelon, and cardboard-tasting pizza—all washed down with giant cups of iced-cold soda pop.

Not on our budget, I reminded myself, ignoring my churning gut.

We sprinted off to the Trabant, a devilish ride that used a spinning motion like a penny spun on its flat side. As if it wasn't enough that the ride spun quickly in circles, the platform raised and tilted midway into the journey. Even the most iron stomachs were sure to be tested on this sadistic contraption. We looked at each other.

"Let's ride the Carousel," Cockroach suggested, his eyes pleading for a consensus.

"Not a chance," Wally said.

"Not happening, baby boy," I added.

Bravely ignoring us, Cockroach still jumped on.

Wally turned to me. "Let's just leave him here."

Considering it, I decided against it. "Too many strangers around, Wally," I said, "and if something bad happened to him…"

"I know," Wally interrupted. "I know. Ma and Pop would kill us."

Hand-painted panels along the outside roof depicted murals of yesteryears, while hundreds of mirrors and clear light bulbs decorated the inside. Though the majestic carousel had lions and tigers mixed in, horses posed in various positions were the coveted prize. As a brass bell sounded the beginning, the sweet notes of a calliope and the beat of a marching band set them off on their course. Cockroach was smiling like he'd just stepped into the living room on Christmas morning.

Damn, Alphonse, I thought, *even with all those brains, you're still just a little boy.*

Attempting to redeem his childish sense of honor, Cockroach jumped off the Carousel before it came to a complete stop. "That was terrifying," he joked, hoping we'd laugh.

"It was even harder to watch from here," Wally said, his face serious, "trust me."

I started laughing. "Do you want to head for Kiddie Land next, Alphonse?"

He shook his head.

"Are you sure?"

"Stop being such a hoser," he snapped back.

This time, Wally laughed. "I don't think you used that word correctly, Cockroach," he said, "but I like your spirit."

As we walked the busy midway, I realized that—even this early in the season—people came in droves to experience the thrill rides and crooked games of chance. Many our age were sporting bright neon colors or novelty T-shirts of popular rock bands like AC/DC and Queen.

At a sprint, we headed toward the Flying Cages.

This test of strength and endurance usually catered to adult men. The idea was to stand upright within the heavy steel cage and work its weight back and forth by pushing against the padded bars at the front and back. Each time Wally, Cockroach, and I pushed, the cage climbed higher toward the top in a circular motion. If enough momentum was gained, we'd be able to muscle our weight, as well as the weight of the cage, right over the top—and keep going.

There's no way we're ever going to make it over the top, I thought. *Men twice our size can't power the cages to go all the way around.*

I was right. Although we managed to reach the peak a few times, we were never able to push the steel contraption over. As a souvenir, Wally's hands got torn up pretty bad.

Damn it, he muttered, looking at his raw mitts. *I'm gonna have to hide these when we get home.*

The Round Up was a twisted invention designed for the brave of heart. The three of us stood back and watched for a minute.

It looked like a UFO turned sideways, red and yellow lights spinning out of control, human screams escaping from within. Essentially, each rider stood upright while the ride spun in circles so fast that gravity sucked them flush to its steel-caged wall.

"Let's do it, boys!" Wally said, egging us on.

There was a pause.

"You big chickens," he said.

Against my better judgment, I jumped in line. *Oh boy,* I thought, *there's a good chance I'm gonna barf on this one,*

Cockroach, however, stood on the sidelines once again. Seeing this, I started to wonder whether he had more courage than I did. *At least he's not caving in to this stupid peer pressure,* I thought. The line moved closer, making it nearly impossible for me to change my mind and bail out.

Starting at a tilt, the ride lifted vertically until our bodies were parallel to the blurry ground beneath us. Wally pulled his Velcro wallet from his pocket and held on tight. Two minutes later, the world was one big smudge. *What a mistake!* I thought.

Before the ride came to a stop, I felt like I was going to start projectile vomiting. Wally managed to turn his head to look over at me. Through the queasiness, I managed a fake smile.

"You okay?" he yelled at me, being sarcastic.

"Go ahead and laugh," I yelled back. "Your face is the same color as the Jolly Green Giant's."

His grin disappeared.

"Okay, Alphonse," Wally said, as we rallied back on the midway, "even though you don't deserve it, we'll give you a break and go check out some of the arcade games."

The first signs of relief appeared in Cockroach's face.

What a bullshit artist, I thought, studying my older brother. *He's the one who feels sick and needs to take a break.*

Lit up with neon, like a mini-Las Vegas, the penny arcade hosted a popular game called Fascination. Each player rolled small balls under a plate of glass and into holes to form straight or diagonal lines. Though winners were paid in coupons to be redeemed for prizes or cash, each game cost ten cents and proved much too expensive for our young Velcro wallets. Instead, we settled for a few rounds of skeeball and the newest video games.

At the end of the arcade, kids squirted streams of water into a row of clowns' mouths until the first balloon broke. The squealing winner picked a small stuffed polar bear. Wally snickered before hurrying off to race the remote-control cars at the park's miniature speedway.

Wally's got a real need for speed, I thought.

As we walked out of the arcade, Cockroach spotted a crank machine that completely removed Abe Lincoln's face by stretching pennies and stamping the words *Lincoln Park* into the center of them. As he opened his mouth to share his idea, Wally and I bombarded him with ridicule.

"Stop being such a Nancy," I told him.

"I swear, Cockroach," Wally said, "just because you still have your baby teeth…"

"I don't have my baby teeth," he argued.

I nodded. "You do," I said, instigating him more.

"I don't have baby teeth," he mumbled under his breath, as we stepped out of the neon playground.

"Sometimes I wonder if you should have been born a girl," Wally told him.

"You guys suck," he barked back, "I wasn't even going to…"

"Sure you weren't, Nancy," I interrupted. "If you want to press a penny, we'll head down to the railroad tracks."

We approached the Scrambler, located across from the Ferris wheel.

"It's the Ferris wheel for me," Wally announced.

"Okay poser," I said, jumping into the Scrambler line. "Go ahead and pick the lame ride, if you want. I'm hitting the Scrambler."

"Whatever," he said, while Cockroach reluctantly tagged along with him.

Surrendering to another spinning ride was a terrible risk, but I was more than happy to take it. One of my greatest fears—remaining well concealed from my brothers—was the dreaded Ferris wheel. Although I'd labeled the ride 'lame,' I always feared I'd get stuck on it—all the way up top—while my maniac brother rocked the car back and forth. *What if we can't get off?* Even the thought of it caused a wave of panic to swell inside me.

The wait wasn't long for either ride, and while the world became a blur for me once again, I concentrated on trying to watch my brothers. As they ascended in their purple swaying car, as expected, Wally began rocking the car back and forth at the top. *Cockroach must be freaking out,* I thought, picturing him clenching the bar tight. *I know I would be.*

A few torturous minutes later, we met in the middle of the midway again.

"Wally's a jackass," Alphonse reported.

"I saw."

"Such a donkey," he repeated.

"Say it one more time," Wally said, "and I swear I'll..."

"Let's hit the roller coaster," I said, cutting him off to save our brother.

Although Cockroach cringed, Wally grinned. "Now you're talking my language, Herbie. Let's do this!"

Turning south, we marched the length of the midway—past Kiddie Land with its WhirlyBird helicopters, Big Ducks and Mother Goose rides, and tiny motorboats that went round and round in four inches of filthy water.

The moment of truth has finally arrived, I thought, already struggling to beat back my growing fear.

The Comet was a rickety old wooden roller coaster from hell, which had long served as a rite of passage and the greatest test of courage for children in southeastern New England. Standing in the middle of the midway, with the kiddie coaster on the right and Mini-Golf on the left, the only real decision of the day needed to be made.

"I'll watch you guys from here," Cockroach said, plopping down on another green bench, with no intention of going anywhere. Wally and I looked at each other. While little kids chased each other in circles on The Flying Jets—raising and lowering their planes but never getting an inch closer to the jet in front of them—the decision was made. *I need to do this.* The time had come to take the risk and overcome another one of my fears.

"Let's do it!" I blurted, feeling once again like I might throw up.

I stepped up to the wooden cutout of a boy who announced that each rider needed to be at least his height to ride. *Drats!* I'd made it. *I'm finally tall enough.* As Wally and I stepped in line, others filled in behind us. More fear took hold. *We're trapped*, I thought. With sweaty palms, I took a few steps closer. As the coaster shot its latest riders up and down its steep hills, the rickety wooden structure creaked and complained. Each step took me deeper into a war being waged between my heart and mind. Everything inside me begged my legs to flee. My pride, however, held on—just barely. People screamed on the ride.

This is supposed to be fun? I thought.

Before long, Wally and I stepped up to the final platform's worn boards. *Thousands, maybe even millions of people, have done this and survived,* I told myself. It was no consolation. As my mind raced, I recalled Ma and Pop speak of those who rode the coaster with reverence and respect. Swallowing hard, I took another step forward. I wanted that respect.

Our French grandfather, Pepere, suddenly spotted us. Lifting the soft hat off his forehead, he addressed us past his half-chewed cigar. "Your mother know you guys are at the park today?" he asked.

While I said, "Yes," Wally simultaneously went with the truth. "No," he admitted.

"Actually, I told her just before we left the house," I blurted, compounding the lie.

The old-timer studied our faces for a few moments, scanning back and forth like some police searchlight. Finally, he shot us a wink, letting us know that our secret was safe with him.

Considering how seldom the man speaks, I thought, *it's a pretty good bet that we won't get busted.*

Wally and I stood before the tracks, while the train of old cars fired down the home stretch and screeched to a sudden stop. Everyone's faces were white. While the passengers climbed out onto unsure legs, I swallowed hard again. It was time to get aboard. Wally went first; and though I followed, I felt like crying.

"Good luck," my big brother joked.

"Same to you," I replied, before pulling a steel bar across our laps.

As Pepere bent to tug on the safety bar, my frightened eyes searched his for help. He winked at me again, offering a grin that said everything was going to be fine. He walked slowly and with purpose to his podium. With one last look at the cars, he pulled on a long wooden handle that caused the train to belch out a gasp of air. He then pulled on a second handle, and the cars began to coast forward. White knuckles threatened to crush the safety bar. There was time for a brief prayer, and then the hyperventilating began.

Through a short patch of forest, the cars rounded the first bend. A thick steel chain grabbed the front car and jerked it violently into control. There was a brief, merciful pause, and then the cars began to ascend slowly toward heaven, the chain clicking off each final moment of life. The sky was blue, spotted with a few marshmallow clouds. My body felt numb. My mind rushed from primitive panic all the way to surreal acceptance. Perhaps shock had already set in. I gave one quick look toward Wally, my riding companion. Fake smiles were exchanged. At the top, the cars paused briefly again. This time, it felt cruel.

I held my breath. Like a nightmare come true, the car plummeted down the notorious first hill, straight toward the earth. The fall lasted no more than a moment and no less than a lifetime. The hill was longer than expected and lasted well beyond the screams of those who chose to exhale. On empty lungs, we hit bottom before being catapulted back up to an invisible turn. *Oh shit!* Thinking we were going right off the track, I struggled to roll myself into the fetal position. The lap bar would not allow it. The turn was just another sick joke from the ride's inhumane designer.

Gravity took over. While the wooden boards swayed and moaned from the weight of the cars and their uncontrolled momentum, premature questions of life and death were considered. The train of cars then rolled home, where Pepere was waiting to apply the shrieking brake.

On rubbery knees, we climbed out. I was breathing again, thrilled to be a survivor. *Yes!* I screamed in my head. I'd finally conquered the giant, and so much more than that. The entire experience was exhilarating, filled with equal amounts of fear and excitement.

Wally turned to me and grinned. "Go again?"

I nodded. "Oh yeah!"

We went four more times, checking in on Cockroach between each ride. I couldn't understand it, but the little man was content to sit in the shade and watch.

After our last run, Pepere asked, "Have you guys eaten today?"

This time, both Wally and I went with the truth.

The old timer reached into his back pocket and pulled out a worn leather wallet. Retrieving a ten-dollar bill, he handed it to Wally. "Make sure all three of you get something in your bellies," he said, "and split it evenly."

Out of Pepere's earshot, Cockroach suggested, "Let's just split the money."

Wally nodded. "We've waited this long to eat. What's another hour or so?"

After making change at one of the vendor's booths, I pocketed my third. "I wonder what Ma's making for supper?"

Cockroach nodded. "Whatever it is, it's free."

It was nearly dusk when Lincoln Park lit up with neon. There were so many flashing lights that they actually generated heat.

"We need to leave," Wally told us.

Without any objections, we hustled off toward our bicycles.

"Make sure you lick your hands and wipe those handstamps off before we get home," Wally further instructed us, "or we'll definitely get pinched."

"Says the guy with the giant blisters on his palms," Cockroach muttered under his breath.

It was getting dark when we started pedaling for home—double time. My bike and Wally's bike—Schwinn and Huffy—were outfitted with lights and baskets for newspaper routes. These steel horses were used for work, as well as for pleasure. Atop his banana seat, Cockroach rode in the middle of our convoy, like the third member of C.H.I.P.S. While Wally illuminated the sidewalk ahead of us, my bike provided a taillight, keeping speeding cars from running us down and killing us all.

"Keep up!" I kept yelling at Cockroach's rear tire, even when he was doing good.

"I am," he yelled back.

"Keep your head straight," I barked at him.

I then watched as he lifted his right hand off the handlebars to throw me the bird.

You little bastard, I thought, smiling. *It's about time.*

•••

We returned home later than planned.

Standing at the stove, Ma nonchalantly looked our way. "Go wash your hands," she said, "supper will be on the table in a few minutes."

Looks like we're in the clear, I thought.

I stepped into the bathroom, where the freckled linoleum was now yellowed and severely worn. A small shag carpet wrapped around the toilet, with a matching swag covering the tank lid. The seat was made of faux wood. A brown wicker hamper housed a mix of rancid smells; when opened, it emitted a similar scent of a diaper Genie. We became impressively quick with our dirty deposits. Besides the lion claw tub, there was an old porcelain sink, which had been stained to off-white over many years.

Cockroach was washing his hands like he was preparing to perform surgery. I quickly surveyed his scrawny arms hanging from his tank top. He was wearing tattoos now; they were temporary, but high end. *This kid's too much,* I thought.

Dirty and tired, Pop returned home from work and plopped down into his kitchen chair. The Formica kitchenette table, surrounded by six pleather chairs—two of them mended with black electrical tape—was the family hub.

Good thing we washed our hands, I thought, when I spotted Wally wearing a pair of winter gloves with the fingers cut off. *Oh brother.*

Pop gawked at him. "What's up with the gloves, Michal Jackson?"

Before he could answer, Ma asked, "So where have you boys been all day?"

Oh crap, I thought. She wasn't making eye contact with any of us. My hackles rose. *This feels like a trap.*

"We went down to the railroad tracks and played," Cockroach said, still too young to understand the dangerous game.

Ma looked at Wally.

He's got no choice, I thought. *Wally has to cover Spaz's lie.*

Placing his gloved hands beneath the table, my big brother nodded that it was true.

Ma slammed the pot of spaghetti and meatballs onto the table. "Is that right," she said, her voice a full octave higher, "because that's not what your Pepere just told Memere!"

Damn that old man! I thought, feeling more disappointed than afraid. *What the hell was that wink for?*

"You guys were at Lincoln Park all day, weren't you?"

Pop finally looked up from his daze, amused.

"And you all lied to me," she said, furious. "That's it, you're all grounded!"

I began to open my mouth when Pop saved me from making things even worse.

"Stop bullin', Emma," he said, clearing his throat, "I think you should cut these boys some slack. Summer's just started and they were only…"

"They were two towns over, Walt," she hissed, interrupting him, "and they should be punished for it."

Pop looked at us. "Did you guys stay together today?" Before we could even answer, he gestured toward Cockroach. "Did you watch after your brother?"

Wally and I vowed that we did.

Our father studied our eyes until he was satisfied that we were now telling the truth. "Okay then." He looked toward our mother. "If we're voting, then I say this'll be their one and only freebee for the summer."

That gets my vote, I thought.

"But Walt," Ma objected.

"You don't think we should give them a break just this once?" he asked her.

I looked at my brothers. From their faces, they were just as shocked. It felt like we'd hired Atticus Finch to defend us, and he was starting to win our case.

Ma remained silent, a miraculous sign that she'd succumbed to his argument.

Pop's head snapped our way. "Don't you dare lie to your mother again, you got me?" he concluded, his tone louder and seemingly angry.

Three grinning heads nodded.

The old man's just putting on a show for Ma now, I decided.

"If you're men enough to head out of town for the day, then you should be men enough to own that decision."

I took a bite of Ma's homemade meatball, which was basically her mini-French onion soup meatloaf. I thought about this for a few moments. *He's right,* I realized.

"I'm sorry we lied to you," Cockroach said, breaking the silence.

"Yeah, sorry Ma," I added, while Wally surrendered with a few nods.

She dished out more food. "Just don't let it happen again," she sighed.

There was silence for a few moments, everyone eating.

"I rode The Comet for the first time today," I finally announced.

"You did?" Pop asked, looking across his suspended fork at Wally.

My big brother nodded. "He did—five times."

I nodded. "It was one of the scariest things I've ever done, but I did it."

Whether she wanted to show it or not, Ma matched Pop's smile—making me do the same.

So, this is what respect feels like? I thought, realizing that the pay-off was worth every second of torment.

I was still basking in the warmth, when Wally removed his gloves and showed his bloody palms to our parents. "And I got this from the Flying Cages."

Ma gagged at the sight of it.

"Did you get the cage over the top?" Pop asked.

Wally shook his disappointed head. "We almost did, but..."

The old man snickered, halting any further explanation. "Give it another year or two," he said. "You'll get it."

• • •

Each night, without fail, I talked to Donna for ten minutes on the telephone. It would have been much longer, but my mother had imposed the time limit. Our drab green phone was her best friend, and she hated to be away from it for long.

Although the spiral cord on the kitchen's rotary phone could reach the living room, it still wasn't long enough for me to enjoy a moment of privacy—not ever.

Calling out is such a pain now, I thought. The telephone company was now requiring that everyone dial seven numbers instead of five.

"Hey Donna," I said when she answered on the first ring.

"Hi Herbie, I'm glad you called."

"I did it," I blurted, trying to sound cool.

"Did what?" she asked.

"I rode The Comet today for the first time."

"What's The Comet?"

I laughed, thinking, *You must be joking.*

"Seriously, what is it?" she asked.

"The giant roller coaster at Lincoln Park." This time I sounded cocky, even though I didn't mean to.

"You did not."

"I did."

"You're serious, aren't you?"

"Yup."

"You're nuts." she said, "I don't care how old I get, I don't think I'll ever ride that coaster. That thing looks so scary." She paused. "How bad was it?"

"It was pretty hairy, that's for sure, but I survived it—five times."

"My hero," she purred.

I was just starting to beam when I heard Ma call out, "Okay, Herbie, time's up!"

I immediately covered the phone's receiver, so Donna wouldn't hear my mother's rant.

"You've been on for more than ten minutes already," she added, getting louder with each word, "and I need to talk to Aunt Phyllis."

Need to talk to Aunt Phyllis about what? I thought. *Whatever went wrong in her life today?*

"Are you still there?" I heard Donna ask, yanking me back into our conversation.

"Yeah, sorry. Listen, I have to go. My mother has a *very import-ant* phone call she needs to make."

Ma sneered at me.

"Oh, okay," Donna said. "I'll talk to you tomorrow."

"I can't wait," I whispered.

Stepping closer to me, my mother extended her hand.

Hearing the dial tone, I handed the phone over to her. "All yours, Ma."

She nodded. "That's right, Herbie, it is all mine and you'd be smart to remember that."

Although I still couldn't understand why, Ma talked to Aunt Phyllis for about an hour on the telephone every night. "Guess where my three little angels went today without permission?" she asked. Lighting a fresh cigarette, she nodded. "So, Ma already told you, then?" She took a long drag. "Can you just imagine the gall of these boys to just head off without..."

That does it for me, I thought, dashing off to the safety of my bedroom. *I don't need to hear another word about it.*

CHAPTER 4

JUNE 1984

JUST BUMMING AROUND

We slept in, as usual—which was awesome because we really enjoyed sleeping as late as humanly possible. I could never understand why Ma allowed it. *I guess when we're sleeping, we're quiet.*

Ma tried everything she could to slow us down from the mountains of breakfast cereal we devoured. She began buying the Jumbo assortment pack from Kellogg's, eighteen individual boxes of cereal: Raisin Bran, Sugar Pops, Cornflakes, Cocoa Krispies, Sugar Smacks, Apple Jacks, Frosted Flakes, Froot Loops. Of course, the heavily sweetened cereals went first, followed by Cornflakes, Rice Krispies, and Special K, each one requiring two teaspoons of granulated sugar before a drop of milk ever hit the pastel Tupperware bowl.

It's probably a good thing we're back to the basics for a while, I thought. The week before, I'd eaten a full box of Boo Berry cereal. It was one of my favorites, until I'd forgotten I'd eaten it and started pooping blueish-green the following day. *Now that'll freak anyone out.*

Without a clue as to where he was going, Wally jumped onto his Schwinn ten-speed and pedaled off into the neighborhood, leaving Cockroach and me in his dust.

"When did you realize that we were poor?" Cockroach asked me without warning.

"The third grade," I told him right away. I didn't even have to think about it. It was stupid, I knew, but the spelling bee that I'd lost in the third grade still haunted me. I could picture that fateful day as vividly as when I'd suffered it.

. . .

I'd outlasted the entire class and was now head-to-head with Paula, the brainiac in the class.

"Spell cheese," Mrs. Parsons told me.

I smiled, thinking, *Easy one.* "C H E E Z E."

Mrs. Parsons shook her head. "Sorry, Herbie, but that's incorrect."

What? I thought. *It can't be.* My mind raced to visualize every cheese product in my house. *C H E E Z E*, I repeated in my head. *I'm right!*

Emerging from my fog, I listened as Paula delivered a different version. "C H E E S E."

Mrs. Parsons nodded. "Congratulations, Paula, that's correct. You're our new spelling bee champion!"

Half the class—specifically the girls—erupted in cheers.

No way! I thought. *Can't be!* I still couldn't believe it.

Returning home, I scoured Ma's kitchen, studying one cheese by-product after the other. The truth suddenly dawned on me. I was being raised in a low-budget, generic household. *Damn*, I thought, *fake 'cheeze' cost me the spelling bee title.*

On the upside, I suddenly learned that I respected intellect much more than brawn or athletic ability.

•••

I returned from my brief stroll down memory lane and looked at my little brother. "Definitely the third grade," I told him.

He shrugged it off. "So, what do you want to do today?" he asked, grabbing one of his tiny plastic paratroopers from his front pocket.

I shrugged. "I don't know. Maybe…"

Cockroach threw the green, faceless soldier straight up into the air. The soldier's arms and legs flailed, the parachute's thread-like strings tied to the rings sprouting from its poor plastic head. For years, we threw these brave warriors airborne, watching them float back down to earth. Every time I witnessed this, I couldn't wait to grow up and join the army. *And wipe out all the bad guys!*

Suddenly, it came to me. "Let's play lawn darts," I told him.

He nodded.

We hustled off to the shed to grab the dangerous game.

While some kids played dungeons and dragons, my brothers and I never did. For us, the nerdy game wasn't physically violent enough. Besides that, my brothers and I didn't possess the intellectual capacity. We were more of a 'lawn darts and blindfolds' kind of a crew.

When we reached the shed, we had to pull several items—a Christmas tree stand, a heavy box of tangled lights, a pair of old winter boots—off the flat box. The Lawn Darts game, or Jarts, had come in a colorful cardboard box that claimed, *A game of fun and skill for all ages.*

I sometimes wondered what Ma was thinking when she'd gift wrapped the lethal toy. "It's for all three of you," she'd announced, as she did for every large gift we unwrapped on Christmas morning.

As I carried it out of the shed, I read the caption on the back: *Lawn darts is a lawn game for two players or teams. A lawn dart set includes four large darts and two targets. The game play and objective are similar to both horseshoes and darts.*

I chuckled, thinking, *Yeah, right!*

Hula hoop-like plastic rings were supplied as targets for the long, heavy darts. Instead, we used those for wrestling props or piggyback harnesses—anything but their intended purpose.

The days of playing in Ma's clothesline, amongst her drying laundry, were gone. The days of her yelling at us, however, were still alive and well. I made sure we played where she couldn't watch us from any of the apartment's second-floor windows.

As if the lawn darts were small plastic soldiers, we hurled them straight into the air as high as we could. We then tracked their path back to the earth, squealing with delight and running out of the way—except for the few times when we lost the dart in the sun's blinding glare. During those thrilling and heart-stopping moments, we had to gamble on which direction to flee. There were a couple of close calls, but those only seemed to make the game that much more exciting.

"We should probably be wearing helmets," Alphonse suggested.

I nodded. "I agree, if we owned helmets."

"Can you imagine if one of us got hit with one of these things?" Cockroach said.

"You probably wouldn't even know what hit you," I said, turning it back on him.

"What do you mean?" he asked.

"You'd probably be on your way to meet Grampa before you ever knew what hit you," I said, trying not to grin.

My little brother's eyes became distant, as he contemplated whether to add lawn darts to his long list of fears: the old butcher at the grocery store, aliens coming through the window and abducting us—*thanks, Close Encounters*—and that weird person watching him through our second-floor bedroom window while we slept.

"You want to quit?" I asked him.

He shrugged, surprising me. "Nah," he said, "I miss Grampa. It'd be good to see him again."

I laughed. *Good for you, brother,* I thought, while he giggled. *You're growing up.*

Without warning, he hurled a lawn dart straight into the air, making us run for our lives.

"I'm coming, Grampa!" he screamed, nearly collapsing me in the kill zone from laughter.

Cockroach and I were taking a break, grabbing a drink from the garden hose, when we heard a familiar screech.

The hose was still running when we dropped it and ran for the front of the house.

Ma was calling from the window, loud enough for the deaf lady who lived a few houses down to hear her. "Alphonse!" she called out, desperately, "Alphonse!" Once again, she sounded like she was in real distress.

We're gonna hear this all summer, I realized.

Abandoning the game, our little brother high-tailed it for the house.

"Hurry up, baby boy," I teased him, walking back to the hose.

He stopped, looked back, and smiled. "I need to restock anyway."

Curious to see the shyster at work, I told him, "You know what, I think I'll tag along with you for this run." I hurried to shut off the hose, so I could shadow him.

Back in the house, Ma placed her order. "Get a gallon of milk and a pack of hamburger buns," she told Cockroach, "I'm making Steak-Umms later." She looked off into the distance, clearly running through a list in her head.

I love Steak Umms, I thought.

She nodded. "And grab me three packs of..."

"Carlton 100s," Cockroach finished for her, hurrying out the door to run up her tab.

Time for Ebenezer to restock, I thought, following him. *I can't even imagine what Ma's tab is up to now with this little criminal doing her shopping.*

Considering that Cockroach was a frequent shopper at the school's lost-and-found box, scoring some very nice items throughout the year, I knew that nothing was beyond his reach. I laughed, considering my brother's bargain hunting. *At first, Ma questioned where he'd gotten the new clothes—gloves, hats—but he just told her that he'd borrowed the stuff from a friend.* I shook my head. *She doesn't even ask anymore.* I laughed, knowing that Cockroach had probably been in the main office at least once a week during the school year, browsing for new stock.

I returned from the daydream and snickered. *The little conman must be fleecing Ma blind.*

• • •

The corner store—R&S Variety—sat on the corner of State Road and Wilbur Avenue, the place where we got our discreet fix for a bad sweet tooth. Outside, a Coca-Cola machine and a pull-knob cigarette machine stood guard on either side of the front door, while a padlocked Sunbeam Bread bin—with a young, red-headed girl painted on the front—sat on the side of the small brick build-ing. *Old Man Sedgeband is a greedy weasel,* I thought. *The cigarette and Coke machines are making money for him, even when this dump is closed.*

The heavy door swung open, triggering a brass bell that warned Mr. Sedgeband that he had a customer. As usual, it took my eyes a few seconds to adjust to the darkness. The store's windows, papered in old advertisements, were so filthy that only a few shards of sunlight were able to finagle their way in.

Beyond the candy case, old plank floorboards led to outdated displays that offered even more outdated goods. The short stacks of cans and bottles were covered in several seasons of dust. The mag-azine rack was ancient, though it hardly mattered when it came to the comic books. A toy selection included paddle balls, jacks, yoyos, whiffle ball bats, and balls. For last-minute gifts, you could choose from nail clippers, plastic combs (though no one bought them because they looked used), nylons, playing cards, or corncob pipes. The one-shelf pharmacy offered feminine supplies and condoms, causing embarrassed giggles. There was also aspirin, band-aids, and rubbing alcohol. For some of the neighborhood parents, Sedgeband carried rolling papers and cheap wine. For our parents, he was kind enough to stock quarts of Narragansett, Schaeffer, and Miller High Life beer, as well as cartons of Carlton 100s.

At most convenience stores in town, shoes and shirts were

required. *But not at R&S Variety. Only cash is required here—the more, the better.*

The geezer was standing behind his scarred wooden counter, playing a game of checkers with his mute friend, Oscar.

"Hi Mr. Sedgeband," Cockroach called out.

I'm not sure how, but the wrinkled old goat scowled even more. *I wonder how much money it would take to make the android smile?* I thought about it for a moment. *I bet it would cost a mint.*

While my brother headed toward the back of the shop to do Ma's bidding, I bent at the waist to gawk into the penny candy case. Wax lips, root beer barrels, pixie sticks, Swedish fish, fireballs, Bazooka bubble gum—all the old favorites were there. Even the wax bottles, where you bit off the tip and sucked out the few drops of colored sugar water, were in stock. For the first time in my young life, I scoffed at the tiny sweets housed within the magical glass case. Snickering to myself, I smugly moved on to the full candy bars. *I'm a working man now*, I thought. *Penny candy is for kids.*

"Are you gonna make a decision today?" Old Man Sedgeband asked, waiting behind the counter with a small brown paper bag.

I looked up at him. *If it wasn't for the Coke bottle glasses and those overgrown bushes sticking out of his ears, he might even look like a nice old man,* I thought, smiling at him. "I am," I answered, continuing to take my time.

R&S Variety was the land of passive-aggressive behavior—from both sides of the counter.

While Cockroach continued to shop, I paced back and forth a few times, weighing my options. I looked past the tasteless flying saucers, black licorice gum, and rolls of paper dot candy, until finally deciding on a pink can of Bubble Tape, a box of Lemonheads, two packs of Pop Rocks, a bottle of RC Cola, and a sleeve of Mentos, the last two items intended for a long overdue science project.

As I placed my loot onto the counter, Sedgeband's alien eyes followed my every step. With a huff, he dropped the small brown paper bag onto the glass penny case and dragged his feet over to his humongous cash register.

While he rang up my purchases, I couldn't help but smile. *No tab for me*, I thought, still excited over the novelty of earning my own money. *I pay cash.*

Cockroach stepped up behind me, both of his arms full. *Holy crap*, I thought, shocked at his level of greed. Although he held Ma's gallon of milk and pack of hamburger buns, the rest was for him: A pouch of Big League Chew—*which I'd never even considered throwing on Ma's tab*—a pack of Bottle Caps and a grape whistle pop. He also had a package of Funny Bones, a yellow bag of Fritos corn chips, and a glass bottle of Yoo-hoo chocolate drink.

You've gotta be kidding me! I shook my head. *Maybe he's opening his own store?*

"And give me three packs of Carlton 100s," he told the undertaker behind the brass register, "all on my mother's tab."

Old Man Sedgeband offered a couple shakes of his disgusted head. "If I don't get a payment soon, you and your mother are shut off."

"No sweat," Cockroach said, sounding like a seasoned mobster, "I'll get you your money."

I could feel my bottom jaw drop open.

"Alphonse, you're too much," I told him, stepping back out into the blinding sun, "and you take way too much."

"You used to put things on Ma's tab when you ran to the store for her!" he said, quick to defend himself.

"Yeah I did, but I wasn't looking to land her in the poor house." I was surprised to hear my mother's own words return to me. "I can't even imagine what her tab's at now."

He was silent.

"What is it?" I prodded.

He half-shrugged. "Just over forty bucks," he said.

"Oh, my God," I gasped, adding a whistle. "She's gonna lose her mind."

"Not if she doesn't find out," he said, searching my face for a promise of discretion.

"She won't hear it from me," I vowed.

He exhaled deeply, obviously feeling relieved. "It's not like you didn't leave me your debt when I picked up the store runs from you," he reminded me.

I stopped in my tracks. "Get real! When I handed it over, Ma owed just over nine bucks. That's it! You're the one who decided to commit highway robbery."

"Whatever, Q-bert," he said.

"Let me get a sip of that Yoo-hoo you stole from Ma," I told him. He hesitated.

"Better for me to ask you here than when we get home, Gumby."

"Fine," he said, aggravated. "Just a little one." He pulled the bottle of chocolate water out of the large paper bag, cracked it open and took the first sip—a long one. Although it was killing him, he handed over the sweet drink.

With his eyes peeled on me, from the time I put the cold glass to my lips, I started chugging. "Herbie!" He went off like a steam whistle.

It was the first time he ever fought me—or attempted to anyway. I finished the drink in two long chugs, pivoting my body away from him with each chug, while he wailed away on my sides and back.

I was so proud of him that I marched right back into R&S and bought him a new one.

"It's about time you stuck up for yourself," I said, handing him a fresh Yoo-hoo. "Wally's gonna be proud."

Still panting in the heat, he took his first sip, grinning the proudest grin I'd ever seen him wear. *Good for you, Butch Cassidy*, I thought, *you little thief.*

• • •

I was preparing for our latest adventure in the middle of our yard when I heard some loud music approach. I paused to investigate.

Vic rode his bike with an old boom box duct-taped to the handlebars, Def Leppard's *Photograph* rockin' hard from his iron steed.

"It's Fish Stick," Cockroach announced.

Very observative, I thought, snickering.

My best friend sped into our yard, Miami Vice-style. I watched as he jumped off the bike, turned off the radio, and retrieved a switchblade comb from his back pocket. For the next minute or so, he ran that comb again and again through his panther-black hair. I had to laugh, thinking, *Nobody's a bigger fan of Vic than Vic.*

As he dismounted, I noticed that he'd been riding barefooted. Given that the bike's pedals were made of steel with razor sharp teeth, it was a real commitment to cruise around shoeless.

Barefoot but fully groomed, he approached. "What are you dorks up to?"

"We're going to do a science project," Cockroach told him.

"Screw that," Vic said. "We just got out of school a few weeks ago. There's no way I want to…"

"It's a different kind of science project, dweeb," I clarified.

He took a knee beside me, where I showed him the sleeve of peppermint Mentos and a liter bottle of RC Cola. "Oh, I'm in!" he said, already giggling.

We were easily amused and just as easily satisfied.

Unwilling to waste the entire bottle, we each took a long sip of the cola. That's when I was unanimously nominated to drop a couple of Mentos into the narrow neck of the bottle. *I got this*, I thought, thinking I could just slip the candy discs into the plastic two-liter before back-pedaling a safe distance away. Boy, was I wrong. No sooner did I drop in the candy, when the instantaneous reaction produced the most glorious geyser we'd ever seen—and worn. While Vic and Cockroach were sprayed with the sweet, sticky liquid, I was saturated. There was no way I could have run fast enough—or far enough away—to avoid the syrupy shower.

Vic licked his arm. "I love RC Cola," he said. "What a waste."

As Old Faithful simmered down to a pathetic dribble, Wally rode his bike onto the lawn, skidding to a sideways stop right in front of us.

I jumped away from him like a skittish cat. Summer had just begun and my shins were already black and blue from banging into steel bike pedals.

"You guys are such ass clowns," he said, surveying the scene.

"We considered the superglue and toothpaste prank, but figured you'd have a cow," Cockroach confessed.

Wally's eyes went wide. "Consider yourselves lucky then," he said.

The rest of us nodded.

"Do you wanna take a tour of Oriental Pearl?" Wally asked out of the blue.

"Yes!" all three of us answered.

"I was talking to Herbie," he said, drawing two wounded moans. "I'll take you when you're a little older," he told Cockroach, ignoring Vic like he was less visible than Casper the Friendly Ghost.

"Of course I want to go," I said, trying to temper my excitement. *Is this real*, I wondered, *or is it Memorex?*

Cockroach and Fish Stick groaned again, unhappy they'd been kicked to the curb.

"Then go change your shirt," he said, "I'm not taking you anywhere looking like that."

Okay, Ma, I thought, hurrying off to the house to grab a dry t-shirt. "You guys clean up," I yelled back to Vic and Cockroach.

"Clean what up?" Vic asked.

"Just get rid of the evidence, you knucklehead."

The Oriental Pearl's exterior neon sign pulsated with a giant pearl that hovered between two fire-breathing dragons.

Happy to show off, Wally kicked off the tour of his new workplace. "Just keep your mouth shut and don't touch anything," he warned me.

Yeah, whatever, boss, I thought. "You think you're the cat's ass now," I muttered under my breath.

"What's that?" he asked, instinctively shuffling his feet to take an aggressive posture.

"Nothing," I mumbled.

Inside the heavy glass doors, a thick plush carpet with swirls of red and orange covered every inch of the floor, while red and gold foil—accented in jade green—papered the walls. Big-belly Buddhas and tall bamboo plants complemented the décor throughout. Light fixtures were made of hand-painted rice paper, or some material fabricated to resemble it. The bamboo partitions, separating several dining stations, were covered in the same material. Paper place-mats printed with the Chinese horoscope allowed folks to discover whether they were born during the year of the dog, rat, pig, or snake while they waited for their bowls of steaming lo mein and crispy egg rolls. And it was always loud in the place. Adult laughter was aided by empty Mai Tai glasses and scorpion bowls for two, while most children were essentially left unattended to play and scream.

I'd been in the place a hundred times, but this time felt different. *Gaudy can't even begin to describe this joint*, I thought. Yet, it was a favorite restaurant in town and a frequent stop for our family. In all my years of enjoying the flaming pupu platters and shrimp fried rice, I'd never imagined seeing where and how it was made. *This is so rad*, I thought, my excitement growing with each step forward.

Past the front counter—its glass case featuring souvenirs such as Geisha girl dolls, scroll calendars, Chinese fans, and boxes of fortune cookies available in both chocolate and cardboard flavors—a ramp led to the kitchen. Red swinging doors opened into the bustling kitchen, where a maroon tile floor was covered in a film of grease. I quickly realized that I needed to watch my step.

Wally headed straight for the dishwashing area, where an older teenager was working hard. The guy was tall, maybe 6'2", on a wiry frame. He had brown hair and eyes, and short cropped hair that was tapered in the back, with sideburns sculpted in the shape of long, sharp fangs. He also had straight white teeth; beneath those, a scraggly goatee; a patch of facial hair that was clearly meant to hide his chin acne—and failing miserably.

"This is Billy Baker," Wally said, introducing the guy who was obviously training him.

Billy took a quick break, wiping his wet, shriveled hands onto a stained white apron. "What's up, little brother," he said, shaking my hand, "it's good to meet you."

"You too," I said. Without thinking, I wiped my hand across the front of my pants.

Catching it, Wally shook his head. Thankfully, he said nothing about it. "Billy's training me," he explained.

I nodded.

"We share the weekend shifts."

I nodded again before learning that Billy and my brother washed dishes for thirty dollars each Friday and Saturday night—sixty whole bucks for slaving away an entire weekend. Each night started at five o'clock and ended at two o'clock in the morning.

The money sounds pretty sweet to me, I thought, *but I can't imagine having to break my back for all those hours.*

I watched closely for a while. No matter how hard Billy worked—and it had to be hard to keep up—he never made any real progress. He busted hump to spray down the dishes, load them onto the rack, and slide them through the washer. From there, he made stacks according to geographic location within the vast kitchen before scurrying around to put them all away. Silverware sorting was the most time consuming, while glassware went quickest. Then, just when it appeared that he'd made a breakthrough, he had to start all over again.

"Crazy busy, huh?" Wally said to him.

"Nuts," Billy groaned, nodding.

Wiping the sweat from his forehead, Billy looked up to see that the dirty silverware tub was overflowing. As he sorted them face down onto the faded plastic rack, Wally said, "Listen, we're gonna fly. I just wanted to bring my little brother by to show him the dump."

Little brother? I repeated in my head, snickering.

"Dump is right," Billy agreed, chuckling. But he never stopped working, and he never lifted his head off his work.

Damn, I thought. *Billy's right. This is nuts.* I then considered that Wally was jumping through the same hoops during his shift. Although it was hard for me to admit it to myself, I'd just gained even more respect for my stupid brother.

Wally slapped the stainless steel shelf in front of Billy. "Later, bro," he yelled.

"Later on," Billy said, his eyes remaining on his work.

At the end of the strange field trip, Wally and I made our way out of the kitchen. Without even realizing it, I began ogling one of the pretty waitresses. *Wow,* I thought, unable to peel my eyes away, *she's wicked choice!*

"You're not tall enough to ride that ride," Wally told me, breaking my lustful trance.

"Wha…what?" I asked, managing to close my mouth.

"Stop staring," he said, "I work here."

"Oh, sorry," I told him, stepping out of the place.

"No worries," he said, laughing. "She's smokin' hot."

I nodded, thinking, *Hotter than any pupu platter I've ever enjoyed.*

As if he were reading my mind, my brother laughed again.

• • •

As we stepped into the apartment's stairwell, Wally and I could hear Cockroach screaming his head off. "Oh God…please don't!" Sprinting up the stairs, we threw open the kitchen door.

Home from work, Pop was sitting at the kitchen table, removing a splinter from Cockroach's hand. "Stop your squawking," he told our little brother, squinting at the tweezers. "If the splinter gets into your bloodstream, it might reach your heart and then you'll be in some real trouble."

Oh my God, I thought, *don't tell him that, Pop! His fear list is already full.*

As our weary father concluded his surgery, Ma began dishing out Swedish meatballs and Rice-A-Roni. It wasn't my favorite dish, but at least I could keep it down.

"So, how'd it go today?" Pop asked no one.

"Wally took me to Oriental Pearl and showed me around," I offered.

"So lucky," Alphonse mumbled, cradling his cherry-red finger.

Pop looked up from his half-eaten meatball. "Is that right?"

Wally shrugged it off as nothing.

"So, no bike rides a couple towns over today?" our father teased.

Wally chuckled. "Not today, Pop."

"I spent the day cleaning this pigsty of a house," Ma said, "not that anyone in this ungrateful family would ever care about that."

"I care," Pop said, shoveling a giant forkful of rice into his mouth.

"We played lawn darts today," Cockroach said, needing to be in on the conversation.

"You need to be careful with those," Ma said. "I don't know why

Santa brought them for you guys. They're so dangerous."

We all stared at our mother.

"Santa?" Wally blurted.

She just shook her head. "He should have never brought them," she added, still refusing to take any credit or accountability. "Just be careful, okay?"

"Oh, we are," Cockroach lied.

As we put a dent into Ma's San Francisco treat, Pop nonchalantly dropped the hammer. "Well, it looks like the TV's finally shit the bed," he announced from out of the blue.

"So, we're getting a new television?" I asked, excitedly.

He glared at me like I'd just taken a swing at him. "Are you daffy?"

I started to answer, but he cut me off.

"Do you know how much it costs for a new TV?"

Wally said, "Probably somewhere around…"

"How many overtime shifts that you guys don't have to work?" he asked, interrupting again. Shaking his head, he looked toward my mother. "Call the repair man, Emma," he told her, "and tell him that we need to replace the tube on the Zenith. See if he has some time to get it done next week."

"Next week?" I blurted. "We're not going to have a television for a full week?"

Pop's squinted eyes slowly returned to me. "I guess that depends on how much money you and your brothers can pony up." His eyes narrowed, causing my backside to pucker. "My guess is nothing… so yeah, it'll get fixed next week when your mother and I have the money to pay for it." He took a bite. "That's how the real world works."

"I'll call him tomorrow, Walt," Ma said, getting up to grab more food.

That was the end of the discussion.

Now to figure out how we're going to watch the Dukes of Hazzard and The A-Team, I thought. *This is so whacked.*

• • •

Alphonse had learned to play his plastic recorder, which was a miracle, given that Wally and I threatened to snap it in half every time we heard a single note come out of it.

He was playing the nasty noisemaker when I walked into our bedroom. "You might not want to go on Star Search just yet," I told him.

He immediately placed the instrument into his toy box, swapping it out for the cutting-edge NFL electric football game by Tudor. Essentially, the entire game was a colorfully detailed square of sheet metal that vibrated, making the tiny, helmet-wearing players dance across the board—fans and all.

This lasted for all of five minutes before he locked it back into his wooden chest.

Although I chuckled, I understood his need to do something to pass the time. Not having a working TV in the house didn't seem like a big deal, until there was no working TV in the house.

"What do you want to play?" he asked me.

I smiled. "What about Twister?"

"No way," he said, "it just turns into a pig pile with me on the bottom."

I laughed. *That's true.*

"I'll play with you, tough guy," Wally said from within the shadows on the other side of the room—startling me.

Tiny hairs on the back of my neck jumped to attention, warning me against accepting the invitation. Foolishly, I paid no attention. "Cool," I told him, "I'll play."

Wally stood and approached me, clearly looking forward to playing the masochistic game.

Taking turns, we spun the arrow, doing exactly as instructed: right hand on red; left foot on green; right foot on blue.

There was nothing stranger than getting into a fight, because my left hand on yellow suddenly put my backside right smack in Wally's face. *He's lucky it wasn't taco night,* I thought.

Wally didn't care. "Friggin' nasty," he said. "You're so grody." Suddenly, I felt his fist hit me dead center in the turd cutter, sending tremors up my spine and shaking my organs.

In response, I involuntarily swung my right leg to escape the plastic board, cracking the goon in the face on the way. *Now it's on,* I realized, just as soon as I heard the thud of my foot on Wally's cheek.

His second punch caught me on the back of the upper thigh, causing a piercing pain and then temporary paralysis. As I rolled to my right, I was already launching a counterattack with a flurry of quick jabs—Jean Claude Van Dam-style. A few of them actually pelted him, making my knuckles sting like I'd plunged them into a hornet's nest. I knew Wally had to feel the same, because I watched in terror as his eyes changed from angry to maniacal. *Oh no…*

"You're so dead," he hissed.

From that moment on, I decided to play defense; I rolled into the fetal position and turtled up, while he punished me with one body blow after the next. Finally, I screamed, "Okay, okay… enough!" I knew that tapping out by announcing my defeat would allow him to stand the victor. *It's my only way out.*

"I win," he said, getting to his Fred Flintstone feet.

By then, multiple parts of my body were sending pain messages to my brain. As I slowly emerged from my cocoon, I noticed that I'd bloodied Wally's nose during the scrap. *Good enough*, I thought, struggling not to smile. Bloodying my thug brother was enough— even though he'd pummeled me pretty good. *Good enough,* I repeated in my throbbing head, *I hope your schnoz bleeds for a while.*

• • •

Once we turned in for the night and silence took hold, I called out in the darkness, "Goodnight, John-Boy."

"Enough with that crap, Herbie," Wally barked.

There was silence.

"It is getting old, Herbie," Cockroach mumbled from the top bunk.

My fists instinctively clinched. "Shut your pie hole, Alphonse," I hissed.

There was more silence.

"Well, it is," my little brother whispered.

"One more word and I'm gonna give you an Indian sunburn until your arm bleeds."

Wally was still laughing when I finally nodded off.

CHAPTER 5

JUNE 1984

MALL RATS

After a long wind sprint, Cockroach and I caught up to Gus's banged-up ice cream truck, panting like two out-of-shape Beagles.

Cockroach jumped in line first, knowing that he'd be making everyone wait—and he had no problem with it.

"Don't take all day," I told him.

"Why," he said, "where do you have to be?"

"The mall," I reminded him, "and if you don't shut your mouth, you'll be hanging out all by yourself tonight."

"I'll have two Creamsicles," he told Gus.

"Two?' I asked, surprised.

He half-shrugged. "Ma likes Creamsicles, too."

I laughed. "Good for you, Alphonse," I said, "scoring brownie points, while working off some of the guilt. Very clever."

"It's not like that," he said, double counting the change he received from Gus.

"Of course it is," I said, stepping up next. "Any screwballs, sir?" I asked the ice cream man, trying my best not to stare at his atrocious comb over.

Adult Chucky shook his head. "I need to start ordering more," he said, shrugging.

"No worries," I said, making sure he heard me. I glanced at the menu, where most of the pictures of the cold novelties were faded by the sun. *Ice cream sandwiches, Bomb Pops, popsicles, Fudgsicles, Creamsicles, strawberry crunch bars, chocolate crunch bar, Nutty Buddies…* "Strawberry crunch bar," I blurted.

Gus withdrew into the van window, quickly reappearing like a puppet returning for an encore. "You got the last one, kid," he said.

"Lucky me," I muttered, making sure that I smiled wide, so he didn't think I was being a smartass. I was still shaken by the nightmare and didn't want any chance of reliving it.

Jamming the pink ice cream into my gob, I stepped away, leaving Cockroach to walk home alone. Although I tried to ignore the ice cream goblin, I kept looking over—mesmerized by his dancing hair.

• • •

The Godzilla zit that I'd suffered over the winter had cost me too much time. While I awaited the monumental eruption, Donna began talking to Steve Pimental, a cocky punk that I despised since elementary school. For a while, it was rumored that they were "going out together." Unsure of their actual status, I was tormented for weeks.

Within my twisted mind, I imagined that Steve Pimental and Donna Torres had become an item. I pictured them roller skating together. I saw them going to the Snowball Dance together. I worried for months that I wasn't even in Donna's blind spot. It was pure anguish, each painful and fabricated detail quite vivid in my mind.

At one point, I even smashed my Magic 8 Ball, spilling the sacred purple liquid onto the bedroom floor.

But when I finally mustered the courage to give Donna the letter I wrote her—and then ask her out—she confirmed that none of the rumors were true. "Steve asked me out a few times," she admitted, "but I never agreed to go out with him."

A few times? I repeated over and over in my head, fueling my hatred for Steve the Moron.

I called Donna at our agreed-upon time. After some small talk, I held the phone receiver tightly to my ear, drumming up the courage to ask her, "So what's up with that kid, Steve Pimental?" My heart was in my throat. "I heard he's been sniffing around, still trying to get with you," I finished, trying to keep my voice even.

"There's nothing to worry about, Herbie," she said.

"Are you sure, Donna?"

"I'm sure," she said, firmly. "It's no big deal. He likes me. But I like you, end of story."

I started breathing again. "That...that's good to hear," I stuttered.

"Herbie, there's nothing to worry about," she repeated, taking a pause. "I really like you," she whispered, "and no one else but you."

I breathed even easier. "So, you still don't think your mom will let you go see a movie with me, huh?"

"I've brought it up a few times with her, but she keeps saying that I'm too young to date."

"What about going together as friends?" I asked.

"Is that what we are?" she teased.

"I'd like to think we're more than..."

"That's enough, Herbie," Ma called out.

As usual, I covered the phone's receiver.

"I'm late calling your Aunt Phyllis."

Unreal, I thought.

"You need to go, huh?" I heard Donna ask, stopping me from spiraling any further.

"Yeah, sorry. It's my mother's turn to use the phone."

She giggled. "No worries, Herbie."

"Not that I want this call to end," I whispered, "believe me."

I could almost feel her smile on the other side of the phone. "I know," she said, "me too." After a brief silence, she said, "You hang up first."

"No, you hang up first," I told her.

"No, you," she purred.

"You," I whispered, realizing that if anyone in my house overheard this exchange, I'd be ridiculed for all eternity.

"Let's do it together on three, okay?" she wisely suggested.

"Okay."

"One," she said.

"Two," I added.

"Three," we said together.

I heard a dial tone and smiled. *God, do I love her.*

"Herbie," Ma wailed again.

"I'm off, Ma, okay?" I yelled back. "Are you happy now?"

"Another word out of you, and you won't use this phone for a week," she warned. "I swear it."

Although my lips instinctively parted, I was smart enough to choke on my next words. *I can't imagine what my life would be like if I couldn't talk to Donna for a whole week.*

I stepped into my bedroom to search for my Magic 8 Ball. Finding it, I took it into the privacy of my bottom bunk. I shook the smooth plastic ball three times. "Is Donna telling me the truth about only liking me, and not Steve?" I whispered.

I flipped the ball over to peer into the circular window filled with purple fluid.

The triangle read, *Cannot predict now.*

Not good enough, I thought.

"Does Donna like Steve, yes or no?"

I shook the annoying toy harder. When I flipped it over, I lost my breath.

Very doubtful.

"Herbie the Love Bug," Cockroach called out. "Our show's coming on soon."

I could smell Ma's hand-cut French fries before she'd even salted and bagged them. *There are times when life can be perfect,* I thought, emerging from my funk. The TV had finally been repaired, and a new episode of the Dukes of Hazzard was less than five minutes away.

While Cockroach headed for the living room, I gave the 8 Ball one last shake.

"Am I the only one for Donna?" I whispered, sucking in a deep breath, before flipping it over and looking into the fateful window.

Signs point to yes.

Perfect, I repeated in my head, before happily joining Cockroach on the living room couch.

While Ma paced from ashtray to ashtray, smoking one cigarette after the next, she was still able to multi-task and get things done. "I'm frying French fries for the boys, Phyllis," she said into the olive-green receiver, "because they like munching on them while watching their stupid show." She took a drag.

Stupid show? I thought, grabbing a plastic tumbler of diluted lemonade. *More like totally tubular show!*

She looked at me. "That cup stays in here, Herbie," she said, "I don't want any more spills in that living room."

Whatever, I thought, swallowing down half the cup.

"No, no," she said, "I was talking to Herbie. He was trying to…" She paused to listen. "I told you already, Phyllis, I don't know who this guy Geoffrey is. Aren't you a little old to have a crush on someone and not be able to tell him?" Ma took another drag of the cigarette and listened. "Then just tell him you like him, Phyllis. Who knows, he might even like you too."

I gagged on my drink, nearly spitting it out.

Ma looked at me again, her eyes narrowing. "These boys haven't been home from school for a month, and they're already driving me crazy."

How can we drive you crazy when you're already there? I wondered, smirking.

She glared at me like she could see inside my skull.

My smirk disappeared.

"They're out of the house," Ma said, lighting another cancer stick, "from dawn until dusk." She smirked at me this time. "Maybe I should send them over to your place for a few nights to cool their jets?"

I downed the rest of my bland drink. *When hell freezes over,* I thought, making a beeline back to the living room where it was much safer.

• • •

"Can we go to the mall?" I asked Pop, who had become one with his recliner.

"Go ask your mother," he said. It was his sacred mantra.

Off to the kitchen, I repeated my weekly plea. "Ma, can we please go to the mall?"

She sighed heavily. "Go ask your father," she said.

"We just did, Ma. It's why we're here, asking you."

Wiping her hands on her flowered apron, she shook her head. "I never imagined having to do this parenting thing alone," she muttered under her breath, before heading into the living room. "Walt," she said, "the boys need a ride to the mall."

"So take the car and…"

"Fine, but you'll have to finish supper while I'm out," she said, heading back toward the kitchen.

He looked at us like we'd just betrayed him.

Why do we always have to go through this dance, I wondered, *when it always ends the same way?*

We never wore cutoff shorts or ratty tank tops for our Saturday afternoon ventures to the mall. We got dressed in our best jeans, or parachute pants that hosted more zippers than the urinal trench at Fenway Park. Our graphic rock t-shirts advertised the Rolling Stones' big lips, AC/DC's signature lightning bolt, and Pink Floyd's badass prism. Our kicks of choice were nothing less than Chuck Taylors. The look was finished off with white braided bracelets that Ma soaked at the beginning of summer, which quickly sun dried snug to our wrists. Everyone knew that by the time the yellow school bus arrived, we'd be cutting them off to see how much sun—and dirt— had accumulated. As always, Cockroach took it one step further with his attire; he began sporting a shark-tooth necklace, resurrecting his dreaded nickname, "Phonsie"—derived from the character Fonzie on Happy Days.

"Ayyyy," we teased him in the back seat.

"You're just jealous," he snapped back, pretending that the nickname didn't bother him.

Pop cleared his throat, ending the banter. "So, what do you guys do in there for all that time?" he asked, pulling up to the mall's grand front entrance.

"We walk laps," Cockroach reported, being honest, "lots of laps."

"And grab something to eat at the food court," Wally said.

"Your mother has food at home. Why are you guys going to waste your money?"

No one answered him.

"We also play video games at the arcade," I added, attempting to derail the famous 'wasted-money' talk.

"You don't have video games at home?" he countered, reaching for a cold beer in the small red cooler on the passenger-side floor. "I didn't work a couple of overtime shifts so you boys could have your own Atari?"

Wally leaned over the seat and spoke softly, as though he was sharing some secret with our old man. "We come here to meet girls, Pop."

The old man nodded. "Well, all right. Now I get it," he said, without further interrogation or judgment. "Go do your thing then."

We piled out of the station wagon.

There was air conditioning at the mall, which was good, considering the number of laps that most of us hoofed. The first lap was always walked at a pretty brisk clip, scouting out the pockets of friends—specifically potential female friends. Most girls were dressed in brightly colored jumpers, their big unruly hair roped in by matching scrunchies or large hair clips.

Subtle nods and smiles set the tone for flirting later in the night—and hopefully, a phone number.

The piped-in music was our soundtrack for summer: *Working for the Weekend* by Loverboy, *Down Under* by Men at Work, *I Melt with You* by Modern English, *Dancing in the Dark* by Bruce Springsteen, *Say It Isn't So* by Hall & Oates, *The Reflex* by Duran Duran—the incredible list went on.

Like mindless zombies, we put in our laps for the first hour—past the Glamour Shots store and Regis Hair Salon. I always liked the smells and wished I could afford a haircut there. We slowed in front of Claire's, because that's where the girls hung out. Browsing at Sharper Image and Spencer's Gifts, however, were strictly selfish pit stops.

"I love the posters here," Cockroach said.

"I'm surprised," I told him, "the women are wearing bathing suits." I held up a can of peanuts that concealed a spring-loaded snake. "I'm thinking about getting this for Pop's birthday."

"He'd rather have a scratch ticket and a couple Slim Jims," Wally said, stepping up beside me with his best friend, Owen.

I still didn't like the rehabilitated bully and stepped away, creating some distance between us. "What about rubber dog poop?" I asked Cockroach, holding up the plastic prank.

He shook his head. "Waste of money," he said, "you can get all the dog poop you want from Roscoe in the neighbor's yard." He grinned. "And it's free."

I laughed. "I'm not sure Pop would appreciate the real stuff."

"I know," he said, "but it might be funny as hell."

Sam Goody Record Store, Zales Jewelry Store, Kinney Shoe Store and KB Toys were up one side of the mall. On the other side were Structure, Debs, American Eagle, and the Candy Stop, a coin-operated candy crane and a small carousel, sitting just outside of the busy shop.

"You wanna take a ride?" I asked Cockroach, pointing toward the children's ride.

"Nah, I'm good."

"It's not as thrilling as the one at Lincoln Park, but I'm sure you'd still…"

"I'm good," he repeated.

If you were able to make a connection with the opposite sex, it usually required the assistance of a wingman, a good friend who was willing to suffer time with the girl's pouting sidekick.

I'm glad I don't have to sweat this craziness anymore, I thought. *Donna's the only girl for me.*

For all the other guys, it was a real game of cat and mouse, with any girl they thought was cute. If she smiled your way, it was stalking time. The hunt was on—past Radio Shack, Hickory Farms and Walden Books straight into the food court: the land of high prices and heartburn. Pizza at Sbarro's, Chinese food at Hoy Tin's, pretzels at Auntie Anne's, iced coffees at Dunkin' Donuts—the expensive options were plentiful.

Cockroach and I had just reached the Food Court when I heard some guy use the cheesiest line on one of the dozens of big-haired girls, "Can I buy you a drink?"

If she says yes, I thought, *then it's two Orange Julius's.* From there, small talk led to a nice slow stroll across the mall to the Pet Store to see the puppies and kittens. *I can't imagine how many telephone numbers have been exchanged in front of whining puppies.*

"Just don't call after nine o'clock," more than one girl had said. "My dad gets nuts."

We logged in miles before the night was done, always ending at The Dream Machine, the mall's packed arcade. *If we didn't eat first, we'd starve*, I thought, as the arcade always drained us of whatever money we had left—whether it was dollar bills or loose change.

The Dream Machine lured teenagers in with the lights and sounds of an Atlantic City casino. Pinball machines—which I still enjoyed because I could get my quarter's worth out of them—lined the back wall on the bottom floor. There were two floors, with red carpeting covering both levels. The counter, with a change maker sitting behind it, was located at the front.

A BMX bicycle hung from the ceiling, as though it was a real prize available to be won. But it had hung there for years. After only a few visits, it was clear that there was nothing to be won in this neon den of smoke and mirrors—*except for maybe a top score or the occasional date.*

On the upside, the music was an amazing soundtrack that rarely repeated songs. *Time After Time* by Cyndi Lauper, *Against All Odds* by Phil Collins, *Jump* by Van Halen, *Ghostbusters* by Ray Parker, *Missing You* by John Waite—the wonderful list went on for as long as we were feeding the machines with quarters.

On the downside, the acne-faced burnout who ran the counter was a useless moron. When we reported that one of the flashing machines had eaten our change, or was broken altogether, he simply fashioned a cardboard sign—*BROKED*—and taped it to the front of the culprit.

Broked? I thought, shaking my head. *This is exactly why Ma wants us to finish school.*

When the Centipede game was up and running, Wally continued to maintain the top score at the arcade—while also beginning his quest to dominate Space Invaders. He was an arcade god, making me think, *I can't even imagine what the title has cost him?* It must have claimed a good percentage of dishwashing wages.

As I watched him play, I considered that we were well into the era of remote controls with wires and all-night marathons of Asteroids, merely a training ground for Wally and his supernatural friends. *I wonder if I'll be as good as them when I get to their age.* I shook my head. *I doubt it. It's just not worth the time and money.*

Video gaming was hardly a spectator sport, so Cockroach and I usually camped out at the air hockey table.

By the second score of the first game, I'd already gotten him good.

"Ouch," my little brother screamed, throwing his stinging fingers into his mouth and making me laugh hysterically.

It was inevitable. One of us always got hurt by a flying puck, which rather than the score, usually defined the winner.

"Stop your belly aching," I told him, as Kenny Loggins sang *Footloose.* "You're embarrassing the both of us."

"I don't friggin' care," he said, sucking on his digits like they were a baby's pacifier.

That a boy, I thought.

We also played Skee Ball. The Dream Machine was almost as good as the arcade at Lincoln Park—*almost.* While we bowled for strings of tickets to the song *When Doves Cry* by Prince, a few of the preppie girls I knew from school crammed themselves into the tiny curtain-drawn photo booth to waste handfuls of quarters on vertical strips of black and white photos—each displaying silly faces and ridiculous poses.

"Now that's what I call wasted money," I whispered to Cockroach.

"Air hockey's a much better investment," he said, nodding, "until someone breaks a finger."

"Always so dramatic," I told him, wondering if his finger was actually broken.

My brothers and I were walking out of The Dream Machine, when Steve Pimental and one of his punk friends appeared.

"Asshole," he muttered, locking eyes with me.

"What did you just say to me?" I barked back, feeling confident with Wally standing at my side.

"You heard me," he said. "Listen, if I were you, I'd stay the hell away from Donna Torres. You know I'm into her and…"

"Screw you!" I roared, furious.

"If you knew what was good for you, you'd stay away from her, asshole," he threatened, taking an aggressive step toward me.

Although I could feel a ball of fear growing in my core, a wave of anger was becoming even more dominant. "And if I were you, I'd step off, bitch!"

"Oh, I'll step off," Steve said, "and give you the worst beating of your life."

While my adrenaline began to rush, my forehead beaded in sweat. My hands started to tremble—with equal amounts of fear and rage—and my breathing quickened.

Steve's beady eyes darted back and forth between me and Wally. "You know what, meet me tomorrow at the D.A.V. parking lot on Faulkner Street," he said.

My mind immediately filled with the same anxiety I'd watched Wally go through over the winter. *I don't think so,* I told myself. *If we're going to do this, then let's get it to hell over with.* "Why wait until tomorrow," I asked him, "when we're both here right now?"

"Oh, so you want me to beat you right now?"

"Actually, I'd love it if you just stopped talking." I raised both fists.

"Oh shit," I heard Cockroach say.

Wally was smiling from ear to ear. "Brazen."

By now, a good-sized crowd had encircled us.

It felt like the entire world had shrunk, with only me and Steve facing off. As we circled each other, I could hear my heart pounding in my ears. Fear engulfed my chest. My mind raced with a thousand jumbled thoughts. And that's when I threw the first punch, landing it square on Steve's cheek, making his eyes go wide with surprise.

He countered, throwing a right hook that landed square on my left cheek just under my eye. Although it stung, it didn't bring nearly the same devastation I'd predicted. In fact, the shot was child's play compared to what Wally usually dished out.

Oh, you're so done, bitch, I thought.

I grinned, watching as my opponent's fear was betrayed in his eyes. And that's when I began throwing one punch after the next. I figured it was much better to be the hunter rather than the hunted. I don't know how it happened, but it felt like a switch had been thrown—the last slivers of fear dissolving into pure rage. I preferred the latter.

Before the fight was over—not two minutes later—I earned myself a black eye, as well as a clear victory.

"If I were you," I told Steve, as he rolled himself into the fetal position, "I'd stay the hell away from Donna." I stood over him like the prodigy of Steven Seagal. "And if you don't, then this is only a taste of what's coming next."

Teenagers were still cheering for me as my brothers and I walked away, passing two responding mall cops.

As we headed for Pop's station wagon, Wally told Cockroach, "That's how you get it done." He nodded a few times. "That's how you stand up, Alphonse, and be a man."

It was the greatest compliment that Wally had never given me to my face.

Donna and I are a couple, I decided, *and no one's ever gonna come between us.*

"Just so you know," Wally told me, "you've got quite a shiner."

I looked toward Cockroach. "Oh, it's a good one," he said, giving me a thumbs-up.

I grinned, thinking, *I earned it, I guess.*

• • •

"How was the fishin'?" Pop asked when he picked us up from the mall. "Catch anything?"

Wally laughed. "We had a few bites, Pop," he joked, "but we didn't land anything." He looked at me and winked. "Well, maybe a few right hooks, but…"

"What's that?" Pop asked, looking in the rearview mirror.

"He said we weren't using the right hooks," Cockroach said,

quickly covering Wally's sloppy tracks.

As our father laughed from his belly, I realized how witty my little brother was. His mind really did fire like a well-oiled piston.

"So, you don't think it was the bait, huh?" Pop asked between laughs.

"Not a chance, Pop," Wally said.

While everyone laughed, I spent the rest of the ride hiding my face. I wanted to enjoy the moment and not have to explain it. *At least not yet.*

As soon as our father parked the station wagon in the driveway, I was out of the car and hurrying off to get my paper route done. Cockroach also hustled off to grab Ma's corner-store order.

I grabbed my newspaper bundle in front of R&S Variety, counting twice to make sure Old Man Sedgeband hadn't ripped me off like he sometimes did to Wally, I threw the papers into my cross-shoulder canvas bag and jumped back onto my bike. I was struggling to balance the one-sided load, when I caught my reflection in the smudged glass window. *Wow,* I thought, throwing my foot out to stop myself from falling. *That's a pretty good shiner, all right.*

Although I'd felt a nearly overwhelming rush of fear just before the fight with Steve, once it started, most of that went away, replaced by an intense focus I'd never experienced before.

I turned my head from side to side, admiring the purple and yellow welt under my left eye. *He definitely got the worse of it,* I told myself, feeling my chest swell with pride. I felt like a man now, or at least as close to being a man as I could at my age. *I'm so glad we duked it out right there and then,* I thought. *At least it's over and I don't have to think about it anymore,* I leaned in toward the dirty glass, taking one final look at my battle wound. *I'd rather catch a bad beating than spend weeks worrying about one.*

Standing up on my left bike pedal, I pushed down hard and was off to work.

Our family sat for an early supper, because Wally had to work. Ma was just starting to serve her cheap steak and scalloped potatoes, when she spotted my eye. "Oh, my God," she squealed, nearly dropping the cast iron frying pan. "What happened to your face, Herbie?"

"I got into a fist fight at the mall," I confessed.

Pop looked at me, his face in shock.

"With who?" she asked.

"Some punk named Steve," I said.

Ma's face filled with disgust, while Pop simply grinned.

She caught the old man's smirk. "I don't want the boys fighting, Walt! You know that." She placed the heavy pan onto a potholder sitting in the middle of the kitchen table.

"No Emma, you don't want the boys starting fights." Still wearing his grin, he looked me straight in my good eye. "But if someone comes looking for a fight, then by God our sons had better stand up."

The room went silent.

"Who threw the first punch?" Pop asked.

"Me," I admitted.

The old man shook his head. "I thought we talked about not being the one who starts a fight, Herbie?"

"He brought the fight to me," I explained. "I just beat him to the first punch."

Pop looked toward Wally.

"It's true," my brother reported. "The kid brought it to Herbie." He smiled. "And then he wished he hadn't."

"Well, all right then," Pop said, grabbing for the ladle to fill his plate with creamy potatoes.

Ma said nothing; she just looked at me and shook her disappointed head.

Sorry, Ma, I told her in my head, *but I had no choice on this one.*

We were about to dig in, when Pop noticed Cockroach chewing gum. My younger brother had a new addiction with Freshen Up gum and began chewing it by the truckload.

"Throw out your gum," Pop told him. "We're about to eat."

"But I just started a new piece, and it squirts in your mouth when you bite into it."

Pop raised one eyebrow but said nothing. He pointed toward the closet door where our trash barrel was.

Scooping potatoes into his plate, Pop commented, "Every time I see this kid lately, he's chewing gum. He must have started a good job that I don't know about."

"He goes to the corner store for me," Ma said, quick to come to her little boy's defense.

Pop stopped in mid-motion to look at his wife. "Have you thought about how much he's spending at that store?"

While Cockroach's face went white, I stopped breathing.

Wally grinned wide. "I like gum," he commented. "Can I get a piece from you later?" he asked, glaring at our little brother.

"Alphonse is fine," Ma said, ignoring Wally's input. "I tell him when he can get himself something."

Although Pop shook his head, he went quiet.

I started breathing again, while some color returned to Cockroach's face. We exchanged a glance across the table.

He'll be chewing gum in secret now, I thought. *There's no way he's stupid enough to get questioned on this again.*

"Groceries went up again, Walt," Ma said, completely changing the subject.

He looked at her, awaiting the bad news.

"A dozen of eggs are up to a buck now, and a pound of bacon is $1.65."

"Whoa Nellie," the old man said, whistling.

"And that rib-eye steak you're eating tonight," she added, "was $3.89 a pound."

"Don't waste it, boys," Pop said. "this meat's what you call expensive."

I looked down at the gristle beef. *You've got to be kidding me?*

We were toward the end of the meal when Pop slid a big, juicy piece of steak fat to the edge of his plate. He turned to me and grinned.

I looked away, afraid I might dry heave. I was so finicky when it came to some foods that I'd gotten a bad rap for it from my family. But I couldn't help it. Certain foods made me sick; split pea soup, the fat found on the edges of steak and pork chops—the list was fairly lengthy.

While Ma got mad at me, Pop used it to his amusement. "Okay, Rocky Balboa," he said, smirking, "I have a deal for you."

I gave him my undivided attention.

"Eat this piece of steak fat and keep it down for at least five minutes, and I'll let you keep this twenty dollar bill," he announced, slapping the wrinkled bill onto the table.

"And if I can't?"

"No such thing as can't," he said. "You know that."

I stared at my nemesis—all juicy and white and making my throat constrict. *But twenty bucks is some big scratch*, I thought.

"But remember, you have to swallow it and keep it down for five minutes," my father confirmed.

I looked to my mother, who gave me a subtle nod. "You can do it," she mouthed, grinning.

At least Ma's rooting for me, I thought, happy that she'd chosen my corner over my father's. Sucking in a lung full of air, I tried my best. I really did. But it was a texture thing; feeling the fat sliding around in my mouth made me immediately nauseous. *Come on, Herbie,* I told myself, *you can do this!* I gagged and gagged, my eyes watering to blindness. Still, I did everything I could to swallow it. I think it got halfway down before my body violently rejected it, hurling it out of my slobbering mouth.

"That is absolutely disgusting," Ma said, turning away from the spectacle.

My brothers laughed hysterically. Even Pop was laughing when he swiped the twenty off the table and jammed it back into the front pocket of his worn dungarees.

I couldn't believe it. *Twenty bucks lost!* The entire experience gave me the piss shivers, and I was still trying to shake it off. I looked at my mother, afraid I'd disappointed her.

"Like they say," she blurted, "there's no such thing as courage without fear." She looked at my dad. "And you'd better give Herbie something for giving it a try."

Pop chuckled. "I'll give Herbie something, all right." He grinned at me. "How 'bout a swift kick in the ass?"

Ma sighed. "The next time you run to the corner store for me, Herbie, you can get a little something extra for yourself."

Both of my brothers nearly choked on their supper.

"Thanks Ma," I said, feeling the guilt from years of shameless embezzlement.

"How 'bout I take that bet?" Wally told Pop, referring to the steak fat.

The old man shook his head "Not a chance," he said between bites. "You'd choke down horse hooves for half that money."

Everyone laughed—except me.

I was still trying not to ralph from the gelatin feel in my mouth. *Deadly.*

Finishing his final bite, Wally stood. "I hate to chew and screw, but I've got work."

"Watch your mouth," Ma scolded him, "or I'll wash it out with soap."

This time, we all laughed. *Ma would never waste a bar of Ivory soap on Wally's cussing.*

My big brother hurried out the door for his shift at Oriental Pearl.

• • •

The kitchen phone rang twice before Alphonse answered it.

"Yellow?" he said, trying to sound cool.

I took the green phone from my smirking brother.

"I heard that you and Steve Pimental fought at the mall," Donna said, as soon as I put the receiver to my ear.

I couldn't tell whether she was upset or angry. "Yea...yeah," I stuttered. "He didn't give me much of a choice. He came at me, so I had to go."

There was a pause.

"Who told you?" I asked, breaking the deafening silence.

"Paul Collura's little sister, Regina. She saw the whole thing. I just got off the phone with her."

"And what did she tell you?" I asked.

"That Steve started it, and that you guys really went at it good." Donna sounded upset now. "She told me there was blood."

There was another pause.

"Not much blood," I hurried to clarify. "We'll both live." I took a deep breath. "Did Regina tell you who won?" I asked, trying not to sound too happy about it.

"She said you did. But I don't care about that, Herbie. All I know is that I felt sick to my stomach when I heard, worried that you'd been hurt or…"

"I'm fine," I confirmed, cutting her off.

"I hope the fight wasn't because of me," she said.

"It wasn't," I lied. "This day's been coming for a very long time." I nodded to myself. "And now it's done."

"I hope so," she whispered.

"Done," I repeated.

After saying our long goodbyes, I told Donna, "I'll meet you in my dreams tonight."

"I'll be waiting," she whispered.

I hung up the phone to find Alphonse staring at me and shaking his head. "Gag me with a Ginsu knife, dude."

"Whatever."

"I think I might throw up in my dreams tonight," he added, unwilling to let it go.

"You'll never understand until you have a girlfriend," I told him.

"A girlfriend?" he repeated. "I was hoping for more than just one." He smiled wide, showing off his pearly whites.

I laughed, thinking, *I have no doubt, brother.*

Right on my heels, Ma snatched the phone off the hook and dialed Aunt Phyllis. "Phyllis, it's Emma," she said, lighting a long, white Carlton. "You're never gonna guess what happened today."

Here we go, I thought.

"The landlord went up to $350 on the rent." She sucked in some nicotine. "Of course, a month."

What? That's a lot of money.

"And if that wasn't enough, guess who got into a fist fight this afternoon?" She took a drag before shaking her head. "No, not Walt!" she said. "Why on earth would you think my husband's been in a fist fight? He's a grown man, for God's sake, and..." She paused to listen. "Well yeah, I know Walt's no saint, Phyllis, but..."

Tapping out, I closed the plastic accordion door behind me. *Sweet dreams, Ma.*

CHAPTER 6

JULY 1984

POP'S VACATION, WEEK 1

Before we knew it, it was already the first week of July, and the start of Pop's annual two-week vacation. He never looked so happy. Even young, I realized that our father worked to live, and not the other way around. The old man kicked off the festivities by bringing home fish and chips from Higson's Seafood.

As we tore through the greasy meal, we discussed options for the week.

"We should go to the beach," Wally suggested.

"We will," Pop said, "before summer's out."

My brothers and I exchanged hopeful glances.

"Seekonk Speedway," Cockroach said.

Pop nodded, while shoveling more fries into his mouth.

"I've always wanted to see a Red Sox game," I said, knowing that I was tiptoeing out on a limb.

"I like that idea," he said.

My brothers and I exchanged glances again.

"Lincoln Park?" Cockroach listed.

"Didn't you guys already cross that off your summer list?" Ma asked.

Our father laughed. "Listen guys," he said, washing down the last of his supper with some fermented suds, "we'll do as much as we can, but keep in mind that your mother and I aren't made of money."

He's starting to sound like Ma, I thought.

"We might have to stay local this summer, but we'll have fun just the same."

"That's right," Ma said, "as long as we spend time together, we…"

I drowned out the rest of her spiel, thinking, *We usually just go on day trips, anyway, never straying too far from the house. It doesn't make a difference to me. I love it when Pop's on vacation, and the family's together for two whole weeks.*

"Okay guys?" Ma asked.

I nodded. "Sounds good to me, Ma."

• • •

On day one of vacation, after a packy run for beer and scratch tickets, Pop brought us to Kartway, located two miles down the road from our house. It reminded me of Seekonk Speedway on a much smaller scale. Bright red, green, and yellow Go Carts, with numbers stenciled on the front hoods, idled in two lines—waiting to be abused.

Yes! I thought, as the three of us scrambled out of the station wagon. I loved how the smell of gas and burned rubber filled the warm air. We waited for Pop. He stayed in the car.

Wally stuck his head into the passenger window. "What's up, Pop?"

Cockroach and I crouched down to see what was going on.

The old man grinned. "Alphonse is old enough to ride alone now," he said. "You guys don't need me getting in your way." He lifted a large glass jar, his change jar, which originally held dill pick-les. There had to be two inches of quarters in it. "Ride until the jar's empty," he said, "and make sure everyone gets the same number of turns, okay?"

"Absolutely, Pop!" Wally said for all of us.

Unscrewing the lid, Pop placed the jar on the passenger seat. "Come back and refill your pockets when you need to."

We took turns reaching in to grab handfuls of cold silver, thank-ing him as we ran off. "Thanks, Pop," I said, realizing that at fifty cents a ride, we were in for a long, fun-filled day.

He cracked open his first beer. "You got it, kid," he said, before putting the can to his lips and taking a healthy swig. "Now go have fun."

We stood in the short line, which guaranteed we'd all get on the track. And that was the plan for the day. "We all ride together," Wally said, "or we wait until we can."

Cockroach and I agreed.

The sounds of two-stroke engines screaming side by side on the black asphalt track pushed waves of adrenaline through my blood-stream. I suddenly imagined being David Hasselhoff in *Knight Rider*.

"I don't see you boys winning one single race today," Wally said, popping my bubble. I looked back at him. He was smiling wider than I'd seen him smile in a really long time.

"Oh, we'll see Dale Earnhardt," I said. "It's on!"

Cockroach nodded. "It's on," our little brother echoed.

I looked at him and grinned. *This ain't gonna be some stupid little Big Wheel race in the cellar*, I thought. *This is the real deal.*

When the racers on the track slowed down to park, I took a deep breath. *This is so righteous. Thanks Pop!*

The different colored carts were also numbered on the side. Once the gate opened, allowing us onto the track, I sprinted for number eleven—my favorite number. I even let one kid jump in front of me so he could grab number seven. Once he was out of my way, I sprinted toward my blue race machine, knowing I'd be doing the same for as long as Pop's quarters lasted—whether number eleven was parked at the head of the line or in the rear.

Once the green flag dropped, I planted the gas pedal to the floor and never let up. As far as I was concerned, the brake pedal could have been missing, and it wouldn't have made a bit of difference.

Racing felt so exhilarating: the wind in my face, my eyes focused on catching up to my brothers and passing them. I picked off Cockroach first. "Get out of my way," I yelled at him, as I brushed past him.

He yelled something back, which I believe rhymed with the word 'truck.'

I laughed, but then concentrated on Wally's back bumper. For the next four laps, I hugged the turns trying to make up ground. But Wally was too skilled, maintaining his distance.

Damn, I thought, as we finished the race and pulled into the pits.

Climbing out of our carts, we sprinted to get back in line.

"Told you," Wally said.

"That was only the first race, Yosemite Sam," I reminded him.

As we stood in line again, I surveyed the white-lined track. *This isn't Seekonk Speedway,* I thought. *It's actually better.* I smiled. *We get to drive here and not just watch.* I glanced over at Pop. He was kicked back in his seat, drinking his beer and enjoying the view—Conway Twitty's voice blaring from the station wagon's eight-track player. We locked eyes. I nodded my appreciation to him.

He threw me a thumbs-up. From his body language, he was in no hurry to leave. I realized that my father didn't have to sneak in any beers here, the sleeves on his flannel coat tied off with heavy twine so that he could slide three or four cans into each. In Kartway's gravel parking lot, he could drink in the open at his leisure.

This is so clutch, I repeated in my head.

The gate opened again, permitting us back onto the track. I nearly ran over two smaller kids to get to blue number eleven. I looked around. Wally was positioned two carts behind me. *Sweet!* Three seconds later, I jammed my right foot to the floor and could feel an actual squeal escape my throat before I began giggling like one of the kids I'd nearly bowled over.

No matter what I tried, I couldn't fend off my older brother. He won again. *Damn it!*

The pickle jar was nearly empty, my hopes of beating my brother dwindling, when Wally and I lined up, side by side. *It has to be now, Herbie,* I told myself. *This race!*

We were three laps in, when something struck me from the rear. I looked back. Wally was smiling like a maniac. "Move over, Pinocchio," he yelled.

"I don't think so, Geppetto," I screamed back.

"No bumping," the silver-haired man that ran the track yelled at us, "or you're both getting tossed!"

Wally went to the outside. I swerved to defend my position. He dove inside. I did the same. I felt another tap on my back bumper.

"Last warning!" the portly man roared.

It was the last lap, when Wally ran into the right side of my bumper, nearly spinning me out of control. I don't know how, but I was able to recover and drive over the finish line ahead of him.

"Yes!" I screamed. *Victory at last!*

The track owner took his long steel hook and caught the back of Wally's bumper, slowing him to a stop. "You guys are all done for the day," he said. "I warned you."

Wally climbed out of his cart and nodded. "My apologies," he said.

This is perfect, I thought, *I finally won, and we're almost out of quarters anyway.*

The man showed us to the gate.

Back at the station wagon, Pop sat up straight and turned the key in the ignition. "You got kicked out, huh?"

"Yup," Wally said, trying not to laugh.

"Any quarters left?" Pop asked.

We all nodded, closing the back doors.

"Put whatever's left back into the jar," he said, backing out of the parking lot.

We did. "Thanks for today, Pop," Cockroach said, "it was so much fun."

The old man peered into the rearview mirror and nodded. "You're welcome," he said, "and when you're talking about it later at the supper table, you might want to leave out how this fun day ended."

We all nodded again.

Understood, Pop.

• • •

For a few weeks, Ma served us either English muffin pizzas or cucumber sandwiches slathered in mayonnaise, like she was earning a commission.

It's a quality lunch, either way, I decided.

And with each Tupperware pitcher of lemonade she made, she used less and less of the yellow granulated powder. As I took a long swig, I read the giant canister: *Country Time Lemonade Flavor Drink, with natural lemon flavors.* "Tastes like good old-fashioned lemonade," I read aloud, "not too tart, not too sweet." I took another sip and snickered. *I wonder what good old-fashioned lemonade actually tastes like? I'm guessing it's a lot better than this crap.* I downed the rest of the tumbler. *By the end of summer, we'll probably be drinking colored tap water.*

"Pop, where are we going today?" Cockroach asked.

"To the backyard," the old man said. "It's already paid for."

We stared at him.

"What do you think," he asked, "that we're going to spend money every day?"

Spend money? I thought. *We emptied your change jar yesterday.*

When we were bored—which was more often than not—we made up games that usually leaned toward violence or mayhem. This seemed to be more innate than concocted.

Jarts were gigantic lawn darts, with long sharp tips, their red and yellow plastic fins making them aerodynamic. And they were a lot of fun to play with—until they weren't.

We'd just dug the box out of the shed, when Vic suggested, "Why don't we hunt squirrels with them?"

Wally glared at him. "Why don't we hunt you instead?"

Vic's eyes went distant; he actually considered the suggestion.

Wally looked at me. "Is he tapped in the head?"

I shrugged. "No more than we are, I guess."

Everyone laughed.

"Why don't we just use those plastic hoops that come with the game?" Cockroach asked, foolishly trying to introduce logic.

I shook my head. "Too boring. We could use…"

"…some of Cockroach's action figures as targets," Wally said, finishing my sentence.

"No way!" our little brother yelled.

"Shhhh, bro," I hissed at him, "there's no need to bring any heat on us."

"Yeah, man," Vic agreed, looking around.

"It beats throwing the darts into the air as high as we can until one of us gets whacked," Wally said.

It's true, I thought. The potential for maiming and disfiguring ourselves was ever-present.

"You have a few G.I. Joe dolls that are pretty beat up," I added, "and for all we know, we won't even end up hitting one of them."

Cockroach continued to shake his head.

"Come on, Alphonse," Wally said.

Vic grabbled his arm, nodding at him. "It'll be fun."

"Fine," he finally surrendered, "but only one."

Wally nodded. "Sure…to start," he said. "We'll see if we need more."

Two hours later, G.I. Joe and two of his action figure comrades had been maimed beyond recognition. In turn, Cockroach was warned to keep his mouth shut or else face "a dirty beating."

• • •

It was early Friday night. After a family vote of where to grab take-out from—Frates, McCrays or The Carnival—Pop had us tag along with him to our favorite summer haunt, McCrays Clam Shack. They served fried clams, clam cakes, and French fries; three items, that was it.

The double line—a parade of anxious customers—snaked out as far as State Road; the gravel driveway was filled with old Buicks and Cadillacs.

"Look at that Caddy," Pop muttered, his eyes growing distant, a grin threatening to crack the side of his mouth. Our father's dream was to own a brand-new Cadillac one day; a day he knew would likely never come.

Someday, Pop, I told him in my head, as we waited in line for clam cakes. *Someday, we'll be able to buy you a Caddy in whatever color you like.*

Every time someone emerged from the tiny clam shack, juggling their red-striped boxes, all eyes were on them—people nodding jealously, licking their lips in the hot sun.

Forty minutes later, Pop paid for our dinner and turned to us. "Let's get this food home to your mother before it gets cold."

After we ate, while Ma stayed home to "finish her show," Pop drove us to Silver Screen Video. While we piled out of the car like circus clowns, the old man stayed in the station wagon, sipping his beer. "Don't rent any movies that your mother will give me hell for, or this'll be the last time I bring you here. Got it?"

"Got it, Pop," I said.

I had a copy of *The Outsiders* in one hand and *Risky Business* in the other, trying to decide which one would upset my mother less. When I looked beyond the rentals in my hands, I spotted my little brother hanging around the black curtain in the rear of the store—the *Adult Section*. Although Wally and I talked about sneaking in there, Cockroach had clearly plotted a plan and was about to put it into action.

There's no way he's gonna…

The velvet curtains parted, with Cockroach quickly disappearing behind them.

I'll be a son-of-a… I was thinking, when I saw Mr. Deschenes rushing toward the rear of his shop toward my ballsy brother. *Oh no!*

The man wasn't two steps from the *Adult Section* when Cockroach returned from the unknown—smiling. His eyes were glazed over, as though he'd just emerged from some unforgettable dream.

Busted!

Mr. Deschenes grabbed Cockroach by the arm, spinning him sideways and nearly yanking him off his feet. He bent down to look him in the eye. "What do you think you're doing back here?" the angry man asked.

"I…I got lost," Cockroach stammered.

"You got lost, all right," Mr. Deschenes said, becoming even more upset.

"I'm…I'm sorry, Mr. Deschenes," my brother stuttered, "I'll never go in there again." Cockroach's eyes swelled with tears, and I couldn't tell whether they were real or part of his defense strategy.

"I know you won't," the store owner said, "especially when I tell your mother what you just did."

Cockroach's face bleached white, and suddenly, I could feel his fear—like I was the pervert who'd just gotten pinched. "Let's go," I told my brother.

Mr. Deschenes released his arm.

"I'll take care of this, Mr. Deschenes," I said, trying to speak with authority, "and don't you worry, I guarantee this little deviant won't ever pull a stunt like that again."

The man studied my face, trying to decide whether he was being conned.

"Now get out of here!" I yelled to my brother. "Just you wait until Pop hears about this."

I nodded once toward Mr. Deschenes before marching my stunned brother out of the shop, the two of us empty-handed.

We were at the door when Cockroach whispered, "Herbie, you're not gonna…"

"Relax, crocodile tears," I told him. "Let's just get out of here before Mr. Deschenes follows us out and has a talk with Pop."

We jumped into the station wagon to make our getaway. As he turned the ignition, Pop's brow furrowed in the rearview mirror. "No movie rentals?"

Cockroach was trying to breathe when I shook my head. "Nothing we haven't seen already, Pop."

"Really?" He grinned like he'd just chewed on a fresh lemon. "Ain't that something," he said, like he knew something was wrong but didn't have the energy to investigate.

I nodded. "We'll just watch *Airwolf*," I said, "or *Different Strokes*."

He put the shifter into Reverse. "Let's go then," he said, taking a swig from the beer can concealed between his legs, "and you can give me my money back when we get home."

"Sure, Pop."

We pulled out of the parking lot and onto the road before the color returned to my brother's face.

"So, what did you see behind that curtain?" I whispered.

Cockroach's eyes were as big as Frisbees. "Shhhhhh…"

We were a mile down the road when I tapped him on the shoulder. He looked at me. "Well?" I asked.

His smile finally returned. "My future," he whispered.

I laughed the rest of the way home.

· · ·

Not every "day trip"—as Pop called them—was legitimate. Some were nothing more than errands that he tried to sell as fun little getaways.

The entire family—minus Wally, who'd come up with some new excuse—had piled into the station wagon when Cockroach excitedly asked, "Where are we going?"

"To S&H Green Stamps," Pop announced, "where your mother's looking to purchase some new dinnerware."

Ma nodded, raising her purse, which was bulging with books of stamps.

Pop chuckled. "You boys are gonna love it there. It's a real shithole."

Ma slapped his arm. "It is not, Walt."

"S&H what?" I asked.

"Green Stamps," Pop said. "Whenever I fill my gas tank or your mother buys groceries at the market, we earn a sheet or two of stamps." He then explained that the little green stamps were distributed by various retailers as rewards for shoppers. Customers received stamps at the checkout counters of supermarkets, department stores, and gasoline stations, among other retailers, which could be redeemed for products in the catalog or at one of their redemption centers.

Ma explained, "All you have to do is lick the stamps and then stick them into a book." She smiled. "And when you have enough of those books filled, you go down to their store and turn them in for everything from small appliances to housewares." She handed back one of the filled books.

Cockroach slid over, so we could look at it together. As explained, the stamps were collected into booklets—the backs had an adhesive similar to postage stamps—then the booklets were redeemed for "rewards" ordered from S&H catalogs or picked up at the store in Fall River.

So that's where we're heading? I thought, *Shopping?* I looked at my little brother and shook my head.

He looked as disappointed as I felt.

We handed the book back over the front seat.

"So how many stamps would you need to buy…say, a toaster oven?" I asked, going along to get along.

Pop chuckled. "I'd have had to fill this car with enough gas to get us to the moon and back."

Ma slapped his arm again. "That's not true, Walt," she said, looking over her shoulder. "You'll see."

As Pop parked the wagon, Ma said, "The inspiration for the names 'Starsky and Hutch' came from S&H Green Stamps, which stands for Sperry and Hutchinson."

Is that supposed to make us feel better? I wondered. *You've brought us shopping, end of story.*

One step into the place and I turned to Cockroach. "Pop was right," I whispered, "the place is a shithole." It was an old mill, converted into a redemption center with worn wooden floors and rows of steel shelves that were arranged in some sort of category: Housewares, Sporting Goods, and so on. "It's definitely not Bradlees or Zayre's," I added.

I can't imagine saving for months for a carving knife or a bath towel, I thought.

Ma pushed an old steel carriage—shaky from a nervous wheel up front—smiling like she'd just won a shopping spree. The first item she set into the carriage was a good-sized box; an Anchor Hocking Tulip beverage 24-piece set, which included eight 8-ounce juice glasses, eight 8-ounce rocks glasses, and eight 12-ounce beverage glasses—all in blue. "This cost me two and a half books of stamps," she announced, proudly.

"Nice glasses," Cockroach commented.

She nodded. "And they're for company only, Alphonse. You boys will still use the plastic tumblers I bought you from Tupperware."

"Gee, thanks Ma," I mumbled.

"Just once, I'd like to have something nice," she huffed, "something you boys won't break."

Cockroach took off to go hang out with our father, who was wandering aimlessly around the shop.

New glassware is something nice? I wondered.

She then placed a tie tack set into the cart.

A birthday gift for Pop, I guessed. *But when does he ever wear a tie?*

This was followed by a bottle of English Leather aftershave, which cost one full book of stamps.

"Don't tell your father," she whispered, looking around to make sure he wasn't watching.

"Your secret's safe with me, Ma," I told her, snickering. At that point, I was done following her and decided to break off on my own and do some browsing.

The Health-O-Meter oval bath scale was four and a quarter books, the same amount as a large square hassock—*which we could really use for our Saturday morning wrestling matches.*

The place had watches, electronics, housewares, sporting goods, kitchenware—you name it. In the toy section, I checked out everything carefully: 3-D magnetic puzzles, TootsieToy truck sets, Placo Super Dart Target set, Gabriel Airplane set, Oil Paint by Number set, Play Pal Banks in either Mickey, Donald Duck, or Pinocchio.

A few years earlier, I would have begged Ma to share one of her books of stamps, I realized. *But not now.* I was beyond that.

I looked up to see my little brother standing beside me. *Although I'm sure Deputy Dawg here will try to score something for himself.*

"Ma's heading for checkout," he said, showing me the Presto Magix Picture Magic Dry Transfer Game that he was holding, the Star Wars version.

Easy as one, two, three, I thought, picturing the commercial that played around the clock during the holiday season. *Just trace it with your pencil and then pull back the plastic sheet, revealing your masterpiece.*

"I'm gonna ask Ma if she'll get it for me," he said, making one of his eyebrows dance.

"Of course you are," I told him, before heading out of the place to join Pop in the station wagon.

Another successful field trip, I thought, sarcastically.

• • •

That night, Cockroach locked himself in the bathroom with Mr. Bubble. He loved that smiling bubble on the pink box.

"Hurry up," I yelled at him through the door, "I have to use the bathroom."

"I'm taking a bubble bath, Herbie," he said. "You'll have to wait."

My entire body pulsated with angry blood. "I can't wait," I yelled, pounding even harder on the door. "Now unlock this door!"

I could hear him get out of the tub and shuffle across the linoleum. With a bath towel wrapped around his waist, he slowly opened it.

"You're lucky I don't…" I started to tell him, sprinting for the toilet.

"I can't even take a quiet bath around here anymore," he muttered, before heading for our bedroom.

It was late when Wally and I conspired to scare the hell out of bathing beauty.

"Did you hear about that kid who got rushed to the hospital?" Wally asked me.

"No," I said, fighting off a smile, "what happened?"

"I guess he was taking a bubble bath and got some soap in his peehole."

"So what?"

"I heard he got a bad infection and needed to get a shot."

"Bullshit!" Cockroach called out from his bunk. "You guys are just trying to scare me."

"You wish," Wally said. "I know I'm not going to take any more bubble baths and risk it."

"Bullshit," Cockroach repeated.

Both Wally and I knew that our fib would spell certain death for Mr. Bubble in our house.

• • •

"Are we going anywhere today?" I asked our father the following day, hoping he had some kind of plan in mind.

"We're going to relax today, Herbie," he said, "that's what we're going to do." He shook his head. "We don't have to do everything in the first week, do we?"

What? I thought. *You took us to the Go Karts.*

"It's me and Mom's vacation too, you know."

I didn't realize it at the time, but all Pop wanted to do was relax during his two weeks off. He busted his hump for the family the other fifty weeks of the year.

At Ma's strong suggestion, we prepared to spend the night at the drive-in movie theatre to see *Splash.*

"A mermaid movie?" I questioned, before deciding it was still a night out.

Heading to the drive-in meant packing Pop's steel cooler with a jug of Country Time lemonade, two cans of Tab, and a can of Fresca for Ma. The rest was jam packed with golden cans of beer for the old man.

Three multi-colored Tupperware tumblers were packed in Ma's cloth bag, along with a large bag of Jax cheese curls, M&Ms with peanuts—because they melted in your mouth and not in your hand—Doritos, and a half dozen paper bags of popcorn Ma had popped in her beloved microwave. The bag of Spanish peanuts and beef jerky were solely intended for Pop. Although the box of Cosmic Brownies was meant for everyone, I planned on tearing through most of them as early as possible. I'd been seduced by Little Debbie at a very young age and couldn't manage to escape her spell.

Although we were a bit too old to wear pajamas to the movies, we were just as comfortable in cut-off jeans and t-shirts. A full lather of bug spray later, we locked the apartment door behind us.

The whole family—even Wally—piled into Pop's wood-paneled station wagon, excited for the night ahead. Pop had his usual beer resting between his legs, while Ma sucked on one of her cancer sticks in the passenger seat. The three of us sat in the back seat, vying for every inch of vinyl real estate we could. All four windows were rolled down, creating a refreshing wind tunnel in the back. The ride might have even been enjoyable if it wasn't for Pop's choice of music.

The old man eased down the lane to the drive-in's guard shack, where he stopped. "Still charging by the carload, I hope?" he said.

The ruddy-faced kid nodded. "Yes, sir," he said, accepting the money in exchange for a ticket. "Just put it on your dashboard."

"You got it, kid," Pop said.

I imagined that poor ticket being buried under a layer of dust in no time.

Pop turned to Ma. "Your great idea just cost me fifteen smack-aroos," he teased.

"Big deal," she huffed, "we all know you got it."

Still shaking his head, Pop turned right. Parking the car toward the middle of the theatre grounds, he hung the silver speaker onto his slightly rolled-up window. "Show time," he said.

Ma checked her watch. "Not for another fifteen minutes." She turned sideways to address us. "You have time to play on the swings if you want," she said. "Just make sure you put on more bug spray, or you'll get eaten alive."

Wally snickered.

"What?" she asked him.

"Are you kidding, Ma," he said, "I'm sure there's people here I know."

"So?"

"So, I don't want them to see me here with you guys."

That was my cue to leave, with Cockroach on my heels. We took off running toward the swing set in front of the massive movie screen. *I don't blame Wally*, I thought. *I won't be playing on any swings when I'm old enough to take Donna to the drive-in.* As I claimed an empty swing. I felt some serious déjà vu. *I think I've had this very same experience before.*

CHAPTER 7

JULY 1984

POP'S VACATION, WEEK 2

Before we knew it, we were already into the second week of Pop's vacation.

Our father treating us to Butlers Donuts on Sunday mornings was hardly a special event. He took the drive, making it a weekly stop over the summer. Although they served the best glazed, chocolate frosted, jelly and apple filled donuts, their signature item was the Long John; this long, thin pastry was filled with real cream and strawberry jam—a lot like a Flaky Puff pastries, but fresh. Through the years, I witnessed Wally choke more of them down than Coney Island hot dogs, which was really saying something.

We were still licking our fingers and wiping the powdered sugar from our mouths, when Pop announced, "I have a surprise for you guys today."

"What is it?" Cockroach asked, finishing his glass of coffee milk.

"It wouldn't be a surprise if I told ya, right?"

"Is it a thing or…" Wally began to ask.

"It's a place," Pop said. "I'm taking you guys somewhere this morning."

While Cockroach and I remained excited, Wally gave it some thought, weighing his options. "I can't go, Pop," he finally announced, pushing his chair out from the kitchen table. "I have work later."

I knew my brother well enough to know that he wasn't willing to wage his free time for a long shot on our father.

"Your loss," Pop told him.

"Will we be back in time for my paper route?" I asked, still on the fence.

He gawked at me. "You're coming, Herbie," he said, "I'll get you back in time."

Twenty minutes later, we pulled into the parking lot of the White Eagle Soda Company.

Cockroach looked sideways at me.

I shrugged. "At least it's not a dump run," I whispered.

"Not yet," he said, shaking his head, "but his vacation isn't over yet."

Only on the rarest of occasions—holidays and the like—were my brothers and I allowed to drink soda. "Too much of that crap will rot out your teeth," Pop sometimes stuttered.

My brothers and I always exchanged baffled looks. *What about all the beer you swill?* I wondered.

Although White Eagle delivered to our house whenever Ma called in an order, Pop obviously had different plans in mind.

"You guys can pick the flavors today," he said, leading us toward the small factory, "as long as I get two bottles of ginger ale and your mother gets her cream soda."

Our family was about to enjoy a full case—a wooden crate of two-liter bottles—of White Eagle soda pop. *Sweet!* I thought, strangely excited.

"Okay Pop," Cockroach said, clearly less impressed by this big surprise.

Two steps into the building and Pop was already talking to the middle-aged woman at the front desk. "Any chance these boys can get a quick tour of the factory?" he asked, gesturing toward us.

She began to shake her head. "Ummm, that's not something we normally…"

"It's their vacation," he added, cutting her off, "and they've been begging me to bring them in here for years."

"Ummm…"

Leaning in closer, the old man lowered his voice. "The younger one suffered a bad head injury over the winter and we're still not sure about the amount of damage." He shot her a wink. "It sure would mean an awful lot to him."

The woman finally nodded. "Okay," she said, "I think we can make something happen."

Holy crap, I thought, pushing down a laugh. Watching Pop in action was like being able to take a peek behind the Wizard of Oz's curtain.

"What did he just say to her?" Cockroach asked me in a whisper.

I shrugged. "I think he told her we'd really enjoy a tour."

He nodded.

"When were you thinking…" the woman began to ask.

"No time like the present, I always say," Pop said, winking down at us.

As we were reluctantly allowed behind a set of double doors, the first thing that struck me was the noise level. The place was loud, machines and conveyor belts clacking and buzzing away. Following along the assembly line, we watched as the clear glass bottles were quickly filled with different colored soda pop. From there, the clanking bottles traveled down a wider conveyor belt to another machine, which stamped on the metal caps.

It looks like it'd be really cool to work here, I thought. Yet, all of the men in their gray coveralls looked miserable. I just couldn't figure it. I was still too young to understand the monotony associated with manual labor on an assembly line.

The entire self-guided tour took no more than ten minutes before it ended.

Pop was a man of his word, allowing Cockroach and I to fill the order with the flavors we preferred—grape, strawberry, and orange. Of course, he got his ginger ale, and Ma got her cream soda—even though everyone knew she preferred her store-bought Tab and Fresca.

Walking out, Pop carried the case of mixed soda bottles. "What a pit," he commented. "I'd hate to work here."

What do I know? I thought.

We got back into the station wagon and headed for home.

That shithouse tour can't be it? I thought, keeping my disappointment to myself.

"Did you boys have fun today?" Pop asked in the rearview mirror, clearly proud of himself for running an errand that he was able to peddle off as a field trip.

"It was okay…I guess," Cockroach answered.

Looking out the side window, I shook my head. "I hope we still have time to head over to the pharmacy to pay the electric and gas bills," I told him.

The old man's smile vanished. "Ingrates," he muttered, while we buried our laughter in the blanket that may have never seen the inside of a washing machine—ever.

If we're lucky, I thought, *maybe Pop will take us to K-Mart for the chopped ham sandwiches on blue light special.*

• • •

Feeling nostalgic, I peered into the penny candy case at R&S Variety, gazing at the enormous selection. "Give me ten Fortune Bubbles, ten Now or Laters, five Swedish Fish and five Lemonheads," I told Old Man Sedgeband.

He was a scarecrow of a man, with serpent eyes that peered out from Coke-bottle glasses. Abandoning his checker game, he snapped open a brown paper bag and begrudgingly filled my petty order.

I placed thirty pennies onto the counter; these copper beauties had been earned and not vacuumed up from one of our parents' pitch games.

Sighing heavily, Sedgeband snatched up the change with his gnarled fingers, making a quick recount to ensure I hadn't cheated him. After throwing the change into his massive, brass cash register, he began to return to his game.

Just then, Cockroach placed a pair of Push Pops and a Sugar Daddy onto the cloudy glass counter. "What Ma doesn't know won't hurt her," he whispered to me.

"You just keep telling yourself that," I told him.

"Hey, I learned from the best," he said, grinning.

I nodded. "My bad," I agreed, "but I should have also taught you that…someday, it's going to catch up with you."

Ignoring me, he told Old Man Sedgeband, "And give me two packs of Carlton 100s on my mother's tab."

"Sure, just as soon as your mother forks over a payment." He never moved an inch toward the cigarettes. Instead, the zombie grabbed his green, spiral notebook.

My brother yanked a twenty-dollar bill out his pocket and handed it over to the fluffy-eared store owner. "This should hold us over for a bit."

"Not for long," the geezer said, marking it in his notebook.

"I didn't know Ma gave you money to…" I began to say.

"She didn't," he explained in a whisper, "that twenty was mine."

"What?" I was in shock.

He shrugged. "I don't want it to catch up with me, Herbie," he said, grinning.

Hmmm, I thought, knowing it would take me quite some time to process this one.

As we left the store, I looked at Sedgeband. *Later, loser.*

• • •

McDonald's introduced the salad to its menu in the summer of 1984. For whatever reason, it really pissed my father off. "What the hell will they come up with next," he groaned, "breakfast burritos?"

I didn't understand his anger. "It's on the menu as an option, Pop," I told him. "No one's forcing anyone to eat the rabbit food."

Vic nodded like some deranged bobblehead. Pop had allowed him to join us for supper. *Even the old man feels bad for him*, I thought.

My father looked back at me. "Well, it shouldn't be on the

menu," he said. "This is a burger joint. They should stick to burgers. You don't see KFC serving anything but chicken, do you?"

Whatever, I thought, considering my own options. The McDLT had also just premiered, served in a double Styrofoam container. *It looks good*, I thought, but it was an unknown. *I'll try it*, I finally decided, placing my order behind Wally's.

Vic ordered the same as me, careful not to overstep.

Although there was some assembly required, the hot side stayed hot, while the cold side stayed cold—just as the commercials promised.

I slammed it down in five or six bites. With every chew, I couldn't decide whether I'd made a mistake. *It's delicious,* I thought, *but it's not the Big Mac.*

I looked at Pop, who was already tearing into his second Quarter Pounder with Cheese. "How was it?" he asked between bites.

I shrugged. "Better than a salad, I guess."

He shook his head. "Salad," he repeated, "who eats salad for dinner?"

Clearly not us.

"Where's the beef?" Cockroach said, referring to the popular commercial.

I laughed, thinking, *Funny, but wrong restaurant.*

"Best burger ever," Vic announced out of the blue. "The best!"

My father looked at him, and then over to me. "This boy needs to get out more."

I nodded in agreement, thinking, *Except, he never has a dime on him.*

• • •

The following day, as we played in the backyard, I asked Wally, "Hey, do you want to play rundown?"

Without the expected wisecrack, he headed straight for the shed—where all of our broken sports gear was stored.

It seemed funny to me because using sports equipment made no real difference to us. Sometimes, two trashcan lids and a tennis ball were all we needed for a full day of playing rundown.

"Alphonse runs first," Wally said, handing me a glove and baseball instead.

"Fine," the little man said, "but no crisscross this time. I'm not taking another baseball off the head."

I laughed again. Of the three of us—although he was the youngest—Cockroach was the best ball player. Like anything else, he had to try so much harder and the extra effort served him well. As a result, he already wielded the best glove in the family.

"Because I swear to God, I'll bean you off your noggin when it's your turn to run," he yelled over to Wally.

Wally and I laughed, as we warmed up our arms with a light game of catch.

"If you keep running that mouth, I'm gonna tell Ma," Wally said. "You don't want to end up at the orphanage, do you?"

I laughed again. Whenever we were misbehaving—which was always—Ma threatened that she and Pop were going to drop us off at some mythical orphan's home. "Let's see if they can do something with you animals," she'd tell us, "cause God knows I'm at the end of my rope." Sometimes, she'd even pick up the kitchen phone and pretend to call the scary home, requesting that they come pick us up right away. Although this never worked on me or Wally, it usually straightened our little brother right out.

Cockroach shrugged. "You know what, I'm ready for that orphanage whenever they want to come get me," he said. "No matter how bad it is, I'm sure it'll be better than living in this nuthouse."

As Wally and I started laughing again, our little brother took off running, sliding into the opposite base. "Safe!" he screamed.

"Cheater," I yelled at him.

"One to nothing," he announced, smiling wide.

We were an hour into playing rundown, when both Pop and Ma joined us in the backyard.

This is weird, I thought.

None of us could believe it when Pop announced, "What do you say we play some real ball, boys?" To our further surprise, this went beyond a simple game of catch. "Get me a bat and I'll hit you some pop flies."

I felt my entire insides heat up from excitement.

A wire fence separated our yard from the Portuguese family that lived beside us, most of them unable to speak a word of English. Fortunately, we usually had Vic to serve as our translator. He always laughed, saying, "These people really hate your family."

For the next few hours, Pop hit us fly balls, which we happily shagged.

As we played, Roscoe, the neighbor's dog—chained to his makeshift coop—walked as much of the fence's perimeter as his chain would allow. He had a small plastic kiddie pool just outside of his doghouse.

"I hope you guys don't play in that pool," Pop teased us, "because that's not lemonade, you know."

We were laughing, when Pop hit a high fly ball that landed just over the fence.

Waiting in the shadows, the old Portuguese lady stormed out of her house and made a beeline for our baseball. She suddenly spotted my father and stopped. For a moment, it appeared to be a stand-off, with both of them sneering at each other.

"Go get that ball, Wally," Pop yelled, "and make it quick! We need it more than she does."

Wally jumped the fence, snatched the ball, and successfully hurdled back.

Shaking her fist at us, the old hag screamed something in Portuguese, presumably a swear word.

I looked toward Vic.

"Oh, that's a bad one," he confirmed, whistling.

As morning bled into afternoon, Ma paid Gus for as much ice cream as we could stomach. And it was plenty, leaving the stout ice cream troll with a smile on his face.

I can't imagine a better day, I decided.

We played for hours, loving every minute spent with Pop.

Ma watched us from her orange vinyl-woven lawn chair. While we shagged one fly ball after the next, she occasionally shagged us plastic cups of ice-cold lemonade—or at least what she tried to pass off as lemonade. Her transistor radio played the oldies—her and Pop's 50s music—but we didn't care. *It beats listening to Country and Western*, I thought, though not even that could have ruined such a magical day.

Even with all our experience, Alphonse was the best fielder by far. It wasn't even close. At the crack of Pop's bat, the youngster was already on the move, homing in on his high-flying target. No matter how long we played, Cockroach never missed a single fly ball.

"That's how you do it, boys," he yelled, as the slap of leather echoed from his glove.

The afternoon began darkening into night. While Ma headed upstairs to the apartment, we sat under the willow tree with Pop. As the old man sipped his Miller, he shared a story that I knew I'd never forget.

The back power window in Pop's previous station wagon had been broken since he'd picked up the second-hand junker. Had it worked, all you'd have to do is put the key into the rear hatch and turn it; this would automatically open or close the back window, depending on which way the key was turned.

"That damn window was broken from the day I owned the car," he explained. "Anyway, one day, I helped Aunt Elizabeth by giving her a ride to the hospital." Pop's Aunt Elizabeth, our great aunt, was a saintly woman who'd been bedridden for years. "So, I handed the keys to Darrell, her son, to unlock the car. He had no idea that the rear window was broken, so he tried it—looking to store his mother's wheelchair in the back of the rig." Pop shook his head in disbelief. "And don't you know, the damned thing worked!" His eyes misted over, bringing us even deeper into the story. "It was a miracle, boys," he claimed, "an honest-to-goodness miracle."

Considering that our father wasn't a very religious man, the story gave me goosebumps, while also confirming Ma's claims about the power of faith.

Pop took another sip of beer and laughed. "Elizabeth's late

husband, my Uncle Fred—who you guys never got a chance to meet—was a real strange duck."

"How's that?" Cockroach asked, enjoying story time with our father as much as I was.

"The old coot loved warning me and your Uncle Skinny about the craziest things." Pop chuckled. "He once told us, 'You fellas know that holly berries are poisonous, right?' Before we could answer, he said, 'So don't be eatin' any of 'em.'" Still laughing, Pop shook his head. "I remember thinking, *Yeah Uncle Fred, holly berries are my favorite snack…when I'm not munching away on pinecones.*"

My brothers and I laughed hard. It was such a treat to see this side of our father.

"Another time," Pop said, clearly on a roll, "me and Uncle Skinny were at the kook's house visiting Aunt Elizabeth, when Fred pulled us aside and whispered, 'I just sprinkled some rat poison under the porch, so make sure you boys stay out of there. It'll make you real sick.'"

Wally and I laughed again.

Pop joined us. "Skinny and I started to laugh, too, thinking that Fred was joking because the porch was no more than a foot off the ground." He shook his head. "But he wasn't."

We laughed harder.

"I remember telling Uncle Skinny, 'What a bummer 'cause I was hoping to jam my head under that porch and lick some of that powdered sugar off a few leaves.'"

While Wally and I kept on laughing, Cockroach shook his head. "Good thing you didn't, Pop, because you would have been rushed to the Emergency Room to get your stomach pumped."

Wally and I exchanged stunned glances.

What an airhead, I thought.

"You can't be serious?" Wally said to him.

"I guess there was only one way to find out, Alphonse," Pop said, playing along. "I should have had your Uncle Skinny lap up some of that powdered sugar."

We all laughed.

"No wonder Darrell is such a weirdo," Wally commented.

Pop's head spun toward him. "We don't live in a house without mirrors," he reminded my brother, "so you might want to watch who you label *weird*."

Wally said nothing.

"I'm telling you, if you'd ever met his father, you'd know why Darrell was touched in the head."

I couldn't wait to hear more. For whatever reason, I loved hearing stories about our family—good or bad. We were hypnotized.

"Although Fred was crazy, he really had no nuts when it came to other adults," Pop said.

What?

He smirked. "A squirrel could have shimmied up his trousers and starved to death."

I laughed so hard I thought I might wet my Levi's cutoffs.

"But when it came to his son, there were times when he could be a cruel bastard." The old man shook his head. "One time, when Darrell was a kid, he spilled a pan of scalding water onto the floor, some of it landing inside his rubber boots." Pop looked at each of us. "Do you know that Fred made him dry that damned floor before he allowed Darrell to take off his boots." He shook his head again. "Poor kid suffered second-degree burns and limped around for months after that."

"Oh, my God," I said, "that's gnarly."

"You never know why people are the way they are," Pop said, looking sideways at Wally, "so you might want to lock that away in your memory bank."

My older brother nodded.

· · ·

"Nice Rolex," I told Cockroach, teasing him about his candy watch. If he waited too long to eat it, it was guaranteed to turn his skin different colors. It was a ridiculous piece of edible jewelry, even if it did tell the right time twice a day. The matching candy necklace was a nice accessory, though. Cockroach just needed to stretch it into his mouth and start chomping away.

"No more candy jewelry for me pretty soon," he announced, grinning.

"What do you mean?" I asked.

"I'm buying the Casio calculator watch this weekend when Pop gives me a ride to the mall."

"What?" I repeated, always surprised that my little brother had money to spend.

"I was thinking about shelling out the thirty bucks for a Swatch watch, but I like the calculator watch more."

Since his first Speak & Spell, Cockroach loved any new technology. He stayed up on all the latest trends—compact discs and PCs—and even had his eyes on the new Nintendo gaming system, featuring some game called Mario Brothers.

"How much is the Casio?" I asked him.

He shrugged. "A few bucks more than the Swatch watch."

Damn, I thought, still in shock. My brother was as tight as two layers of wallpaper. *But calculator watches are the rave right now,* I realized, *especially the digital ones with an alarm.*

Whether it was a candy watch or calculator watch, Cockroach was punctual.

• • •

It was Wednesday afternoon when I found Ma standing alone at her stove, already starting supper.

I leaned in to take a whiff. "What are you cooking?" I asked her.

"It's a bit of a mixed bag tonight," she admitted.

I waited to hear more.

"I'm making tri-colored pasta salad, mini-wieners, and deviled eggs," she said.

"Smells good," I lied. "Where's Cockroach and Pop?"

She took a break from cooking. "Your father's finally taken Alphonse for a ride 'to have the talk.'"

"Oh no," I said, laughing. As though it had happened yesterday, I could still remember that same dreadful ride with my father. My mind immediately went back.

"Okay," the old man said to me, "Tell me everything you know about sex, and then I'll fill in the rest for you, okay?"

"But Pop…" I'd never felt so embarrassed.

"It's just you and me, kid," he said, "and remember, there ain't a thing that you've thought and felt that I haven't already thought and felt. Understand?"

Reluctantly, I told him what I knew. He looked surprised at how much I already had down. As promised, he then filled in whatever details I needed to understand. It was shocking at how cool Pop was with the awkward conversation, explaining everything without jokes or judgment. He was thoughtful and considerate, and respectful. It was a different experience with him all the way around. "Don't be in such a hurry to grow up, Herbie. You have your whole life to have sex," he told me, "and just remember that making love with someone you actually love is so much better than just having sex with someone you couldn't care less about." One of his eyebrows rose. "Though your Uncle Skinny might disagree with me there."

Although I laughed, I couldn't even imagine how filthy this same conversation would have been with Uncle Skinny.

Returning to the present, I headed to my bedroom to bring Wally up to speed.

He laughed harder than me. "Poor Cockroach," he said, shaking his head.

"How doesn't Pop know that we have a stack of Playboy magazines hidden in the cellar?" I asked.

Wally shrugged. "Especially since I stole half of them from his stash."

We both laughed.

Looking to kill off boredom, I picked up my Magic 8 Ball and gave it a few shakes, while considering a good question.

"That thing is so bogus," Wally commented, "I can't believe you still play with it."

I shook it once more. "Will Pop get his facts straight about the birds and the bees this time?" I asked the shiny plastic toy.

I turned it over and peered into the small window. "Outlook hazy," I read aloud.

Wally remained silent.

"Will Alphonse teach Pop something he didn't know?" I asked, shaking it even harder.

"Definitely," I read.

A smile broke through Wally's stoic gaze.

One more, I thought, giving the black globe a few more shakes. "Will Alphonse put his teachings to use right away?" I asked the Hasbro advisor.

I slowly turned it to read the message on the floating triangle. "Yes!" I announced.

Wally was sent into a fit of hysterics. "Damn," he snorted, "I guess that thing is spot on!"

Bogus, huh?

Both Wally and the Magic 8 Ball were right. Our little brother had an inappropriate crush on our twenty-something next door neighbor. Had he been a few years older, I had no doubt that he would have already made a move on her. You could see it in the kid's sparkling brown eyes. When it came to the opposite sex, my little brother was a born hunter.

"Spot on," Wally repeated.

• • •

It was nearing the end of Pop's vacation. After a packy run for beer and scratch tickets, the old man took us to the local scrapyard to redeem four enormous bags filled with aluminum cans for cash.

The bulging plastic bags smelled terrible.

"Whatever we make," Pop announced, "you guys can split." Our father could be crunchy on the outside, but he was definitely soft and gooey on the inside.

We weren't at Mid-City Scrap Iron for two minutes when Pop was already haggling with the guy on the scale. I wasn't sure how much we were getting a pound, but I did know that my one-third cut was $28.40. I felt like we'd hit the lottery.

Why didn't we do this at the beginning of Pop's vacation, so we had money to do a few things? I wondered. It dawned on me again. *Because doing a few things is the opposite of the old man's master plan—being able to relax.* I nodded. *Well played, Pop.*

We returned to Kartway on our bicycles, hoping that enough time had passed that the owner no longer remembered our faces.

He didn't—or at least pretended not to. We raced Go Karts for hours.

• • •

The following day, as Cockroach had predicted, Pop began to bag and box all of the junk that the garbage truck wouldn't pick up with the weekly trash.

"Let's get a move on," he told us. "I need your help."

"Told ya," Cockroach whispered. "We're doing a dump run."

I shook my head. "Are we going on another field trip?" I asked our father, making my little brother smile.

The old man nodded, grinning back. "That's right," he said, "and you're never gonna forget it, Herbie."

Yeah right!

We loaded up the back of the station wagon, as well as the back-seat, with boxes and bags of anything that was rusted solid, broken beyond repair, or stinking to high heaven.

Both Cockroach and I took a seat in the passenger seat up front, our eyes watering from the terrible stench.

"Must be an old pair of your brother's underwear," Pop joked.

I didn't allow myself to laugh, afraid that one of my gags might turn to liquid.

All the way up Route 88, the windows were rolled down, while the country music was turned up. With a cold beer nestled safely between the old man's legs, he looked like he was in heaven.

We took a left onto an old dirt road that stretched for nearly a half-mile into the woods, years of litter and trash bags lining both sides. The station wagon kicked up enough dust to cover our faces and arms. As the road opened up to a massive clearing, Pop pulled up to a giant mountain of trash.

We all jumped out and emptied the car, throwing the boxes and bags as high onto the heap as we could.

"This is so much fun," Cockroach mumbled under his breath.

"Yup, the perfect vacation spot," I joked, looking around.

When we finished our work, Pop yelled, "Alphonse, get in the backseat." He then walked over to the passenger side door, opened it, and took a seat.

I looked at him, dumbfounded.

"What are you looking at me for?" he asked. "Don't you think it's about time you learned how to drive?"

I couldn't believe it. I was scared and excited, all at the same time. *Gnarly!*

I hurried into the station wagon, adjusting the seat so I could reach the pedals.

"Gas is on the right. Brake is on the left," my father instructed.

I nodded. *No duh.*

"Remember, this car's like a gun!" he screamed; he wasn't angry, just making sure he got his point across. "You can kill someone, Herbie, if you don't use your head."

"I get it, Pop," I told him, although I would have agreed to anything he'd said at that point. I was busting at the seams to get the car rolling. At his nod, I put the shifter into drive and pointed the nose straight. *It's happening!* I screamed in my head.

"You don't need a lot of gas," Pop warned. "Go easy."

I was nodding, when I spotted a pickup truck driving toward us. *Oh shit...*

"When you're not sure what the other guy's gonna do," the old man said, "just come off the gas and cover the brake with your foot, so you're ready to stop if you need to."

I nodded.

"Stay to the right of the road and give him room to pass."

"Okay...okay," I said.

"Slow down and hug the right, Herbie," he yelled.

I did just that, nearly coming to a stop. As the truck passed, Pop relaxed back in the passenger seat and took a long chug of his beer.

By the second run, I'd really gotten the hang of it, learning how hard I should press on each pedal, or how far I should turn the steering wheel. *This isn't a whole lot different from the Go-Karts,* I thought. *Just a lot bigger.*

Pop looked sideways at me and grinned at my excitement. "You're doing good," he said. "Just keep your eyes out the windshield."

"Can I change the radio?" I asked him.

To my surprise, he nodded. "The driver's always in charge. It's your call."

I spun the dial to 94 HJY, the local rock station, and while Steven Tyler from Aerosmith wailed "Dream On," I was living it.

With both hands on the steering wheel, my heart raced from pure excitement. I could finally taste the freedom I'd fantasized about for so many years. I could still smell the stench in the car and was swallowing some of the dirt that swirled in through the open windows, but I didn't care. *I need to start saving money for my own car,* I decided.

I took four or five more turns, barreling up and down that long dump road, and loving every second of it. *I wonder if Pop knows how huge this is for me,* I thought. *He was right, I'll never forget this day!*

With his dark shades on, the old man just sat there, one elbow out the passenger window and the other bending a cold beer to his lips. "One more run and then it's your brother's turn," he finally announced.

Even when Cockroach got his chance to drive—sitting in my father's lap and steering the wheel—I was overwhelmed with excitement. I could actually feel what he was feeling. We took a few laps up and back, my little brother giggling the whole time.

When it was time to call it quits, Pop said, "Okay, who wants to drive us home?"

I immediately volunteered.

He laughed. "That a boy," he said, pulling Cockroach off his lap, "but you still have a few more dump road lessons ahead of you before we can take that ride."

Awesome! I thought. *This won't be the last time I'll get to drive this old dirt road.*

We were almost back to the house, when I asked, "Pop, have you ever let Wally drive?"

Finishing his beer, he nodded. "Sure I have. A few times."

"He never told us," I said.

"That's because your brother knows how to keep his mouth shut."

"So do we, Pop," Cockroach said.

The old man cracked open a fresh beer. "Time will tell on that one, I suppose."

• • •

We'd finally reached the end of Pop's two-week vacation and were just wrapping up one of our famous backyard cookouts, when our father announced, "I've been speaking to your uncle, and we both figure it's time for a boys' night out."

We waited for the payoff.

"We're taking you guys to the Red Sox."

"Yes!" we screamed in unison. We couldn't have been more excited.

We're actually going to see Jim Rice, Dewey Evans, Yaz, Pudge, Freddie Lynn, I thought, *all the greats.* Reality continued to set in. *And we're finally going to get to see Fenway Park with our own eyes!*

Cockroach started dancing and hurt himself. "Ouch," he whined, grabbing for his crotch.

Pop caught the whimpers. "What the hell's he bellowing about?"

"Cockroach was dancing recklessly like one of those California raisins," Wally reported, holding back a smile, "and he may have compromised his groin muscles."

"Oh, dear God," Pop complained. "No more hospital visits, please."

During the ride to Fenway Park, Wally and I teased Cockroach.

"How did the birds and the bees talk go with Pop?" I whispered.

He shook his head.

"Well?" Wally quietly prodded.

"I don't want to talk about it," he said. "I'd rather forget about it."

I laughed. "Did you learn anything new?" I asked.

"Please stop," he said.

"It's more like, did you teach Pop anything?" Wally asked, extending his palm to me for a high-five.

We laughed until Uncle Skinny turned around in the passenger seat. "What's so funny, guys?"

"Nothing," Wally said.

We all knew that if we let our crazy uncle in on the truth, then he'd turn it all dark and twisted.

Uncle Skinny shrugged. "Probably for the best," he said, "I'm too sad to hear a joke, anyway."

"Why?" Cockroach asked, still gullible.

"My cat, Mr. Fluffernutter, has been wandering into the Chinese restaurant's parking lot for the past few weeks." He shook his head.

Pop grinned. "Good thing Mr. Fluffernutter has nine lives."

"That's the thing, Walt," Uncle Skinny said, looking legitimately upset.

Maybe he's not screwing around? I thought, leaning forward in my seat.

"Mr. Fluffernutter hasn't come home for two days," our uncle reported.

"Damn," Wally said aloud. I looked over at him. He shook his head. "I'm not surprised," he whispered.

"Worst part is, I won't be able to eat lo mein for at least a month," Uncle Skinny said, his face set like granite.

A moment later, he and Pop burst into laughter and couldn't stop.

"And I love lo mein," our uncle managed between laughs.

"That's so messed up," Wally said.

No kidding, I thought. I loved Uncle Skinny's white and brown cat, Mr. Fluffernutter. *I'm the one who won't be eating Chinese food for a while.*

"So messed up," Wally repeated, while Pop and Uncle Skinny tapped beers in some mock celebration.

After an hour ride—listening to Hank Williams all the way—we ended up at McCoy Stadium, home of the Pawtucket Red Sox, the Boston Red Sox's farm team. As we pulled into the massive parking lot, Pop turned down the music, "Ain't this something?" he said, starting to boast. "Free parking and only six bucks a ticket to sit right near the field." He nodded, proudly. "Beer and hot dogs for a fraction of the price they charge at Fenway."

Yeah, that's just great, Pop, I thought, trying my best not to sulk. I looked at my brothers, who were equally disappointed. *So much for seeing all the greats play at Fenway Park.*

We'd arrived early enough to catch batting practice. Two rows from the field, we were ready with our baseball gloves. As the Paw-Sox wrapped up, Ed Jurak, the team's third baseman, threw a ball into the crowd. Wally leapt to his feet, missing the free souvenir by inches. It flew just over his head.

Quick to respond, Uncle Skinny stood. "I know where we can find more of those, boys," he said. "Follow me."

The next thing I knew, we were standing in the middle of the Souvenir Shop, where our generous uncle bought us each a fitted ball cap. Cockroach opted to go with the tiny wooden souvenir bat. *The resale value must be higher*, I figured.

Unfortunately, we'd missed Wade Boggs by a few years. There were no recognizable names on the Pawsox, except for Pat Dodson, playing first base, and Mike Greenwell, who played in the outfield. Even though the team had a losing record, keeping them down in eighth place, both players showed some real promise to make it to the Big Leagues.

McCoy Stadium held ten thousand fans, with the five of us sitting in some great seats—almost on the field. The advertisements pasted on the outfield walls gave me a great idea. "I spy with my little eye," I said, elbowing Cockroach, "a potato."

"Hasbro's sign with Mr. Potato's Head on it?"

"Yup, you got it."

"I spy with my little eye…" he began.

"Are you guys gonna watch the game?" Pop asked.

"Once it starts," I fired back.

Pop quickly searched my face to see if I was being a smart-ass. I wasn't. He pardoned me with a single nod.

The Syracuse Chiefs were the first to bat—three up and three down.

"Let's go, Pawsox," we began to chant. "Let's go, Pawsox!"

To our collective surprise, Pop and Uncle Skinny joined in and sang a few bars with us.

This is so awesome, I thought.

Besides the hawkers that threw bags of peanuts and passed hot dogs and beer down the aisle from one hand to the next, our trips to the concession stand seemed endless. We devoured sports bar ice cream novelties, popcorn, oversized pretzels, and frozen lemonades—*which actually tastes sweet and tart like real lemonade,* I thought. Pop and Uncle Skinny alternated paying, neither one of them batting an eye. *Someone must have finally hit on a scratch ticket,* I thought.

As the sun went down and the sky turned dark, the field was illuminated by towers of giant lights. In the warm night air, the crowd cheered on the hometown team, with nobody clapping harder than me and my brothers.

"Let's go, Pawsox," we chanted. "Let's go, Pawsox!"

Whether it was the Boston Red Sox or Pawtucket Red Sox, in the end it didn't matter. I finally understood why baseball was America's favorite pastime. *Best night ever!*

On the walk back to the station wagon, Uncle Skinny slurred, "Did you boys know that a few years ago in '81, the PawSox and the Rochester Red Wings played the longest game in professional baseball history?"

We all shook our heads.

"Yes sir," he said, "it lasted 33 innings."

"If I got it right, it took them almost eight and a half hours to play that game," Pop added.

Uncle Skinny nodded. "We should have caught that one." He grinned. "Talk about getting your money's worth."

A few feet from the car, Pop asked us, "Did you boys have fun?"

"Absolutely, Pop!" I said.

"For sure, Pop," Wally agreed.

"Thanks so much for taking us tonight," Cockroach added.

"So, who won the game, the Chiefs or the Pawsox?" the old man asked, grinning.

There was silence, with Pop and Uncle Skinny looking at each other and smiling.

"The Pawsox," Wally blurted.

"Well, you did have a fifty-fifty chance on that one, Walt," Uncle Skinny said.

"And you happened to guess right," Pop said, laughing. "Let 'er go."

Everyone laughed, before being tortured by listening to Kitty Wells—Pop's 8-track player skipping tracks all the way home—with Uncle Skinny at the wheel. He'd been drinking, too, but he was still in better shape than Pop. *At least he can still see straight*, I thought, being hopeful.

CHAPTER 8

JULY 1984

BEACH TRAFFIC

We only had one car in the family, so when Pop was working and Ma needed it, some arrangements had to be made. This meant she had to drop Pop off for work early in the morning.

For a week, she kept reminding him, "I need to borrow the station wagon, Walt. I want to bring the boys to the beach."

"How many times are you going to remind me?" he asked.

"Until you remember," she answered dryly.

The only other time Ma needed the car was when she went grocery shopping, and Pop was happy to make whatever arrangements were necessary, so he didn't have to take her.

Ma alternated her weekly grocery shopping between Almacs on President Avenue and Lees Supermarket on Main Road, depending on their coupons and weekly deals.

Every time she left the house to go food shopping, Cockroach asked her, "Can you bring me home a surprise, Ma…please!"

Although she said no, she usually returned with small trinkets—packs of gum, Slinkys, whatever—for each one of us. Cockroach liked the small toys—like those balsam gliders, some assembly required—while I preferred a simple box of Flaky Puff pastries, filled with sugary cream and raspberry jam. Although there was one exception. On several occasions, Ma had brought home three large balloons attached to long rubber bands. When we finally got them blown up—nearly passing out in the process—we kept punching them like one-handed speed bags, feeling like special guest stars on Romper Room. Of course, this quickly turned violent—bouncing our overinflated balloons off of each other's face.

"Where will you guys be when I get back from the market?" she asked.

"Riding our bikes in the neighborhood," I told her. We lived on our bicycles in the summer. From morning until night, we were off pedaling somewhere toward one foolish mission or another.

"I don't want anyone riding doubles," Ma said, offering a stern warning. She was still shaken over last summer's grisly accident, when Dewey's foot had slipped off the back peg of Vic's bike and got jammed in the spokes, tearing his ankle to shreds.

"We know, Ma," I said. "We have our own bikes."

"Okay." She nodded. "Just make sure you're here to help me unload the car when I get back."

"How long will you be gone?" Cockroach asked.

"As long as it takes."

That's super helpful, Ma, I thought.

As the rear bumper of the station wagon disappeared from sight, I turned to Cockroach. "No use heading off, only to get into trouble later when she gets back and we're not here."

He nodded in agreement.

"We could hang out in the yard and play king of the mountain or even muckle," I suggested, trying not to smile. "Vic should be over soon and…"

"I don't think so, Herbie," he said, without emotion or a hint of possible negotiation.

I nodded. *He's starting to become his own man*, I thought, feeling an inkling of pride for him. "Then what?" I asked.

"We could…"

"How 'bout we set up some bike ramps that we can jump, Evel Knievel-style?"

He thought about it, his eyes lighting up. "And when Fish Stick gets here, we can talk him into laying under the ramp so we can jump over him."

I nodded. "I like that plan a lot," I said, realizing that the pecking order within our backyard gang was slowly evolving.

Ma returned home, the station wagon's back seat stuffed with brown paper bags.

"Let's go, boys," she called out. "Lots to carry this week."

My stomach churned at the possibilities.

"I'm not helping," Fish Stick said, angrily, "that's for sure!"

I turned to him. "Just go home and put ice on it, Vic. There's no way your arm's broken. Cockroach hardly caught it with the back tire."

"You guys are terrible people," he said, storming off.

I watched him for a second, debating whether I should toss him a nasty comeback. *Nah,* I decided, *he's got a good point this time.*

We lugged every bag—two at a time—up to the second-floor apartment, while our mother stood at the fridge filling it with anything that needed to stay cold. We might have been poor by some folks' standards, but Ma's cupboard was never bare.

Back at the wagon, I spotted a box of Flaky Puff pastries. Cockroach and I wrestled over them, while bringing up the last load.

"Did you get me anything, Ma?" Cockroach asked, his voice sounding like a desperate addict. White cream was smeared above his top lip.

She shook her head. "You boys are gonna break me yet." She nodded toward her purse on the kitchen table. "Get me my pocketbook."

In a flash, Cockroach fetched it.

She pulled out three Silly Putty eggs and extended them. "You're welcome," she said.

"Thanks, Ma!"

I couldn't wait to find a Sunday newspaper and transfer the Funnies onto the flattened, pink clay.

We finished helping her as much as we could. Basically, this meant lining up box after box of cold cereal in the kitchen closet: Punch Crunch, Pac-Man, Smurf Berry Crunch, Donkey Kong, and even Mr. T.

"Mr. T. cereal?" I questioned.

She shrugged. "All the new cereals were on sale, so that's what you're eating this week."

I looked at the box. My brothers and I were sugar addicts—professional cereal killers, you might say—but this one was a stretch. *One and done*, I predicted.

As we headed out the door, she reminded us, "Don't make any plans for tomorrow with your little friends. We're going to the beach."

"We won't, Ma," Cockroach said in his overly-sweet voice.

Little friends? I thought.

. . .

Ma had already dropped Pop off when she woke us. "Let's go," she said, "if you want to go to the beach, then the bus is leaving now." She started for the accordion door. "And make sure you brush your teeth, or you're staying home."

"I can't go to the beach with you guys today," Wally announced, swinging his feet off his bed, "I already made plans."

"You're the one who mentioned the beach when we were making vacation plans at the kitchen table," Ma countered, "I thought…"

"But I made other plans, Ma." He yawned.

She laughed aloud. "I couldn't care less about your plans, Wally," she said. "What is it, something to do with your delinquent friend, Owen?" She shook her head. "Nope, I don't care what other plans you've made. You're coming with us for the day and you're gonna like it."

"I am, huh?"

"Yup, we all need some quality time together, and we're going to spend that time on the beach." By now, her mouth appeared crooked, and one of her eyes was starting to twitch.

Ma's losing it, I thought. *Either that, or she's having a stroke.*

"This is such bullshit!" Wally groaned.

"That's what family is," Ma told him, her smile turning insane, "lots and lots of bullshit."

We quickly changed into swim trunks and tank tops—or wife-beaters, as Uncle Skinny called them. We also wore sneakers—high top Chuck Taylors—with no socks, turning them rancid.

While Wally and I carried the steel cooler out to the station wagon, I opened it to see why it was so heavy. It was packed with blocks of ice that Pop had made from Cool Whip containers in the freezer. There were also wrapped sandwiches that Ma had made: PBJs, egg salad—which had a short window—and bologna and cheese with mustard.

"Too bad the bologna's not fried," I whispered to my older brother.

Wally laughed.

The cooler was so heavy that Wally and I had to lug it out to the car by the side handles.

On the second trip, we carried out three large towels, Ma's beach chair and two cloth bags—one overflowing with snacks, the other containing sunblock, a Soap Opera Digest, a small transistor radio, and several packs of Carlton 100s.

Pop's wood-paneled Chevy station wagon with no exhaust had recently been replaced with a newer version of a wood-paneled Chevy station wagon. The biggest difference was that the power window in the rear of the wagon now worked. *It's no DeLorean*, I thought, *but it's an upgrade from the old junker.* I grinned. *I'm sure Cockroach will own a DeLorean someday. Maybe he'll let me pay him a few bucks to test drive it?*

As Cockroach and I jumped into the backseat, Wally begrudgingly joined us. Although there were seat belts, none of us ever wore them; the steel buckles were tucked into the bench seat so they didn't burn our skin after baking in the sun.

"Why don't you sit up front with me?" Ma told Wally.

He shook his head. "It's safer back here, Ma," he said, still pouting.

He just wants to be close to the food and drinks, I thought.

Packed together like sardines in the back seat, lots of excited chatter—in anticipation of the trip—kicked off the long ride.

"I love the beach," Cockroach said.

Me too, I thought, nodding, *though I'm more excited about meeting Donna at the snack shack for lunch.* I checked my pocket to ensure I'd brought enough money. *Good, it's all there.*

"Ma, remember when we went to the beach last year?" I asked, feeling giddy. "We had the best time."

She nodded into the rearview mirror. "We sure did," she said, "but don't lose sight of today, Herbie. This is a new memory we're making, right?"

The car went silent.

"It's fun to visit the past, but make sure you don't stay there too long," she added, "If you linger, you'll miss the present...moments in your life that you won't want to miss." She smiled. "So stay in the present, okay?"

"Okay," I said, hoping this nugget of wisdom would be the last for the day.

While Ma kept both hands on the wheel, positioned at ten and two, a Carlton 100—half of it burned down to a long ash—rested between her teeth. She'd just merged from Route 195 onto Route 88, when a sea of red brake lights illuminated the world before us. She slowed to a stop, changing the radio from her oldies station to 1480 AM, WSAR, to listen for any possible traffic updates.

"It's just beach traffic," Wally said, nonchalantly. "It's always like this."

"Not this far down," she said, still playing with the radio knob. "Must be construction or an accident." She paused. "Oh God, I hope it's not an accident."

Whatever it is, I thought, *they'd better clear it quick. I've made plans to meet Donna at 12:30 pm.* "What time is it?" I asked Cockroach, leaning over to peer at the runt's new Casio calculator watch.

"10:30," he said.

Plenty of time, I thought, as the car inched along a few feet at a time. It was torture.

Happy Hec reported, "Looks like we have some Boston traffic this morning heading out to Horseneck Beach. There's been a multi-car accident just before the stretch of construction. The authorities are on site now, clearing the scene."

An accident AND construction? I thought. "You've got to be kidding me!" I blurted.

"Kidding you?" Cockroach repeated.

I shook my head. "This traffic sucks," I muttered, knowing I'd never let my brothers in on my lunch date plans. This was hard enough. *They'd make it even worse.*

Sighing heavily, Ma suggested, "Why don't we play a game to keep our minds off of this terrible traffic." Smiling, she shrugged. "When life gives you lemons..." she began, launching into one of her philosophical rambles.

"Make real lemonade," Wally said, "and not the fake, diluted crap that we're forced to drink."

She stared him down in the rearview mirror.

"I like the lemonade Ma makes," Cockroach mumbled.

Wally went straight into a solo rendition of kissing sounds, erasing our little brother's smile. Although I would have normally jumped right in, I couldn't. I was too busy freaking out over being trapped ten miles away from Donna—and traveling only a few feet a minute.

Ma's eyes turned to snake-like slits.

Wally's lip-smacking song went silent, inviting Cockroach's grin to reappear.

As the car inched along, we opened the cooler—as well as the first bag of chips—and began our discreet gorging.

"Punch buggy red," Wally called out, punching my arm before pointing at the red Volkswagen Bug that was sitting idle just two cars ahead of us.

Damn it, I thought, rubbing the sting out of my arm, while searching for another VW Bug. *Nothing.*

A few minutes later, Wally called out, "Punch buggy red," and slugged me hard in the arm again.

"Where?" I yelled, already feeling the throb in my bicep.

He pointed at the same red Volkswagen Bug sitting idle two cars ahead of us.

"That's not fair," Cockroach said. "You can't pick the same car twice."

"I can't?" Wally said, playing stupid. He looked over at me and grinned, letting me know that he wasn't finished with the game.

"I swear to God, if you hit me again, I'm gonna punch your face until I hear something break!" I barked. In that moment, I didn't feel an ounce of fear for my brother—only rage.

"Animals," Ma muttered under her breath.

"Relax," Wally told me, his grin turning from masochistic to respectful, "I was just trying to play a game to pass the time."

You're so full of… I was thinking, when Cockroach cleared his throat.

"Let's play Simon," he suggested.

It was a popular electronic game of lights and sounds. To beat Simon, a player needed to remember the color pattern and repeat it by pressing the game's colored pads in the correct order. It started off at a nice steady pace; but the more you played, the more complicated the patterns became. Players—usually Alphonse—tried to hit a new high score by completing the longest sequence possible without messing up. If he didn't complete a sequence successfully, Simon triggered a 'fail' sound before displaying his score; this was merely a series of lights and sounds. Each point was indicated by a flashing green light. When all four lights flashed at once, it meant ten points had been earned.

Although Simon was fun to play solo, it was even more exciting to challenge friends—or angry, frustrated brothers.

"Well?" Cockroach asked, turning on the chiming game.

Four pads—green, red, blue, yellow—were situated clockwise, with four different sounds to match.

"I'm in," I said in surrender.

Quietly opening a bag of Funyuns, Wally simply shrugged.

We started slow, the suspense building with each turn.

Almost immediately, Alphonse was hypnotized by the lights. His intense focus bordered on clinically psychotic.

By the third round of play, Cockroach wasn't just beating the both of us—he was skunking us badly.

"Beat ya," he announced again, wrestling with another proud smile.

"And I should beat you," Wally threatened. His face was crimson red, and it wasn't only from the oppressive heat.

"Well, we all know you can't beat Simon, that's for sure," Cockroach mumbled.

Without another word, the panting brute grabbed the game from Cockroach's slippery grip.

"Relax, Funyun breath," Cockroach said. "You need to take a chill pill."

Wally flipped the game over and removed the batteries before handing it back to Alphonse.

"What the…"

"Enjoy," Wally said, pocketing the two Duracells, "and I'll be keeping these for my boom box."

"The one with the corroded battery compartment?" our little brother asked. "Sure, that makes a lot of sense."

Wally stared him down.

Reduced to playing a less thrilling game in silence, Cockroach pulled out one of his grocery store souvenirs—Wooly Willy magnetic personality—a surprise that Ma had brought him when returning home from food shopping. Within seconds, my little brother was hypnotized again, moving steel shavings with the magic wand, putting a mustache and beard on the bald, clown-nosed man.

"What time is it, Cockroach?" I asked again.

"Ten minutes since the last time you asked," Wally said, shaking his frustrated head.

That can't be true, I thought.

We ate and drank more. Even with all four windows rolled down, it was getting stifling hot in the backseat.

"Ma, I thought all new cars have air conditioning?" I said, feeling more aggravated than I'd ever felt.

"This isn't a new car, Herbie," she said, the back of her neck glistening in sweat. "It's just new to you." She sighed heavily. "This was somebody else's junk that your father was kind enough to take off their hands." She looked into the mirror again, blowing hair off her sweaty brow. "Your dad's good like that."

Pop's new honey wagon was used, or what the car salesman cleverly labeled, "Secondhand."

I glanced at the dashboard. *It's clean,* I thought, *for now, anyway.*

Ma turned the radio louder. "Shhh, the traffic report's back on."

"It's still quite a mess on Route 88," Happy Hec reported, "with three of the accident victims being sent to Charlton Memorial Hospital."

"Oh no," Ma said, "that's just awful." She shook her head. "I hope we don't see any blood when we drive past it."

"I hope we do," Wally muttered, rolled up in a ball, half-asleep.

"What time is it now?" I whispered to Cockroach.

"Are you kidding?"

"Time?" I repeated, this time through gritted teeth.

"11:45," he reported.

My heart sank. *We're not even at the high school exit yet,* I thought, *and we're still just crawling along. I wish there was a way I could contact Donna and let her know what's going on.* A thought occurred to me. *Maybe she's stuck in this mess, too?*

I was just starting to breathe freely again, when reality struck. *She's camping down the beach with her family.* My heart plummeted into my Chuck Taylor's. *She's probably already at the snack shack, waiting for me.*

Just then, two ambulances—lights flashing and sirens blaring—whipped by us on the driver's side of the car.

"Dear Lord," Ma said.

This isn't good, I thought, and I wasn't thinking about any accident victims.

Clearly sick of me, Cockroach jumped into the rumble seat behind us to face some very slow-moving oncoming traffic.

"Flip the car off," Wally whispered to him, like a devil sitting on the poor kid's scrawny shoulder.

"No," he said. "You do it."

"What about showing them that full moon of yours?" Wally suggested in a tone that was barely audible. "Everyone loves to gaze at the moon."

Cockroach grew quiet, while he considered it.

Don't do it, I thought, but when I turned around, he was already sticking his bare ass out the back window.

Wally was sent into a fit of hysterics, while the driver in the black Plymouth Duster behind us laid on his horn.

Ma's eyes jumped into the rearview mirror. "Where the hell do you want me to go?" she screamed, throwing both her hands into the air.

Oh shit, I thought, *Ma never swears.*

Her eyes remained peeled on the mirror. "You can't see that I'm stuck in this God-awful mess, too?"

Wally stopped laughing long enough to dive back into the cooler and snack bag.

I jumped into the seat beside my little brother, making enough hand gestures to apologize on behalf of my stupid brother.

With a single middle finger, the irate driver appeared to accept my apology.

"Stop being such a follower, Alphonse," I told him. "That's how people get into trouble."

"I know," he said, surprising me with his response.

After a bit of quiet, he shared his latest pipe dream with me. "I think I want to try body surfing today."

"Shhh," Ma called out from the front, "it's the traffic report."

"You don't think there's jellyfish in the shallow…" he began to ask.

"Shut your trap!" I barked. "I'm trying to listen to the radio."

"What's your problem, Cuckoo Clock Man?"

I glared at him. "Shut it, Diaper Man!"

"What's going on back there?" Ma asked, lighting a new cigarette off the one she'd just finished.

Oh, dear God, I thought, straining to listen.

"Now for the traffic report," Happy Hec began. "It appears that the accident on Route 88 has…" Suddenly, there was static and nothing else.

Ma turned the radio knob again. "Looks like we're out of range," she said, turning the channel back to the oldies station.

You've got to be kidding me! It felt like my head was going to shoot straight off my shoulders. I'd never felt so stressed in all my life.

Every minute spent in traffic, my level of panic grew. "What time is it?" I kept asking Cockroach, leaning over to peer at his shiny new watch.

"Time for you to get your own watch," he answered.

"Now's not the time to test me, brother," I hissed.

He was smart enough to shut up.

From then on, every time I asked, he just raised his wrist to my eye level. It worked for both of us.

I'm sorry, Donna, I thought, devastated.

Abandoning all hope for our lunch date, I jumped back over the seat to join Wally. I opened the cooler and peered in. *Oh shit,* I thought.

We were still miles away from reaching the coveted sand dunes and we'd already ripped through two dozen Hugs—little plastic barrels of colored sugar water—in the red Igloo cooler. Although we begged for Capri Sun—imagining that these were what the astronauts drank—Ma reminded us that the juice pouches were much too expensive. *Too high end,* Pop confirmed.

We'd also torn through full bags of Fritos, Cracker Jacks, and a large package of Lorna Dune cookies. Each package had a toy in it, pocketed for the future—tattoos and a Frito Bandito pencil eraser—to be paid to Cockroach in lieu of hush money. Ma had packed a half box of Tidbits, cheese crackers, which was now an empty box. The only things that remained were two cans of Ma's Fresca and a large tin can of Hawaiian Punch, which we would have also polished off if we could have stolen the church key from Ma's pocketbook.

"Ma's gonna be so pissed," I whispered to my older brother.

He shrugged. "At least she still has the Circus Peanuts and her Fresca," he said.

Circus Peanuts, I thought, *I'd rather eat packing peanuts.*

"Well, she's definitely gonna be pissed that you ate her sandwich," I told him.

"*We* ate her sandwich," he replied. "*We.*"

Nope, that was you, all by yourself. I shook my hopeless head. *Either way, there's nothing left, and she's gonna be fired up at all three of us.*

For nearly two hours, we sat in traffic on a long stretch of Route 88. With the exhaust fumes seeping up through the floorboards,

Cockroach began dry heaving. It started as a cough, quickly becoming a violent retch.

"Alphonse, just make sure you throw up outside of the car, if you have to," Ma yelled back to him.

Damn, Ma, I thought, my body covered in a film of sweat, *that's cold.*

Cockroach stuck his head out the car like a Labrador retriever puppy.

Just then, Wally farted loud enough to be heard ten cars down. There was silence for a few seconds, everyone looking at him in disgusted disbelief.

And then the smell hit us: a mix of decomposing skunk and sour milk.

"That's it!" Ma screamed, finally snapping. "That. Is. It!" Even in the dreadful heat, she sounded like s steam whistle, bellowing at a wind chill factor of twenty below.

Damn, Ma, I thought, *you need to chillax before you have a coronary.*

"This was the worst idea I have ever friggin' had," she said, her raspy voice sounding like she'd just smoked a sheep.

The car went silent and remained that way, even after Ma broke open her second pack of cigarettes.

"What time is it, Cockroach?" I whispered.

He stared at me.

"Last time, I promise."

He turned his wrist to me.

12:45, I read. *Oh, God.*

Ma threw the three dollars at the pre-pubescent guard shack

attendant. We circled the parking lot a few times—like desperate seagulls—until finding an open spot toward the back.

Wally and I nearly ran the half-empty cooler and Ma's steel-framed beach chair—orange plastic straps covering the back and seat—to an open spot in the sand, officially claiming it as our site. The beach was chock-full of sun worshipers.

Somebody must have just left, I figured, before running off to the snack shack to search for Donna.

She was nowhere to be found. *Please…please…* I kept repeating over and over in my head, panicking as though I'd just lost her forever. *Please let her still be here.*

I circled the snack shack three more times before combing the beach nearby for her. *She's long gone,* I realized. *Of course she is. I'm more than an hour late.* I felt like screaming.

Feeling as disheartened as I can ever remember, I moped back to our beach site. Although my brothers were gone, Ma was sitting there in her flowered moo moo, a pair of Dr. Scholl's on her toe-nail-painted feet. These served as both footwear and her favorite weapon, which she usually threw at us when we circled the kitchen table to get away from her.

"Good thing I love Circus Peanuts," she said, looking up from her Soap Opera Digest, "or I'd starve."

I was lost for words—for so many reasons.

Although Ma was listening to Pop's portable radio, it was nothing more than static. She looked at me and shrugged. "On the edge of the signal, I guess."

I nodded.

"Why are you back here?" she asked. Before I could answer, she shook her head. "Go have fun, Herbie. We don't have much time here."

Who even cares now, I thought.

There were warning signs posted at the beach about an infestation of the Portuguese man-of-war, toxic jellyfish that were pretty much invisible to the eye. *Who even cares?* I kept repeating in my head.

Standing at the surf's edge, I looked around me. From beautiful young women in their skimpy bikinis to wrinkled old grandmothers in their swimming caps, the beach was jam-packed. A few sailboats lined the horizon, while a lone lighthouse stood guard in the distance. Between the taste of salt air, the sound of the surf, and the occasional screech of seagulls, it should have felt like heaven on earth. *Who even cares?*

It wasn't long before the sun's heat became unbearable and I headed for the water in search of relief. The ocean felt cold to the touch. I took a few deep breaths and kept marching. It felt good compared to the oven we were all baking in. Still, something deep inside me felt cold.

I lay back and began to float. The tide rocked me like my mother once did when I was young. Children were splashing. People were laughing. *This was supposed to be a great day,* I thought. Horseneck Beach was famous for its riptides. I imagined getting caught in the undertow and dragged way out over my head. *Who even cares?*

When I finally found my way back to the water's edge, I collapsed onto the hot sand. Looking toward our little campsite, I saw my mother frantically waving me over.

What the hell's wrong now? As I hustled over, I saw that she and my brothers were already packing up to head home.

"What's going on?" I asked.

"It's time to go," she reported.

"But we just got here."

"We've been here for nearly an hour, Herbie," she said. "I'd like to stay longer, too, but we still have to drive all the way back to pick up your father from work."

What a wasted day!

"I just hope we don't catch any traffic on the way home," she said.

Oh, God...please no.

I piled the towels onto my shoulders and trudged through the dunes toward the parking lot. *Halfway there*, I thought, *I hope Donna will forgive me for this.*

Our day at the beach had been reduced to an hour at the beach. *What a nightmare!*

• • •

As soon as we got home, Cockroach announced, "I have to use the toilet!" He rushed toward the bathroom.

"Number one or number two?" Wally asked.

"Number four."

"What?"

"All bodily fluids," Cockroach said, grinning.

"Stop," Ma said, "please just stop."

Removed from my haze for a moment, I was actually impressed with my little brother over the brief exchange. *He's starting to sound as cocky as Wally*, I thought. *There's still hope for him yet.*

Wally laughed a little too hard.

"It wasn't that funny," Ma told my older brother. "You know what, why don't you go do a couple loads of laundry, Wally...seeing as you have some free time on your hands."

I was expecting him to lose his mind.

He surprised us all. "No problem," he said, "I enjoy my alone time in that cellar."

Ain't that the truth, I thought.

When Cockroach returned from the bathroom, I grabbed him by the arm so we could both slither into our bedroom. We quickly closed the plastic accordion door before Ma came up with a chore for us too.

I thought about calling Donna, hoping to explain. *But she's camping for the rest of the week,* I remembered, *I won't be able to explain what happened until she gets back.*

I searched out my Magic 8 Ball. *Does Donna realize that I was stuck in traffic?* I asked in my head. Shaking the ball a few times, I flipped it over.

The message read, *Don't count on it.*

I couldn't believe my eyes. "Oh, that's not going to do," I said aloud, drawing a strange look from Cockroach.

Does she know? I asked.

The black ball read, *Try again later.*

There is no later, I screamed in my head. Without asking again, I gave the shiny mystic three shakes, turning it over to receive my response.

The answer was more direct this time. *No.*

I was heading for a complete meltdown, when Cockroach threw me a lifeline. "Wanna play a game?" he asked, oblivious to my terrible distress.

I must have looked at him like I was wearing antlers.

"Well?"

"Sure," I said, desperate to change my thinking, "whatever."

Perfection had a timer that sounded like a tiny drum roll, announcing our arrival to hell. The game was quite simple; all you had to do is push down the pop-up tray, set the timer, and then place all 26 shapes with tiny handles—ovals, diamonds, rectangles—into their rightful holes in the game tray within 60 seconds. The shapes were mixed and placed next to the game with the handles facing up. If you didn't complete the task and hit the Stop button within the allotted time, then the entire board would pop up, ejecting your pieces and catapulting them everywhere.

My heart pounded. My mouth went dry. I believe I was even starting to develop a tick. And that's when it happened. I had two pieces left when the board popped, tossing them right in my face. "Damn it!"

Cockroach laughed.

It was anything but funny. "Go ahead, keep laughing," I told him.

His face turned serious. "What's your problem?"

Every dark emotion that had been building all day suddenly threatened to break free. Worse of all, this inexplicable rage I felt was of my own doing and I knew it. Playing Perfection was the first time I'd ever felt any real stress or anxiety. *So why would I expect this time to be any different?*

"Herbie, what the heck's your problem?" Cockroach repeated. "It's just a game. There's no reason to…"

My little brother's condescending tone was the final straw. I completely snapped, punching the plastic game as hard as I could, and ripping open my knuckles. Cockroach went silent, while I headed into the kitchen to calm down and wrap my bleeding hand.

This entire day's been a friggin' nightmare!

Wally returned from the cellar with a basket of clean laundry. Stepping into the kitchen, he growled at Cockroach. "Hey Skid Mark," he barked, "do you need me to teach you how to wipe your ass?"

"Watch your mouth!" Ma snapped at him, entering the room.

"Sure Ma, I'll watch my mouth when your baby boy can properly wipe his own ass!" Wally shook his head. "I couldn't decide whether I should just throw out his Underoos or toss them into the wash and hope for the best."

I chuckled.

"And you're not much better, Puddin' Pants," Wally said, glaring at me.

Concealing my wrapped hand behind my back, I chewed on my tongue. *I'm going to bed,* I decided. *I've taken more than enough abuse today.*

Also at the end of her rope, Ma called her sister hours before their normal gossip session. "Phyllis, I doubt you've ever lived through the shit show I had today," she groaned into the telephone, taking a seat at the kitchen table with a fresh pack of smokes, a half-empty ashtray, and her red lighter—the entire survival kit.

How many cigarettes has Ma smoked today? I wondered.

"We never got to the beach on Walt's vacation, so I figured I'd take the boys." She shook her head, blowing smoke out of both nostrils like a raging bull. "But as they say, no good deed goes unpunished."

I headed for my bedroom. Although I was still livid, I realized sleep was still a better option. *I can't listen to this horseshit and live through it again. I'd rather hear Cockroach whine over his broken game and how he thinks I'm gonna replace it.*

CHAPTER 9

JULY 1984

SO NOT FAIR

I finally got a chance to talk to Donna. "You need to let it go, Herbie," she told me. "I was upset at the time; but as soon as I heard about the accident and all the traffic, I felt bad for you." The compassion was palpable in her sweet voice.

"You can't believe how bummed I was that I couldn't meet you for lunch," I told her, "and you can't imagine what torture that ride on Route 88 was. I kept checking the time and..."

"Just let it go," she said, kindly cutting me off. "We're good, I promise."

"Okay," I surrendered, "good."

"And speaking of letting go..." She giggled.

"I know, I know. I'll talk to you tomorrow, okay."

"You'd better," she said before hanging up.

We're good, I repeated in my head. *Thank God.*

Not an hour later, Ma followed us into Silver Screen Video. Cockroach's face was as white as talcum powder from fear. The last time we'd stepped into the place, Mr. Deschenes had threatened to squeal on him to our mother. We headed right for the Action and Comedy sections, while Ma broke left toward New Releases and Drama. It worked best for everyone involved.

"Relax," I told my brother, "you could have stayed in the car."

"Then Ma would definitely know there's something wrong."

I nodded. *Good point.*

Cockroach's eyes stayed glued to the carpet. I tapped his shoulder. When he looked up at me, I pointed toward the black velvet curtains at the back of the store. "Do you wanna take a second look?'

He walked away from me.

I brought Ma a copy of *Airplane II: The Sequel.* "Can we rent it?" I asked her.

As usual, she snatched the boxed tape from me and looked at the cover before turning it over and starting to read. "Any sex or nudity?"

As usual, I shook my head. "Nope." I had no idea.

"Okay," she said, handing it back to me, "but just the one."

At the counter, I watched as Mr. Deschenes caught Cockroach's eye and gave him a wink. *Oh no, we've seen that wink before,* I thought, *Cockroach is dead meat.*

Nearly hyperventilating, my poor brother studied the extra-large candy bars and boxes of Good and Plenty.

As Mr. Deschenes rang us out, he looked at Ma. "Did you find everything you were looking for, Ma'am?"

Ma nodded. "I think we did. Thank you."

My brother and I were holding our collective breath when the store owner punched her card. "That's your ninth rental," he announced. "Your next one is free."

"Wonderful," Ma said, handing me the plastic bag to carry.

As we walked out the store, Cockroach and I simultaneously exhaled.

Wow, I thought, having earned some real respect for the man. *Mr. Deschenes never leaked a word to Ma.* As I slid into the station wagon's back seat, I turned to Cockroach. "Now that's what you call a legit wink," I whispered, "not like that fake wink Pepere gave us at Lincoln Park."

He nodded. "Thank God," he whispered back.

Now we can enjoy Airplane II: The Sequel in peace.

· · ·

On Sunday morning, I picked up the empty box of Indiana Jones cereal on the table. *I never even got a chance to try it*, I thought, realizing that it was always a mistake to wake up later than Wally.

Seeing my face, he laughed. "I tore through that box like a tornado in a trailer park."

I merely shook my head at him. *Good thing for him that I'm addicted to Cap'n Crunch Berries*, I thought.

"What do you have cooking today?" he asked me.

"I want to start my paper route early."

He nodded. "Am I glad those days are done."

For the first time in quite some time, I allowed Vic to tag along with me.

Fish Stick and I set up surveillance, Starsky and Hutch style. It didn't take long before we spotted Old Man Sedgeband dipping into my newspaper bundle. "Oh, it's on," I said, emerging from the bushes and rushing across the street.

"Herbie," Vic called out after me. "You might want to think about…"

"We caught the crook red-handed," I yelled back, "and I'm calling him on it!"

The old geezer had just stepped into his little shop of horrors, when I jumped in front of him—panting.

"Hand them over," I ordered, extending my hand.

"What are you talking about, boy?"

"Those two newspapers you're holding…you just stole them off my stack. I just saw you do it."

"I did not."

"Hand them over," I repeated, my voice getting louder with each syllable, "or I'm going home right now to tell my old man."

The swindler grinned; it was eerie. "You're a storyteller. Everyone knows that. Your father won't believe…"

"Oh, he'll believe me, all right," I interrupted. "Trust me." I returned the cynical grin. "And he'll come right down here to straighten you out, too."

As he considered his options, Old Man Sedgeband's Adam's apple slowly descended. "I…I see that your little brother is even greedier than you are when shopping for your mother." His Grinch-like smile returned. "But you're both thieves."

"And if anyone can spot a thief, it's you," I said. My runs to the corner store had ended when I got my paper route and could buy my own loot. Cockroach gladly took over the scam, charging whatever he wanted on Ma's inflated tab. The only real difference between us was that Cockroach was in the resale business.

"What did you say?" Sedgeband hissed.

"Listen, my father will beat you like a rug, if I tell him that you're screwing with me and my brothers. If I were you, I'd…"

Sedgeband handed over the two newspapers, free of charge.

"That's what I thought," I said, turning on my heels. "Conversation over."

Both Sedgeband and Vic were wearing the same shocked expression—eyes wide and jaw slack—when I turned and strutted away.

"Let's jet," I called back to Vic when I reached the door. I could hear his sneakers scampering across the hard wood toward me. "This place is so tired."

• • •

I returned home from my paper route to hear Wally ribbing our mother pretty good. "You always say that Ma," he said, grinning, "which could probably be considered a sin in itself."

"I told you, we are gonna start going back to church," she said, defensively. "This family needs church." She nodded.

For years, our family had maintained our well-earned holiday Catholic status, while our mother conducted most of the faith training at home—for which I honestly received so much more. As I thought about it, I couldn't help but smile.

"It's so important to have a relationship with God through prayer," she always told us. "You're never alone. None of us are. But there will be times in your life—trust me—when you're going to need God. And it's a lot easier to reach out and ask for help from someone you've been talking to every day and not someone you've been ignoring."

This simple teaching was enough to cultivate and sustain my faith throughout my childhood. *Not to mention, it's really helpful to believe in the afterlife,* I figured, *and that when someone you love dies, it's only a temporary separation.* I believed this more than any church sermon I'd ever heard.

Emerging from my daydream, I decided to defend my mother. It was rare. "Don't listen to him, Ma," I said, "If it wasn't for you, I wouldn't pray or have any faith at all. And I do...both."

Wally looked more shocked than she did. But I was being sincere, and they both knew it.

I watched Ma's eyes glisten over, as though it was a message she'd needed to hear. "We may not be able to make it to church today," she said, "but we are going to your Memere's..."

"But Ma!" we sang in chorus. "Today's the last day for the Westport Fair. If we don't go today, then we'll miss it until next year." We were prepared to beg, if needed.

It was an annual tradition. At the Westport Fair, we ate more than we should, rode every spinning ride we could, and then fought off the urge to puke—riding more rides when our stomachs announced that the coast was clear. The town fair only took place once a year, and we weren't about to miss any of it—no matter how loudly our poor bellies complained.

Ma gawked at us, her eyes distant—her mind obviously weighing both sides.

"Please Ma..." we pleaded.

Not Memere's, I silently prayed. Summer visits at our grandmother's could be a real challenge, her small apartment filled with fly strips and fly swatters. It was like the old woman was at war with black flies, a murderous rage burning in her eyes when she heard one buzzing or spotted one hovering.

"Fine," Ma surrendered, but not before telling us, "Your grandparents aren't going to be around forever, you know. Someday, you're going to regret all the times you could have spent with them and didn't."

Yeah, whatever, I thought, clueless to the truth of her timeless wisdom. Our mother delivered opinions like they were facts. It normally drove me nuts. In this case, however, I sensed she was right.

• • •

We were already halfway through our school vacation, and of the entire summer, the Westport Fair was the most exciting event in town. It was typically the first time everyone saw each other since the last day of school. Cockroach was extra excited, dressing up in a Western shirt—a small white tube of Binaca peppermint breath spray tucked behind the shirt pocket's fake pearl snap—a worn pair of Wrangler jeans concealing his Superman Underoos, and a cruddy old pair of high-top sneakers.

Now that's what you call a half-assed cowboy, right there, I thought, wearing the same stained footwear. As far as I was concerned, it was a blessing when my sneakers were damaged; there was no reason to hold back during play.

A fenced perimeter with steel barriers helped to funnel pedestrian traffic into the vast fairgrounds. It was warm out, but not muggy—*perfect.* The smell of marijuana mixed with other smells—popcorn, vomit, fried dough, cow manure—filled the warm air.

Owen must be here somewhere, I thought, smiling.

Flashing neon threw off electricity—real excitement—with red, white, and blue pennants strung everywhere to create a real sense of patriotism.

Once an open field, the midway had recently been transformed. One day, it was a barren field spotted with grazing cows. The next, that same grass was stamped down to distinct dirt paths, strewn with litter—even though 55-gallon drums had been placed everywhere. Eyes wide, we took it all in.

The ticket booth was the size of a phone booth, where highway robbery was committed in broad daylight. After paying a fee to enter, ride tickets were sold by the books: a twenty-dollar investment, if you were going to experience it all. Everyone knew this going in. Thankfully, our parents had saved for it.

As Ma handed us each a full book of tickets, both she and Pop smiled.

Now these are what I call Green Stamps. Looking down at the tickets, I also noticed that my father was wearing open-toed corduroy slippers. He'd been suffering from a large corn and had somehow decided that it was okay to wear his torn slippers.

Oh no! I thought. *Most of my friends from school are somewhere on these fairgrounds*—kids I hadn't seen since the final school bell rang out.

"Go have fun," Pop told us, "but make sure you keep your wits about you." He then handed us each some cash. "Use this for food."

"And make sure you eat," Ma said. "Don't be wasting the money on those crooked carnival games."

Nodding our gratitude, we bolted as far away from Pop's ratty footwear as we could get.

While Wally went his own way, Cockroach and I made our first stop at Rosie's Racing Pigs. This was an attraction that everyone loved, whether they admitted it or not. A corral of piglets, with names such as Kevin Bacon and Elvis Piggly, raced on a small oval track of wood shavings, making the crowd of farmers and lobstermen go wild.

"I wonder if they're actually betting on these races?" I thought aloud.

Cockroach shrugged. "I can't see any other reason to hang out and watch."

I laughed. "I agree."

The high school marching band was in full regalia, sweating their backsides off. The local beauty queen, walking the fairgrounds to show off her sparkling tiara, made me turn to my brother. "She must have scored extra points during the talent portion of the contest."

He shrugged again. "I don't know," he said, staring at her, "I think she's pretty hot."

"You think every girl's hot."

"What's wrong with that?"

I suddenly thought about Donna, wishing she could have met me here. *Her mother's way too strict*, I thought.

A dunk tank had been set up to help raise money for the high school's PTO. It was the longest line in the fairground when a teacher or principal took a seat in the tank. Wally and his friend, Owen, were standing at the front of the line. Although it was too warm for it, Owen was wearing a light neon jacket with sheen patches of every color in the rainbow.

Looking snazzy, Deney Terrio, I thought, before doing a double-take of the tank's foggy glass. "It's Dr. DeSousa!" I blurted. She was my elementary school principal. I immediately jumped in line for a chance to dunk her.

"Are you serious?" Cockroach asked. "This is such a waste of time."

"I'm dunking her," I told him. *When you stay back in first grade for coloring outside the lines*, I reasoned, *it stays with you.*

Shaking his head, Cockroach spotted two of his school buddies. "I'm going to hang out with Jeff and Mongie," he said, and he wasn't asking.

"Make sure you stay together," I told him, sounding like my parents, "and don't leave the fairgrounds."

"No duh," he called back.

It cost me nearly three bucks before I dropped Dr. DeSousa into the filthy water.

Worth every penny, I thought, shooting the soaked woman a smile.

Beyond the dunk tank was an open barn with 4H animals wearing blue or red ribbons. It was like a giant petting zoo, and if you weren't careful, it could become an interactive petting zoo—where the animals aggressively nuzzled you back. The space was also set up for three elderly women wearing white sashes; they judged everything from steers and canned vegetables to strawberry jam and blueberry pies. There were no cash prizes for the winners, just ribbons of blue, yellow, and red awarded to justify bragging rights for an entire year. I never understood the fuss.

I looked up to see Wally walking by with Owen. We ignored each other. *I should have brought Vic with us,* I thought, also realizing that I would have had to split my ride tickets and food money with him. *Maybe it's best he stayed home.*

Bells rang. People screamed. Carnie music competed with the screech of thrill rides, and the midway was filled with them—each one mobile and dangerous: The Sky Ride, Tilt-A-Whirl, The Scrambler, a Ferris Wheel—which made my skin crawl when I began studying the large greasy bolts holding it all together. There was a mobile Fun House, recently towed by a Kenworth tractor. There was also a tall slide called The Carpet Ride, as well as the Rocket Ride, which flipped and spun screaming kids—all at the same time. After my first pass through, I decided, *The Rocket's definitely the most gnarly ride on the fairway, but it's also the most dangerous.* I shook my head. *If that thing breaks apart, lots of people are dying.*

I kept walking. It seemed like everyone was holding hands, young or old. *I really wish Donna was with me right now,* I thought. *Damn her wicked mother!*

Suddenly, Steve Pimental appeared out of nowhere, startling me. For a long, horrible moment, my nemesis glared at me, while his three friends puffed out their chests.

"Looks like Herbie's all alone," one of them said.

Although my heart thumped away like a rabbit's foot in my chest, I maintained my cocky grin.

"Where's Wally?" Steve asked.

"Oh, he's around here somewhere," I managed. "You want me to get him for you?"

Steve's nostrils flared, while his fists clenched tight.

Even though my mouth and throat were bone dry, I laughed as loud as I could. Then, against my better instincts, I took two aggressive steps forward before squaring up my feet to fight. My breathing was so shallow, I felt like I might faint.

This phony advance made Steve carefully consider his next move. "Whatever," he said, starting to walk away. "This chump's not worth it."

Thank God, I thought, *Thank God.* I stood frozen for a moment, watching red and yellow balloons—tied to baby strollers—bob along the midway. As my breathing returned to normal, teenage girls hugged stuffed animals that cost their boyfriends more than a few bucks to win. Trailers with awnings hosted games of chance where very few people won: Ring the Bottle; a different game where you had to land a rubber frog on a lily pad; Balloon Darts; Shoot Out the Star; Knock 'em Down—the milk bottle game—were all there. Forcing myself to get past the near confrontation with Steve and his brain dead posse, I stepped up to the Basketball Free Throw game. The rims looked twenty feet high and forty feet away. *A setup for failure,* I decided. Even still, there was a line of teenage boys waiting to hand over their money at a shot of impressing their girlfriends—the vast majority losing miserably.

There's no way I'm burning through my paper route money on games I can never win, I thought, knowing full well that it would have been a very different story had Donna been standing beside me.

Instead, I spent a few bucks on a balloon animal kit, which was essentially a plastic air pump and a bag of long, skinny balloons—every color under the sun. *I've always wanted to learn how to make balloon animals. Who knows, if I get good enough, I might even be able to make money at it someday.*

At the end of the midway, a line of food trucks and makeshift booths served any greasy delicacy you wanted: Elephant ears, corn dogs, fresh squeezed lemonade, ice cream, cotton candy, brown paper bags of roasted peanuts, Fried Twinkies and Oreos, popcorn, clam cakes, steak bombs with melty, oozing cheese.

Further down was the pavilion, a sea of old wooden picnic tables facing a large wooden stage. It was one of only two permanent structures on the fairgrounds; the other was the 4-H barn. Unfortunately, country and western bands took turns torturing the large crowd. This area was also known as the "Beer Garden." The vast majority in attendance were dads waiting out the night—and chugging suds— within the safe harbor.

I was just passing through the area, when I spotted my father sitting back in his torn corduroy slippers and white socks, enjoying a cold one.

Oh my God, I thought, quickly starting in the opposite direction.

He spotted me, too, because I heard his distinctive baritone voice. "Herbie, come over here for a second."

I kept walking away, never looking back. I had a decision to make, a true fork in the road. I could either go to my father and risk being seen by my friends, which of course would cause great embarrassment to me, or I could pretend I didn't hear him and hope later that I was convincing enough that he believed me. *Just keep stepping*, I told myself.

"Herbie, come here!" Pop yelled out again. "Herbie…"

I picked up the pace and kept walking, thinking, *I'll take the beating later, if I have to. If I'm seen with Mr. Slipper Socks, I'll never hear the end of it at school.*

The tractor pulls seemed like the safest place to hide out for a bit, so I scurried off in that direction.

The tractor pulls were book-ended by bleachers that had been dragged over from the high school football field. For whatever reason, the ear-piercing sounds and diesel smells of the redneck competition made me smile.

Tractor pulling was a competitive motor sport in which modified farm tractors dragged a metal sled along a long dirt course.

Pure hillbilly, I thought, chuckling. *I love it!*

The distance from start to finish was measured in inches, and the tractor that pulled the sled the farthest distance was the winner. If more than one competitor reached the full pull mark, a pull-off was held to determine a winner. The entire redneck sport was all about horsepower and torque—good old-fashioned American ingenuity.

Although there were eight different classes that competed, I—and everyone else—preferred the giant homemade tractors: 5,000 raw horsepower tractors, throwing off flames and enough noise to wake the good folks resting a few miles down the road in Maple Grove Cemetery.

I sat to watch a few of the locals go head-to-head, pulling the steel sled—stacked with heavy concrete slabs—down the dirt track. As the sled transferred weight, moving the cement blocks closer to the back of the tractor, the front wheels lifted skyward, while the engine screamed out into the twilight sky. The farther the tractor pulled the sled, the more difficult it got. *So sick!* I thought.

"Go…Go!" I screamed for Cappy, an old-timer, who won the face-off by half a foot. I couldn't believe how vested I'd become.

The coast looked clear, so I headed back out on foot. Neon lit up the fairgrounds. Hanging white lights, strung across the darkened midway, created a warm and inviting atmosphere. The patriotic pennants, however, lost their intended effect as the sun dove further down.

Small kids ran around holding sparklers, the stink of sulfur polluting the air. A bum pushing an overstuffed shopping cart—filled with inflatables and stuffed animals on sticks—also sold poppers, which were very popular with the boys. These small white devils helped to scare the girls by throwing the poppers at their feet and making them scream. The Hippie also peddled cap guns and rolls of red caps that the young boys quickly burned through. *I used to love these.* The Hobo catered to most childhood vices. *He even carries candy cigarettes,* I noticed.

As I walked, I couldn't help but think, *I'd give anything to be holding Donna's hand right now.*

When we finally met up to leave, Pop looked at me. "I'm not happy you ignored me, Herbie," he said, his eyes betraying a hint of pain. "It was disrespectful."

"What do you mean, Pop?"

"I was sitting in the pavilion. When I called you over, you pretended like you didn't hear me." He shook his disappointed head.

I looked him straight in the eye. "I never saw you, Pop," I lied, "or I would've come to you."

He studied my face for a moment; it was a terrible moment. He finally decided to let it go with a nod.

That's when I realized that my dirty deed would not go unpunished. I already felt terrible for pretending that I didn't know my own father. *Jackass move,* I thought, scolding myself.

Wally approached us at the front gate. "Can I leave with Owen?" he asked Pop, his best friend standing off at a safe distance, listening in.

I was so happy my brother had changed the subject.

"Where are you guys heading?" the old man countered, while Ma listened in.

"To cruise the Ave in Fall River," Wally said.

"Oh, I don't know," Ma muttered.

Pop nodded once. "Be home by eleven."

So not fair, I thought.

Smiling, Wally started to run off.

Wally thinks he's too cool to hang out with his own family now, I thought, tasting bile in the back of my throat.

"Do you have money, in case you need it?" Ma yelled after him.

Wally stopped. "I'm broke, Ma," he announced, shaking his head. "I don't even have a dime to call home if I need to."

"If you ever got into trouble," Ma said, taking him literally, "just find a pay phone and call home collect."

Obviously anxious to leave, Wally began to roll his eyes, when Pop jumped back into the fray.

"But if you ever call the house collect," he warned, "you'd better have a damned good reason." His eyebrows nearly touched his hairline. "Like you're dying."

"Oh, Walter," Ma said, shaking her frizzy head of hair.

"But a call from jail is free," Cockroach commented.

"Dying," Pop repeated, ignoring his youngest son.

Wally nodded once, before taking off with Owen at a sprint.

We were heading for the parking lot when Ma said, "I'm not sure about that Owen, Walt."

"Oh, he's fine," Pop said.

"Walt, he's the same kid who was bullying our son this past…"

"It's in the past, Em," Pop said. "They're friends now." He shrugged. "That's how it is with guys. You have a problem. You settle it like men. And then you can become friends." He grinned. "It's a respect kind of thing."

"I still don't care for him," Ma said, sighing heavily. "We are who we hang around with."

Although I hated to admit it to myself, I sensed deep down that she was right. *I have some friends at school who are pretty much guaranteed to serve prison time at some point.*

As we marched toward the station wagon, the carnival-like sounds behind us grew more faint.

Wally's gonna cruise the Ave tonight, I thought, snickering to myself. My stomach flopped sideways and it wasn't from too much funnel cake, either. I was instantly filled with a tornado of dark emotions—mostly anger and jealousy—that swirled inside me. *What a lucky bastard!*

As we got into the old station wagon, I told Cockroach. "Push over, you're on my side."

"You're not the boss of me," he whined, staying in place.

I glared at him. "You know what, Alphonse, every time I think you're a cool kid, you come up with some bullshit like that." I offered him my best smirk. "Whether you realize it or not, everybody in this family is the boss of you. Just deal with it."

Without another word, he slid over.

Alphonse was catching the brunt of my bitter jealousy toward Wally, and I knew it. *Oh well,* I decided, *as Pop says, 'Shit rolls downhill.'*

As we drove home, Ma said, "It looked like the PTO raised quite a bit of money for the high school with that dunk tank." She nodded. "Good for them. Hopefully, they help the kids who need it most."

"Yeah, like me," Cockroach said under his breath.

I ignored the comment, and while Pop took the backroads home, I continued to smolder. *Wally's always out and about now,* I thought. *He's hardly ever home, especially on the weekends.* My brother was so lucky, allowed to cruise the Ave in Fall River. Two of his friends had gotten their licenses—*those dumb friends who'd stayed back and were old enough to drive.* I was sick with envy. *Next thing you know, he'll be going to rock concerts.*

• • •

When we finally arrived home, I went straight to my bed to pout. With my fingers interlocked behind my head, I began to imagine how rad it would be to cruise the Ave in Fall River. The more I allowed my mind to wander free, the easier it was to visualize.

I could see it all, the awesome game of cat and mouse—just like at the mall, but at a much higher level. Cars packed with girls, cars packed with guys, and parking lots along the way where they could stop and meet up. Teenagers sitting on the hoods of those cars, smoking cigarettes and sneaking swigs from brown paper bags. A star filled sky. Neon lights. Hole shots or doing donuts in those very same parking lots. The occasional impromptu drag race, from a standstill at a red light, two cars lined up, side-by-side. A simple nod from both drivers and it was on, speeding from one light to the next. The risk of getting chased by the cops or even getting busted was understood. The black asphalt glistening under the streetlights. Cruising lap after lap from the Harbor Mall and Burger King parking lot all the way down to China Royal and back, burning up a tankful of gas—at $1.20 per gallon.

I could picture all of the cars: glistening Chevy Camaros and Novas with chrome-moon hubcaps, the Pontiac Firebirds and Trans Ams, Dodge Chargers, Ford Fairlanes and T-Birds. Even some classic cars patrolled the strip, old hard tops and convertibles. Regardless of what condition the cars were in, they were waxed and polished. Anything made of chrome was sparkling, from the front grilles to the back bumpers. Every window, as well as convertible top, was down—regardless of the temperature. The music blared, a mix of Big Hair rock bands and synthesized one-hit wonders: *Break My Stride* by Matthew Wilder, *Rock You Like a Hurricane* by Scorpions, *Somebody's Watching Me* by Rockwell, *Wouldn't It Be Good* by Nik Kershaw, *We're Not Gonna Take It* by Twisted Sister. Although the avenue was long, the playlist was even longer.

I could only imagine what it would be like to have my own car. *A convertible would be a dream come true.* I could see myself and Vic stopping for a burger, having to eat them outside the car because the rugs had just been vacuumed. I could even taste the chargrilled beef and smell the pine scented air freshener hanging from my rearview mirror.

It was sensory overload, eventually forcing me to shut down the fantasy. Jumping off my bed, I could feel the bile rising from my stomach and burning my throat. *I'd give anything to be there with Wally tonight.* But I knew I was still a year or two away from it. *So not fair!*

Except for Cockroach, the entire family was still up when Wally got home. He was grinning from ear to ear.

"Someone met a girl," Pop announced, nonchalantly.

Ma stepped closer to him to study his face. I did the same. *Pop might be right,* I thought. *Something's definitely different about him.* He was wearing the daffiest smile I'd ever seen on him.

"Did you?" I asked him. "Did you meet a girl?"

Although he refused to tell me, the smile never left his face.

"He did," Ma confirmed, before turning to Pop. "You covered everything when you had *the talk* with him, right?"

Oh, my God.

"What talk?" Pop asked, oblivious.

She shook her head. "The birds and the bees, Walt," she said in a strained whisper.

The old man looked at us. "They know," he said, grinning. "Oh, they know. Every one of them." He dismissed her with a wave of his hand.

Although Pop was right, what he didn't tell our mother was that whatever we did know probably didn't come from him. Most of it came from a stack of hidden Playboy magazines in the cellar, coupled with years of overheard adult conversations—most of which took place during some marathon card games.

I looked back at Wally, thinking, *He wouldn't be able to wipe that smile off his face if Pop paid him.* I didn't know exactly what had happened to him on the Ave, but I did know that I couldn't wait until it happened to me. I wanted nothing more than to wear that same shit-eating grin.

We were getting ready for bed when I smelled cigarette smoke on Wally. I knew the scent well from Ma.

"You smoke cigarettes now, too?" I questioned.

He glared at me.

"Relax, I'm not Alphonse. I'm not gonna squeal on you," I whispered, "I'm just curious."

"Don't ever try it, Herbie," he warned, looking to ensure that

Alphonse was sleeping—and not faking it like the little sneak some-times did. "It tastes like ash and burns your throat." He shook his head before locking eyes. "I swear to God, I thought I was gonna throw up. I don't know how Ma can do it."

"Because she's a professional," I joked.

He shook his head again. "Don't even bother trying it, Herbie," he repeated. "You'll hate it as much as I did."

I thought about it for a moment. *But how do I know unless I try?*

CHAPTER 10

JULY 1984

WORKING THE RIVER

It was very early Saturday morning when Pop woke me from my sleep. "Let's go," he said, startling me, "I need your help today."

A rush of adrenaline ran the length of my spine. I sat up, thinking, *The last time I heard that, we were rushing a bleeding giant to the hospital.*

Pop wore tighty-whities that were so old they looked gray. I caught his backside, as he stepped out of the room. *And that right there is enough to kick off my nightmares again.*

One Flintstone vitamin and a cup of coffee milk later, and I was hurrying out of the house.

In the station wagon, Pop explained, "We're having a big clam boil with the family tomorrow and I wanted to work the river today. I figured we could grab a bushel or so of quahogs."

I nodded. *A bushel or so?*

"Your brothers' feet are too soft, and I don't want to hear all the whining." He looked at me and grinned. "So, you're the right man for the job."

My smile nearly sliced my face in half. Pop had a way of bringing us out alone on separate excursions. It was the most valuable time.

On the ride, Pop flicked his headlights on and off to warn an oncoming car that there were cops hiding in the bushes. "Son-of-a-bitches," he muttered, "they should be out chasing bad guys, not hassling the working man who's just trying to get to work."

It's Saturday, I thought, but kept it to myself.

A few minutes later, the old man did the same thing—flicking his headlights—for a tractor trailer that was trying to slide over into our lane.

He looked at me and smiled. "Just letting him know that the coast is clear and he can slide over without squashing us."

"That's good," I said.

I was expecting Pop to take me to breakfast at the Nite Owl Diner on the corner of Pleasant Street and Eastern Avenue. Instead, we stopped at the Kozy Nook Restaurant in the old pharmacy's plaza.

Tangerine Formica-top tables, bordered by black pleather booths, were filled to capacity. Capable of seating ten people, the counter had two empty seats, side by side.

Big score! I loved sitting at diner counters. It was fun watching people sit down as strangers and leave as friends.

As soon as we took a seat, a steaming cup of coffee hit the counter for my father.

"I'll have a large glass of orange juice, please," I told the gum-chewing waitress.

She shot me a wink.

"I think she likes you," Pop teased.

"Sure she does," I said.

"Women like a man with good manners."

I nodded, trying not to blush.

"Low tide's not for another hour," the old man explained, adding cream and sugar to his large mug, "so we need to shovel some coal into our furnaces before we get to work." He patted his abdomen.

I chuckled.

When the friendly waitress returned, she pulled out her small flip pad and a pen and waited.

"Two soft boiled eggs with white toast, and a side of bacon for me," my father ordered.

She nodded.

"Can I please have a stack of chocolate chip pancakes."

"Short or tall?" she asked.

"Give him the tall one," Pop told her. "I'm gonna be working him hard today."

Grinning, she nodded.

"Thank you," I said.

She winked at me again before heading back toward the kitchen.

"That a boy," Pop said, still teasing me. "Don't let your little brother score all the women."

"I won't," I told him, and meant it.

"Are you enjoying your summer so far?" he asked.

I nodded. "I am. It's going by way too fast, though."

"Wait until you only get two weeks off a year." He chuckled. "You're gonna really love that."

Ugh... I'd never even thought about it.

"Did you guys have fun at the beach?" he asked.

I snickered loud enough for everyone in the place to hear. "It was a nightmare, Pop. We left late. We hit traffic and cooked in the station wagon for a couple of hours. I was supposed to meet a girl for lunch but never made it in time. We stayed for about an hour before we had to break camp and come pick you up from work." I shook my head. "A nightmare," I repeated.

He took a sip of his coffee and grinned. "The way I heard it, you guys slept in." He shrugged. "And your mother was stuck in traffic with three gassy boys."

"Just one," I said, defending me and Cockroach.

"At least you ate lunch," he said, looking at me. "Your poor mother didn't."

I nodded. "I'm sorry about that. I…"

"No need to apologize to me, Herbie. She's the one you should've apologized to."

Feeling bad about it, I nodded that I understood.

Without warning, he placed his massive hand on my thigh and gave it a few hard squeezes, offering me what he called a "claw hold." It tickled and hurt, all at the same time. I jumped off the counter stool, happy that I hadn't screamed out like I sometimes did.

He laughed. "Take a seat and relax, Herbie," he said, drinking more coffee. "We're out here to have fun today."

As I began to nod, our waitress delivered our food with another smile. "Enjoy guys!"

"Eat it all," Pop said, "you're gonna need the energy."

I did exactly as I was told.

Quahogging with Pop was an all-day affair, which was normally a huge downer—but not this time. My brothers hated going quahogging, so it was guaranteed alone time between me and the old man. For that alone, I looked past the cuts I was guaranteed to suffer on the bottom of my bare feet. And they had to be bare, or else I wouldn't be able to feel the quahogs.

The tools were simple: a bushel basket, an inflatable inner tube, and a frayed piece of rope. The conditions had to be precise: low tide, regardless of the time of day. *And we only have two shots at that.*

As we trudged through the thick mud, I could feel something that felt like a rock beneath the ball of my left foot. Leaning over, I yanked it out of the silt, soaking my *Orange Fanta* t-shirt with salt water in the process. *It's a quahog!* I thought, lifting it high into the air to show my father.

"That's a keeper," he yelled over at me. "Good job, son!"

I felt so fulfilled, like I'd actually contributed to the family.

Yet, the entire time I was tiptoeing around in the mud, Pop was digging up five quahogs to my one. *You need to start moving faster,* I told myself.

"Stay here," he yelled toward me. "I'm gonna go work the channel." Pop was a great swimmer.

Returning a half hour later, I noticed that the floating bushel basket was nearly full. Although the permit he pulled from the Town Hall only allowed us to pull a half bushel out of the river, he was prepared to grab four times that. "We don't get down here as often as we should," he said, justifying the piracy.

After dumping out the first bushel into the back of the station wagon, Pop covered the mound with a tattered blanket and then parked the car in the shade. "If they cook too early, then we've just wasted the day," he said, half-joking.

We started back toward the river with the empty bushel basket and inflated tire tube.

"When we're out on the river, it's one of the few times I miss cigarettes," Pop admitted, speaking to me like I was an adult.

I didn't even know you smoked, I thought.

We worked the river a second time, doubling our bounty for the day. Although the silence we shared between us felt important, I enjoyed talking with Pop.

"So, how's the paper route going?" he asked me. "You enjoy being a working man?"

"It's okay," I said, hoping this topic wouldn't lead to a suggestion that he and Ma should hold some of my money. "It's not a bad start, but I don't think I want to make it my career." I had something similar in mind, though. I'd decided that our mailman was essentially an adult paper boy, a career opportunity that I was sure to keep in mind. *I already have the skills.*

My old man laughed. "Career?" he repeated under his breath. "There are a lot of different jobs out in the world. Just make sure you find one you can live with." He took a deep breath and held it for a moment. "Sometimes, it's the difference between a happy life and a miserable one."

I still can't tell which one you have, I thought, trying to read my father.

Pop chuckled before starting in on one of his famous tales. "I had a friend that took a job on a paint crew for the state, painting yellow lines in the center of the road. They'd meet in Somerset at eight o'clock in the morning and drive sixty miles to the Cape. After unloading the truck, they'd take a union break. After a sip of water and two cigarettes, they'd set up and make preparations to paint for the rest of the day. But once they set up, it was already lunchtime. A steel pail of bologna sandwiches and a thermos of coffee later, it was time to get back to work. After returning from lunch, they'd paint for two hours before it was time to pack up the truck for the day and head home."

I loved it when my father told me stories.

"After two weeks of this," Pop continued, "my friend questioned his boss about the ridiculous schedule. 'This doesn't make any sense,' he told him. 'By the time we get painting, it's already time to pack up and call it a day.'

"We have to factor in travel time," the older man advised.

"I get that, but…"

"Listen, you need to stop worrying about it and keep your mouth shut. You're getting paid either way, right?"

"Well yeah, but…"

"I don't care how long it takes to get this job done. We're making the same money either way. Once we finish this job, we're onto another stretch of road that'll look pretty much the same." He placed his hand on my buddy's shoulder. "Just relax."

"On the days he worked too quickly, his co-workers warned him, 'You'd better slow down. You're making the rest of us look bad.'

"'With no good reason to put in a decent day's work, it took an entire summer to paint the centerlines on five miles of road. The only downside was that he was afraid if he got used to the state work, he'd never be able to work at a real job again.' Pop thought about it for a moment. 'Easier doesn't always mean better, Herbie. Remember that.'"

As we continued to work the river, Pop spoke to me as though we were peers—equals. It made every single cut on the bottom of my feet worth it.

The bushel basket was nearly full again, when I realized that we'd be giving away most of the quahogs to our family; they'd use every last one of them to make stuffies; clear quahog chowder; pasta with garlic, oil and chopped quahogs—*my favorite.*

"Let me go get the car," Pop told me. "Stay out of sight from the road. I'll be right back."

As I waited in the shadows for the old man's return, my foot slipped on the muddy bank, and I went straight into the river with a splash. *Oh shit!* I tried to get up, but the weight of the basket floating above me prevented it. A thousand thoughts flooded my mind. Before panic could set in, though, I felt a large hand grab my t-shirt and yank me out.

I wiped my face to see my father looking down at me, grinning. "You need to watch your step around here," he said, without judgment or ridicule. "It's a slippery slope for sure."

Together, we carried the second full bushel basket up the bank, muscling the heavy shells into the back of the wagon—looking around the whole time like we'd just robbed a bank. *No game warden in sight.*

As we slid into the car to make our getaway, Pop opened his small red cooler. After handing me a can of ginger ale, he cracked open a beer, chugging down half of it in one sip. "Now that's what you call a good day's work, Herbie," he said, patting me on the back. "Thank you for the help."

Those simple words meant more to me than money ever would.

As if we were real fishermen, I could still smell the river on us when we arrived home.

Pop counted up the bulky, ribbed shells. "Future ashtrays," he commented, placing several dozen at a time into burlap bags to be distributed evenly to our family.

The whole family will be enjoying chowder and stuffies for the next few weeks, I thought, filled with pride.

Given all the praise and thanks we received, I couldn't decide what I enjoyed more: pulling the quahogs out of the river with Pop or delivering them to the people we loved.

* * *

My brothers and I spent Saturday afternoon hosting a whiffle-ball home run derby in the backyard. Fish Stick and some of the other neighborhood kids were there—Jeff Abrams, Dewey, Stevie Cabral, Grant, Richard, and Abby. We modified the long yellow bat by wrapping it with duct tape so we could launch balls over the bushes.

Our massive backyard abutted an unattended field owned by a Portuguese family that seemed to like goats and cows more than humans—especially young humans like us. In fairness, our little brother probably didn't help with neighbor relations. There were times when the old lady pinned her giant bras and panties onto her clothesline, only to turn and find Cockroach staring at them—hypnotized. She'd scream at the top of her lungs until he emerged from his fog and took off running.

It was unfortunate, as every foul ball we hit into her field instantly became her property. I hated watching the old hag hobble out of her house in her nightgown and housecoat, yell something at us in her foreign gibberish, snatch up the ball, and then limp back into her house—the slammed door echoing through the neighborhood. We spent many allowances on new baseballs, as well as a couple dozen eggs at Halloween to toss at her house.

Even with the Portuguese nightmare lurking in the shadows, we played hard. Each one of us tried to copy a Red Sox player's stance when we were up to bat, while the rest of us leapt into the bushes, trying to steal home runs like we were playing right field at Fenway Park. We were an hour into it, when Wally shattered our last whiffle ball beyond recognition.

"Going…going…"

"Broken!" I yelled, finishing his chant.

Everyone laughed.

Damn, I thought, *back to the store.* At a buck apiece, we kept Old Man Sedgeband smiling.

"Buy three," Wally said, handing Alphonse a five-dollar bill, "and don't put it on Ma's tab." He glared at our little brother.

"But they're only a buck a pop, Wally."

"You still don't understand taxes, huh?"

Cockroach went silent.

"And I want my change back," Wally said.

"I know," Cockroach said.

"Every penny," Wally said in a threatening tone. "I'm not Ma."

Cockroach faced the group. "Anyone want to go to the store with me?"

"I hate that place," Abby Gerwitz said, shaking her head.

"And I hate Old Man Sedgeband," Richard added, "that lizard's a thief."

"Ain't that the truth," Wally muttered.

Vic and I looked at each other and smiled. "If you let him, I guess," I mumbled back.

Everyone looked at me but never questioned the comment.

"Vic and I will go with you, Alphonse," I said. "I'm out of Sugar Babies anyway."

"Oh, I really like Sugar Babies," Dewey commented, his eyes hopeful.

"Good," I said, "because R&S stocks plenty, where you can buy as much as you want."

Everyone but Dewey laughed.

I grabbed the front door handle to R&S Variety and gave it a tug. Cockroach and Vic entered the darkness before me. As usual, my eyes wrestled with the shadows.

With the exception of Old Man Sedgeband and Oscar, the store was empty. *Wow*, I thought, *even on a sunny afternoon, this place is a morgue.* The old codger stared at me through his Coke-bottle glasses. *I wonder if he hates me as much as I hate him?*

After grabbing two bags of Sugar Babies, I watched as Cockroach bellied up to the counter with three new whiffle balls.

The old man took pause, waiting for a punch line. "No candy today?" he asked.

Cockroach shook his head. "Just the whiffle balls."

"Your mother finally catch you skimming off the top?" He grinned.

With a shake of the head, Cockroach ignored the accusation. "How much for the whiffle balls?" he asked, flashing the cash.

Chuckling to myself, I bent down to stare into the glass case. *Maybe I should get a few packs of Fruit Stripe gum and treat everyone?* Although there was no better feeling than making my own money, being able to show off was a close second. *But Fruit Stripe only tastes good for ten seconds, and then it's like chewing on a birthday candle. The whole pack will be gone within minutes.* My eyes made their way across the Jawbreakers and Gobstoppers until reaching a half-empty box of

Safety Pops; these lollipops had a stick folded back into the candy, looking a lot like a baby pacifier. As far as I was concerned, *Safety Pops are just another name for lint rollers.* I looked up at the zombie standing across from me. "I'll take these Sugar Babies, and give me ten sticks of Jolly Ranchers, half watermelon and half green apple."

As Sedgeband reached into the glass case, Cockroach called out, "Make two of those green apple ones cherry instead."

The shop owner's giant eyes looked to me for confirmation.

"That's fine," I said, "even though the cherry ones suck."

We returned to the homerun derby, but the break in action had killed the game's momentum. *At least we're still outside and not stuck in that hot house, playing video games,* I thought. *I don't know how Ma can stay inside all day, living like a spider.*

Suddenly, we were saved by the bell—Gus's ice cream truck.

Spending money at the neighborhood ice cream truck was like dipping our tongues into the fountain of youth.

Gus wore a smile from ear to ear when he spotted most of the neighborhood gang congregated in one spot. He didn't even make us run as far.

It was the same old pictoral menu on the side of the white box truck. *Ice cream sandwiches, Bomb Pops, the red, white and blue popsicles, Fudgsicles, Creamsicles, strawberry crunch bars, chocolate crunch bar, Nutty Buddies, Push Pops. Screwballs.*

Wishful thinking, I thought, *what are the chances I'll ever eat an ice cream again that has a gumball on the bottom?*

When I ordered lemon-flavored Italian ice, I knew Cockroach would want my wooden spoon when I was done with it—like he was planning to become a family physician.

"Say ahhhh..." I told him, trying to jam the tiny tongue depressor into his sealed lips.

"Let me get two Screwballs," Grant told Gus, stepping up in line.

Yeah, good luck with that, I thought, snickering.

"Here you go," the ice cream troll told Grant, handing him a pair of the coveted treats.

You've got to be shitting me! I thought in disbelief. *Why didn't I at least ask?* But it was too late to make an exchange, nor did I have the money to get a second ice cream. *You suck so bad, Gus!*

When everyone had gotten his or her ice cream, there was a collective decision—without a word spoken—to disperse for the day.

"What are you guys doing tomorrow?" Grant asked Wally.

My older brother shrugged. "We'll know tomorrow, I guess."

Grant looked at me.

I offered my own shrug. "And probably not know until we're doing it," I added.

"I get it." He nodded. "See you losers around," he said, heading toward Wilbur Ave.

"Not unless we see you first, you big load," Cockroach joked back.

Shaking his head, Wally gawked at him.

"You need to start amping up your material, Cockroach," Wally said.

"And you need to stop trippin', Ace," Cockroach replied, defending himself.

There was still some sun left in the sky, when Cockroach suggested, "Why don't we play lawn darts for a while?"

Without reply, Wally headed straight to the shed to retrieve the weapons.

Playing lawn darts was not supposed to be a contact sport, but our objective was a bit more devious. Everything we did turned into a contact sport. We figured that Pop carried good health insurance, so we were covered.

It was the only game where we would have considered wearing helmets, if we'd had them. *We're not complete morons*, I thought.

Leaving Cockroach's G.I. Joe dolls out of it this time, we began chucking the darts straight up into the air to see who could get theirs the highest. Higher and higher they went until they were lost in the bluish-purple sky.

"Watch out!" we took turns screaming out, as though we were yelling "Fore" during a golf game—the sharp tips racing back toward the earth—or anything in their way.

Sometimes, the warnings came a few seconds late—the darts landing dangerously close to one of us.

"That one almost landed on my foot," I screamed out, the red lawn dart inches from my ratty sneaker.

"Still not close enough," Wally joked.

"Let's see if we can get it closer," Alphonse said, hurling the second dart right above our heads.

We laughed hard, testing the strength of our bladders.

At one point, Wally launched the yellow dart with such a grunt that he fell backwards onto the grass.

Although we lost the missile in the twilight sky, it landed a safe distance away.

Retrieving it, Cockroach heaved it back into the sky.

Scrambling for cover, we were all laughing, when the little guy let out a terrible shriek, dropping to the ground like he'd just been shot by a sniper.

Oh shit, I thought, hurrying over to him.

By now, Cockroach was alternating between screaming and holding his breath—sounding like a Black Sabbath album skipping on the record player.

I was afraid to even look. *Oh shit!* I repeated in my head, trying to prepare myself for the blood bath.

When I finally drummed up the courage to open my eyes, I saw that our little brother had been impaled, his right shoulder skewered.

In a panic, Wally yanked the dart out and began assessing the open wound. "Oh, that's a lot of blood," he mumbled.

Cockroach screamed his head off, occasionally glancing sideways at his crimson-soaked shoulder.

Pop pulled into the driveway, just returning home from some errand. Knowing something wasn't right—with Cockroach screaming and all—he hustled over.

After a quick field inspection, he said. "It's a puncture wound. They're the worse." He shook his head. "Run and get your mother," he yelled at Wally, "and tell her we're heading to the emergency room again."

We were kind of surprised that he didn't tell Cockroach to "just walk it off" or "rub some dirt on it."

Pop looked at me. "You friggin' guys."

But Cockroach is the one who threw the dart that hit him, I thought, insulted by the implied accusation.

Wally and Ma met me, Pop, and Cockroach at the station wagon. "What happened this time?" she asked, her voice panicked.

"I pulled into the driveway and saw Alphonse laid out on the grass," Pop explained, adding a shrug. "I just figured he'd fallen ass over teakettle. I didn't realize his brothers had shish-kabobbed him."

Shish-kabobbed, I repeated in my head. It took all I had to push down a giant laugh.

"He'll need a shot," Ma said, shaking her disgusted head, "or his shoulder might get infected."

As usual, Cockroach freaked out even more. "No!" he screamed, his defiance echoing through the neighborhood.

"Relax," Pop said, attempting to soothe him, "the hospital needle will be a lot smaller than that damn lawn dart." Grinning, he half-shrugged. "And you took that like a champ, didn't you?"

We rolled our eyes. *He took it like a champ, all right,* I thought, *More like a screaming Mimi.*

"At least I wiped the dirt off the steel tips before we played." Wally reported.

"Isn't that thoughtful," Pop said, his bottom lip starting to curl over his teeth—a clear sign that everyone needed to shut their mouths. The old man glared at my older brother. "Nice work, Tin Man," he said, implying that his firstborn was heartless.

"I didn't mean for this to happen, Pop," Wally said.

"You never do," the old man said, "which makes me feel better every time I have to rush your little brother off to the emergency room."

Knowing how tired Pop was from working the river all morning, I felt bad for him.

As the station wagon left the driveway, Ma promised, "Those lawn darts are going in the trash!" She shook her angry head. "No more accidents!"

• • •

The annual summer clam boil was hosted at Uncle Skinny's place. Everyone was there—our grandparents, Uncle Skinny, Aunt Phyllis. Each summer, sometimes twice, the whole family either gathered on and around the gray weathered picnic bench in our backyard or else -at Uncle Skinny's oasis.

You would have thought that as we got older, it would have gotten easier to greet Aunt Phyllis with a kiss. It was the opposite.

Even the suggestion of her lips—the cold snail—sliding down my cheek gave me the piss shivers. *Why?* I thought, breaking out into a cold sweat, *Why can't she just shake hands like Uncle Skinny does?*

While everyone else was losing weight, Aunt Phyllis was packing it on. Something dark inside me wanted to rub her belly and make a wish. *Gaining weight in the summer seems a bit odd to me*, I thought. My brothers and I couldn't eat enough to put on a pound during the warmer months. Being "big boned," I was grateful. It wasn't Aunt Phyllis' extra weight that bothered me, though. *It's the skin tabs she's started to grow all over her neck and arms,* I thought. *They look like baby nipples*, I thought, feeling my own skin crawl. *Like her moustache isn't enough.*

Swallowing hard, I told myself, *Let's just get this over with,* and stepped up to face my aunt's hideous smooch.

She smiled at me before puckering up, sending ice water through my throbbing veins.

Aunt Phyllis' lips felt exactly as I remembered—like a cold mollusk. As usual, she held it to my cheek just long enough to cause goosebumps, before slowly sliding it down my face like a slug trying to escape from her mouth.

I caught Cockroach out the corner of my eye. His face was filled with terror. *You're up next, baby boy.* It was the only thought that made the horror show bearable.

"So, Alphonse took another ride to the emergency room, huh?" Uncle Skinny said, happy to sprinkle some salt into the fresh wound.

Here we go, I thought, looking over at Wally. *It's a good thing Cockroach is in the bathroom, or he'd be whining like an abused puppy right now.*

Pop shook his head. "We should get a discount by now," he said. "That poor kid will be lucky if his brothers don't kill him before his testicles drop."

"But Pop…" Wally said, kicking off our defense.

"You shut your mouth," the old man barked, staring us both down. "Do you have any idea how many hours I've wasted in the E.R. waiting room because of you two?"

Uncle Skinny chuckled, happy to stir the pot. "What did they do for him at the E.R.?"

"They gave him a tetanus shot, making him scream something awful."

Wally and I both shook our heads.

"That's it?" Uncle Skinny asked.

Pop nodded. "No stitches this time. It was a puncture wound, so they just cleaned and dressed it."

"Well, that's good," our uncle said, grinning at us.

Thanks a lot, Uncle Skinny, I thought. *You're a big help.*

The Boston Red Sox played on the tiny transistor radio. Legends like Dwight Evans, Jim Rice, Roger Clemens, Jerry Remy, Dennis Eckersley, Wade Boggs and Bob Stanley came alive in my mind, the hometown heroes taking the field in the shrine known as Fenway Park.

I wonder if we'll ever get to see Fenway in person?

While I was daydreaming about such a glorious day, my little brother returned to the yard. The adults immediately began to fawn over him, shaking their heads over his newest war wound.

"Half of this boy must be made up of scar tissue by now," Pepere said.

Suspicious looks were cast my and Wally's way.

I finally snapped, spilling the beans. "Alphonse is the one who threw the dart into the air that shish-kabobbed him." I loved the new phrase and was hoping to use it more often.

"But who let him throw it up into the air?" Memere asked.

"Yeah, aren't you guys older than him?" Grandma said. "Shouldn't you be a little more responsible?"

Wally and I were reduced to humble nods.

It's a losing cause, I realized, and went silent.

My grampa's famous copper pot was the star of the day. Pop and Uncle Skinny shared the inheritance after the old man's death, and they both treated the tub with great reverence and respect—sharing the annual cooking to boot.

Instead of clams, Pop used cherrystones—essentially small quahogs—and he was hardly stingy with them. "You can thank Herbie for these," he announced to the family while he cooked. "We worked the river yesterday, and Herbie nearly filled a bushel basket with them."

I could feel my face glow with pride. "It was both of us, Pop."

He waved my comment off. "Nah, these were all you. I might

have grabbed the bigger ones for the chowder—pronouncing it *chowdah*—but these were all you."

It felt odd when the adults took turns thanking me for the summer feast.

Ma made lemonade, throwing an extra scoop of powdered Country Time into the clear pitcher. It actually felt like a small betrayal. *She's just showing off for the family*, I thought, wondering how we drank a very different version at home. I wisely decided to keep my mother's dark secret to myself.

Lemonade aside, we ate like royalty. The clear broth chowder was delicious—loaded with quahogs and diced potatoes, seasoned with salty river water.

Going up for seconds, Wally mentioned that he was inviting some girl to the beach in the upcoming week. "I can't wait," he admitted.

"Oh, *now* you want to go to the beach," Ma said, nearly growling.

"Leave him alone," Aunt Phyllis said.

I wonder if this mystery girl's name is Owen?

"Are you nuts, Wally?" Uncle Skinny said. "Bringing a girl to the beach is like bringing sand to the beach. Trust me, there'll be plenty there." Although he appeared the sage at times, our uncle was the same man who sat in the surf all day, drinking beer and never once using the bathroom to relieve himself.

I started to laugh until a cherrystone slid halfway down my windpipe. *Oh God…* I stopped laughing, so I could cough it up.

While Pop and Uncle Skinny drank cold beer from a stocked cooler, they played horseshoes all afternoon in the shade. They were both so incredibly skilled that my brothers and I didn't even dream of asking to jump in and join them.

Two sand-filled pits, with steel poles sticking up in the middle of both, were located an exact distance of forty feet apart.

They were so closely matched that I really enjoyed watching them play. They were halfway through the first game when Pop threw his first ringer. "Put that in your pipe and smoke it!" he called out, before taking a long swig of beer.

For whatever reason, I tried to picture that—and couldn't.

Uncle Skinny laughed. "Oh, I'm just getting warmed up, brother." The twisted man let his last horseshoe fly. The clang of steel hitting steel announced that he'd topped my father's last ringer.

Pop's eyes flew wide open. "I'll be a son-of-a-bitch," he muttered, chugging down the rest of his beer.

Uncle Skinny laughed hard, causing us to do the same.

"Go get me another beer, Cockroach," Pop yelled out, before handing me an empty beer can. "Don't say I never gave you anything," he told me, grinning.

Alphonse headed for the ice chest, fished one out, and then cracked it open for the old man. As he went to hand it to our father, the wet can slipped from his fingers and fell to the grass.

Eyes wide with panic, Pop collapsed to one knee, saving all but two sips. "That's what you call alcohol abuse right there," he said, shaking his head. "That's what that is."

Uncle Skinny laughed more. "One to nothing, Walt," he yelled out, reminding our father of the score.

Pop nodded. "It's a long day, brother, and the cooler's full."

My uncle nodded back. "One to nothing," he repeated, obviously trying to get into Pop's head.

For old men, I can't believe how competitive they are, I thought, before giving it some thought. *No different from me, Wally, and Cockroach, I guess.* I grinned. *And I don't see that ever changing for us, either.*

I sat in the shade for another hour or so, content to watch the score swing back and forth. *Horseshoes are a lot like lawn darts*, I thought, happy to keep the thought to myself, *only not as dangerous.* I grinned again. *Then again, we've never really played lawn darts the way the game was designed.*

I then watched as Mr. Fluffernutter strutted through the backyard. "You might want to keep clear of Chinese restaurants and stay in the house for a while," I told the brown and white cat.

Wally laughed.

Part of the reason I loved visiting Uncle Skinny's place was the massive tree in his backyard. Over the years, we'd hang old gray tarps over the limbs to create a couple of darkened rooms. Even though it smelled and got hot and steamy inside, there was something comforting about the makeshift shelter. No one ever bothered us. Located only a few feet away from the adults, we enjoyed the privacy to whisper secrets or hide from an inevitable chore.

Unfortunately, we're too old for that now.

Instead, we focused on Uncle Skinny's tire swing, which hung from a long rope. I always thought it was strange—*considering he's never had any children.* We never mentioned it for fear that he'd take the badass swing down.

For the next hour or so, we took turns trying to push each other so high that we'd flip over the thick limb. Once, Cockroach came close, which was enough for him to remove himself from the lineup.

More turns for me and Wally, I thought.

"I'm playing Matchbox cars," our little brother announced, "and you guys aren't allowed to play."

I laughed, while he went off to grab his carrying case filled with miniature collectibles.

Mid-summer, Cockroach had begun collecting Matchbox cars in all styles and colors. He took very good care of them, doing a weekly inventory followed by a thorough dusting. Wally and I believed he would have waxed them, if he could have. We also knew that he'd own the finest collection in Westport by the time we returned to school in September.

"We'll come play with you later," Wally called out to him, busting his chops.

"No, you won't. You're not allowed," he repeated.

We both laughed.

By late afternoon, the family grew tired of watching Uncle Skinny torture mosquitos. Every time one of the insects landed on his forearm and started feeding, he'd squeeze his arm around the mosquito, filling it with enough of his blood to explode it. "That'll teach you, ya bastard," he said.

Disgusted, the adults headed indoors to save the mosquitos and play their weekly pitch game at Uncle Skinny's kitchen table.

For whatever reason, Cockroach and I followed them in.

My little brother was excited about the opportunity to play pilot fish and clean up any of the change that dropped beneath the table. "We can split it," he told me, his eyebrows dancing in synch.

I shook my head. "It's all yours, miser. It's too hot in this house for me." I started back for the door.

"Where are you going?" he asked.

"Back outside."

"Where outside?"

I shrugged. "Anywhere but here."

I sat on the tire swing, happy to veg out by myself. As I slowly spun in circles, my thoughts immediately landed on Donna. It seemed like a lifetime ago when I'd finally mustered the courage to hand her the letter I'd written her. I had read it over so many times that I could recite it by heart.

Dear Donna, I've been trying to write you this letter for a while now. Although it's not easy telling you how I feel about you, I know I'll regret it for a long time if I don't. I like you, Donna. Actually, I really like you and I was hoping that you'd consider going out with me. I think we'd be great together. I hope you feel the same. Herbie.

I smiled. *Not bad, if I do say so myself,* I thought.

Realizing I hadn't written her anything since, I thought, *Maybe I should try writing her a poem?*

For the next half hour, I wracked my brain for an opening line. I kept at it until I finally came up with *Roses are red. Your smile is nice...*

I shook my head hard enough to erase the lame poem from my brain. *Maybe Pop's right,* I thought, *maybe I do have rocks in my head? I'd better just stick to the phone calls.*

I'm not sure how long I sat in that swing, but I really enjoyed the time I had to myself, daydreaming in the dark.

I could imagine going roller skating with Donna on a Friday night, my skate suffering from a nervous front wheel—shaking right to left, right to left—like it was having a seizure. I even pictured turning them in for a working pair of skates.

While a yard full of crickets chattered amongst themselves, my thoughts went deeper—trying to imagine who I'd be as an adult, what kind of man I was going to be.

I have no idea.

It was late when I returned to Uncle Skinny's smoky kitchen. The card game was clearly winding down. *All the grandparents are already gone for the night.*

I peeked under Uncle Skinny's kitchen table to see Cockroach hiding there. He placed his index finger to his puckered lips. *He's always sitting in the shadows, listening,* I thought, *not to mention, who knows how much fallen change he's pocketed.* I nodded, letting the gangly spy know that his secret was safe with me.

Without permission, I claimed Memere's empty chair, sliding it closer to the table. Ma looked at me for a moment before grinning. *She's gonna let me stay,* I realized, suddenly feeling much older than my age. Pop, Uncle Skinny, and Aunt Phyllis never batted an eye at my presence. In fact, the conversation continued on as if I wasn't even there. Feeling accepted, I wasn't foolish enough to open my mouth. I knew that one wrong word would instantly exile me from the adult table. *Mum's the word,* I told myself, enjoying the moment too much to risk seeing it end.

"I sometimes wear men's wooden clogs," Uncle Skinny said in mid-conversation. "As an Irish step dancer, I won't stop moving my feet until I smell smoke."

Everyone laughed.

"Hey, where's Wally been?" Uncle Skinny asked.

At one point during the afternoon, my father had slipped away to give my older brother a ride to work. Pop smiled, proudly. "He's... he's a working man now," he stammered, stifling a beer burp. "He's working for the Chinese now, wash...washing dishes."

Damn Pop, I thought, *you're hammered.*

"Even if Wally wasn't working," Ma said, "I'm sure he'd find a good excuse to be anywhere but here." She shook her head. "Wally thinks he's too old to hang out with his family now, especially where me and Walt are involved."

It's true, I thought, *the only time Wally's with us is when he's forced to be.*

"Do you blame him?" Aunt Phyllis commented, surprising everyone. "When we were his age, did we want to be hanging around our parents?" She laughed. "I know I didn't."

Wow, I thought.

Pop dealt the next hand. "They're saying this winter's supposed to be another bad one... the cold...coldest in U.S. history."

"Who are *they*?" Aunt Phyllis asked.

Pop shrugged. "Don't care. Whoever *they* are, I hope *they're* wrong."

"Yeah, last winter was a pretty harsh one," Ma said.

I nearly choked on my drink. *How would you know, Ma?* I thought. *You were nice and warm while you sent us outside to freeze our tails off.*

Her head snapped my way. Remaining silent, I intentionally avoided eye contact.

"We can survive the cold, but..." Pop said, "but too much snow is another thing all together. If we get..." He burped. "If we get another friggin' Nor-easter..."

Then we'll have more time off from school, I thought, before remembering the week and a half we were trapped in the house together. *I hope we don't have another Nor-easter for a long, long time.*

The deal made its way around the table, with each adult taking his or her turn shuffling the deck. *I really need to learn how to shuffle cards,* I thought, feeling jealous.

"Looks like NASA's gonna head into space again next month," Uncle Skinny said, "with the Discovery."

"The Discovery?" Aunt Phyllis repeated, requesting more information.

"The Space Shuttle," Ma clarified.

"Oh yeah," my aunt said, "they were supposed to launch in June, but I guess they've had a lot of technical issues pushing them back." She grinned, obviously pleased to redeem herself.

I watched her elbow sweep several dimes off the table.

Good for you, Cockroach.

Uncle Skinny got up to grab a couple more beers for him and Pop. "Waste of tax money, if you ask me," he muttered.

"It's called progress, Skinny," Ma said before smirking. "And this time, the crew's made up of five men and one woman!"

Returning to the table, Uncle Skinny handed Pop a fresh brew. "Yeah, but I'm pretty sure they're not crazy enough to let that woman drive the damn thing," he said, mirroring her smirk.

I gagged again, this time drawing the attention I was trying to avoid.

"Are you supposed to be sitting here?" Ma asked.

"Let him be," Pop said, shooting me a delayed wink.

"Well?" Ma asked, staring at me.

"I think I…" I began to reply.

"There's no way in hell they're gonna let her drive," Uncle Skinny reiterated, saving me.

"You know what, Skinny, you can kiss my backside," Aunt Phyllis snapped at my uncle.

"I'll take a hard pass on that one," he said, shaking his head. "There are some things you can't unsee, Phyllis, and I don't sleep well as it is."

Everyone except Aunt Phyllis and Ma laughed.

Pop even spilled his beer on his shirt, soaking the front.

"Talk about alcohol abuse," Uncle Skinny said.

Pop looked down at his drenched shirt and shrugged. "I thought I heard a baby cry and…" He grinned. "…and my body just reacted. It ain't my fault."

This time, even Aunt Phyllis laughed.

"Well, if you want to sit here, Herbie," Ma said, ignoring her inebriated husband, "then you need to keep your thoughts to yourself, understood?"

"But I didn't say anything, Ma."

She never broke eye contact with me.

"Understood," I said.

"Thank you for your support," Uncle Skinny told me, mimicking the popular Bartles & Jaymes commercial.

This time, I was able to conceal my smile.

Out of nowhere, Uncle Skinny began spinning one of his famous yarns. "A couple weeks back," he began, "it was late when I woke up, my stomach torn up pretty good."

"Maybe from all that beer?" Aunt Phyllis suggested.

He ignored the comment.

"So, I got up and headed into the bathroom, leaving the lights off." He shrugged. "I hate bright light when I wake up."

"Me too," Pop said, burping again.

"Anyway, I filled a glass with water, threw in a couple Alka-Seltzers, and waited for a fizz to get going before I swallowed it down."

Uncle Skinny was a gifted storyteller. Everyone was listening attentively.

"I was laying there in the darkness, waiting for some relief, but my guts were still churning something awful." He shook his head. "No relief at all."

This should be good, I thought.

"So, I got up again, headed back into the bathroom, and turned the light on this time." He paused for dramatic effect.

"And?" Pop asked, speaking for all of us.

"I learned that I'd thrown two tabs of Polident into the glass instead of the Alka-Seltzer."

"Oh, my God," Ma blurted, busting out in laughter.

"At least my insides got a good cleaning," Uncle Skinny said, before pushing his top teeth half out of his mouth.

Everyone laughed, cringing at the same time.

"Is that a true story?" I whispered to my father, while he chugged his beer.

"Who knows with Skinny," he said, still laughing. "I stopped asking that question years ago."

I laughed. *Pop's right*, I thought. For as long as I'd known him, Uncle Skinny contorted the truth beyond recognition.

"He's an entertainer," Pop added. "He'll say any damn thing to get a laugh."

The kitchen was engulfed in smoke, as the deal traveled around the table.

"So, what's up with this Live Aid concert I've been hearing all about?" Ma asked, taking her turn.

Everyone shrugged, before looking to me.

I know this one, I thought, waiting for the green light.

"Well?" Ma asked, speaking directly to me.

So much for being seen and not heard, I thought, before clearing my throat. "It's actually a bunch of rock concerts that are happening all around the world to help raise money for people who are dying of starvation in Africa."

"Africa," Uncle Skinny repeated. "Don't we have enough problems in this damned…"

"Enough," Ma said, cutting him off—quelling his ignorance more for me than anything.

"Where?" Aunt Phyllis asked me.

"England, the U.S., Australia, and Russia," I listed.

Uncle Skinny whistled. "Damn!"

I nodded, proud to be sharing the information. "The numbers are crazy. They're talking about 200,000 people at these live shows. And by using satellite link-ups and TV broadcasts around the world, they think there will be more than a billion viewers in 110 countries."

"How much are they hoping to raise?" Ma asked.

"$125 million."

This time, both Uncle Skinny and Pop whistled.

"Do we know any of the bands?" Aunt Phyllis asked.

"Elton John, Hall & Oates, Lionel Richie, Madonna, Paul McCartney, Queen, Run-DMC, U2…" I looked up to see blank looks on each of their faces. I stopped.

"So, no Ernest Tubb or Loretta Lynn?" Pop asked.

I shook my head. "No, Pop," I said, "they're only allowing

talented singers and musicians for this one."

This time, everyone laughed—even Cockroach from beneath the table.

It was the best pitch game I'd never played in. *If only I could learn how to shuffle cards.*

Like trained monkeys, Cockroach and I made our rounds, saying our goodbyes. When it was time to pay our respects to my aunt, I couldn't help but cringe. As I stepped closer to her, although I'd missed it earlier, I noticed that she now had a skin tab on the front of her neck. *Oh my God*, I thought, the discolored growth etch-a-sketched on my brain forever. *It looks like a tiny penis.* With all the courage I could summons, I stepped up close enough to suffer her kiss, a cold snail landing on my cheek and creeping down a few inches before I instinctively pulled away. My eyes, however, wouldn't leave Aunt Phyllis's neck. It was like a bad car wreck. *Just like a penis,* I thought, unable to look away.

With Ma in the driver's seat, the last door closed in the station wagon. I looked through the back window and smiled. Just the thought of my entire clan gathered together warmed my chest, bringing a sense of deep love and security. These quirky people were the characters that helped to define my childhood and narrate my earliest memories. *They're here for me*, I thought, *always here.* Being a pack animal, I felt grateful. They weren't perfect people, I knew, but they were the perfect family for me.

CHAPTER 11

AUGUST 1984

IT'S A FIRST

Before we knew it, time sprinted straight past July and into August. *Why doesn't school go by this fast?* I wondered.

I began spending time practicing my balloon animals. So far, the only options were a sword or an eel. Wally and Cockroach were hardly impressed by my skills.

Taking a break to grab a drink, I spotted my older brother sitting at the kitchen table alone. *What the hell's he doing now?* I wondered.

I stepped closer to witness him mowing through a full tin of Danish butter cookies like he was popping Pez candies.

I gawked at him.

"We need something to put the new cereal toys in," he said, his cheeks bulging like Alvin the Chipmunk's.

I really need to get out of this house, I thought, and I wasn't thinking in the short term.

In the privacy of our bedroom, while Cockroach played quietly with his Mad Libs book, I grabbed the Magic 8 Ball and turned it over. "Are you ready to tell me the truth?" I asked the plastic toy. I shook it a few times before gazing into the purple fluid.

It is decidedly so.

"All right, then," I whispered, "so here it is. Will Donna and I go on a real date before the summer ends?"

I shook the black globe a few extra times and then, as if in prayer, I turned the ball over and peered into the small window.

Ask again later.

"Nope, I don't think so!"

"Don't think what?" Cockroach asked.

"Nothing," I said. "Just talking to myself."

"And you'll probably still lose the argument," he commented.

I let it go. Instead, I took a deep breath and I shook that ball like I was trying to mix lemonade powder that may have settled at the bottom of the Tupperware pitcher. "So, I'm asking again," I whispered to the inanimate guru. "What about me and Donna? Will we date before the summer ends?"

I flipped the ball.

The triangle read, *Better not tell you now.*

While my heart rate quickened, I shook it harder. "Will we finally go on a date?" I whispered.

This time, I turned it slow and squinted to read my future.

It is decidedly so, the plastic fortuneteller predicted.

Oh, thank God, I thought, feeling an instant sense of relief. Then, filled with instant joy, my body flooded with adrenaline. *Hell, yes,* I thought. *I knew it!*

I spent the next few hours lying on my bunk, alternating between daydreams about Donna and fantasies about running wild. I imagined watching the submarine races down at East Beach—Lovers Lane—with her. I couldn't help but giggle. Then I fantasized about partying at Alhambra's or the Car Palace, picturing both places to be much like the toga party in *Animal House.* It's what I imagined college would be like, and I was looking forward to it. My mind swung back to Donna, with me picturing us attending the prom—her dressed in a gown made out of Saran Wrap.

That afternoon, I held the drab green phone to my ear with one hand and crossed my fingers with the other. "Well?" I asked.

"She finally said yes!" Donna squealed, without hesitation.

"Your mom...she said yes?" I asked, crossing my fingers tighter.

"Yes!"

"Way cool!" It took all summer, but Donna had finally talked her mother into letting her see a movie with me at the mall. *Bodacious!*

Donna lowered her voice. "But she made me promise her that it wasn't an actual date."

"Ummm...okay."

"I told her that a bunch of us are going to meet up at the mall," she whispered, "and then go see a movie. That's it...just friends."

"Just friends?" I repeated, my stomach plummeting into my bare feet.

"That's what I told her," she said, "even though we both know better."

I lost my breath. Although the last few words were barely detectable, they were still loud enough to make me feel like I could fly without wings.

"Herbie," Ma screeched, "I need the phone. I have to..."

"...talk to Aunt Phyllis. I know, Ma."

I could hear Donna giggle on her end.

"Listen," I whispered, "I need to go for now."

"I heard," she teased.

"So, Friday night at six o'clock, the Dartmouth Mall?"

"Yup, three days away. I'll be there," she purred.

My next three words got stuck in my throat for a moment. "I hope so."

"I promise," she said, "as long as I get to pick the movie?"

"I couldn't care less what movie we see."

She giggled again. "Just remember you said that Herbie."

"I will."

• • •

Against my better judgment, after finishing my paper route, I stepped into the bowels of R&S Variety.

Atop three stacked milk crates, Old Man Sedgeband sat behind a smudged glass case that he used as a counter, playing checkers with his silent partner—Oscar. Besides the pronounced twitch, Oscar was nearly invisible, forever remaining silent.

Arms crossed, Old Man Sedgeband gawked at me, filling his tiny store with clouds of blue pipe smoke.

"Let me have a blue raspberry slush," I told him, hoping to wash down the dust in my throat.

"What size?" he asked.

"Medium."

I loved a good Slush Puppy and was hoping, for once, that Old Man Sedgeband wouldn't skimp on the syrup and try to sell me a cup of ice for fifty cents.

No such luck, I thought, as soon as he turned around. "That's ridiculous," I told him when he returned to the counter, "and I'm not paying for it."

"But you just ordered it," he said, feigning confusion.

"No," I said, "I ordered a blue raspberry slush." I looked down into the cup. "And I don't see a whole lot of blue in that cup."

"Sometimes the syrup drains to the bottom," he said. "You just have to stir it."

"And sometimes greedy old men like to steal from kids," I replied.

"How's that?" he said, turning his hair-filled, cauliflower ear my way.

"Keep it," I told him, avoiding another award-winning brain freeze that could take a boy to his knees. "I'll go home and suck on an ice cube. It's cheaper." I wanted a box or two of Lemonheads, but I wouldn't give the old conman the satisfaction of taking my hard-earned money.

Sedgeband was sipping the diluted slush when I stepped out of the darkness and back into the light.

You old Barf Bag!

• • •

I had three full days to work out and get into date shape. *And it might not hurt to get into fighting shape for high school, either,* I decided, hanging around down in the cool cellar.

My yellow Walkman had become my new best friend. I loved putting on the foam headphones and disappearing into my own world, where no one could bother me if I didn't allow them to.

Curling the long steel bar—a couple of sand-filled plastic weights stacked on each side—I listened to my *Foreigner* cassette, grunting with each rep. For motivation, I focused on our new poster of Heather Locklear dressed in a crocheted bikini. Heather had recently replaced Bo Derek, and her iconic jog down the beach. It was heart-breaking to see Bo go, but there just wasn't enough room on the moldy wall for both beauties.

I was in the middle of my second set when Pop walked by, searching for his toolbox.

I took a quick break to slide the headset onto my sweaty neck. Resuming the curls, I nodded at him.

He looked at me. "Big guns," he said, grinning.

I forced a smile through the pain. *Pop thinks I have big guns*, I thought, inspired to do a few more reps.

On his way out, he finished his thought, "But no ammo."

I could still hear him laughing, as he ascended the stone stairs into the fresh air.

We'll see about that, Pop, I thought, curling two more and nearly bursting every capillary in my face in the process.

That afternoon, I decided to get some color on my face and arms. This was easier said than done. I'd been terrified of killer bees the entire summer because there were rumors of a massive swarm flying over from Africa. As I tried to address the growing fear, part of my brain found the claim ridiculous. *That's a long flight for bees, isn't it?* Another part of my brain—the stronger part—succumbed to the illogical fear, making me focus on getting it out of my head. It was a vicious cycle, turning much of my idle time into a hellish game of mental gymnastics.

Killer bees or no killer bees, I need to get some color for this date, I thought, and the preparation commenced.

Everything my brothers and I had was traded—even being able to use

Cockroach's boom box, which was still like new—and money seldom played into the transaction. "This is important to me," I told him.

Alphonse thoroughly inspected his mobile entertainment center before loaning it out. For this rental, I agreed to his terms. "Fine, I'll play E.T. on Atari with you for an entire afternoon. We'll figure out which day works best for both of us."

"But it has to be before school starts," he wisely stipulated.

Smart kid, I thought, agreeing to his final term. *A high price to pay, but okay.*

"And you have to use your own batteries," the shrewd business-man added at the end of the negotiation.

"Of course," I said, praying that he was done talking.

Armed with everything I needed for a full afternoon of sunbath-ing—a blanket, a full bottle of baby oil, a half bag of Big League Chew, and a Capri Sun juice pouch that I found buried at the back of the fridge—I brought Cockroach's pristine boom box out to the yard. As I set up camp, I realized how significant this investment was. There was no extension cord long enough to reach the house, so I had no choice but to use eight D-cell batter-ies. At R&S Variety, this meant nearly a four-dollar loss, a good percentage of my paper route's weekly wages. *On top of that, I'll have to spend some God-awful afternoon playing the worst video game Atari ever released.*

Ma didn't have any beach towels, and she would have screamed her head off if I'd used any of her "good" bathroom towels—which were nothing more than a stack of frayed and ratty cotton cloths stacked in the closet.

Instead, I claimed my territory on an old cowboy-themed

blanket that Cockroach had grown too mature for. This certainly wasn't the first time that same blanket had been used outdoors. I laughed, remembering when Cockroach and I once played Lone Ranger and Tonto, *That wasn't all that long ago.* It felt strange, but I was already missing the old days.

The Wild West blanket was badly stained—*probably from Pop changing the oil on the station wagon*—but it had been washed and was clean. I knew this to be true because I was now sharing the laundry duties with Wally.

As I lay prone on my back, the boom box played one hit after the next: *Hold Me Now* by The Thompson Twins, *I Can Dream About You* by Dan Hartman, *Drive* by The Cars, *Sister Christian* by Night Ranger—one awesome song after another. I even caught my favorite tune, *Sunglasses at Night* by Corey Hart.

Barefoot and carefree, I took a few deep breaths and could feel the sun kiss my skin. The sky was sapphire blue, with a few wispy clouds floating by. *A perfect day to get a tan,* I thought, before scanning the sky for any sign of killer bees.

Between songs, the only sound was the hum of passing cars on the hot tar road out in front of the house.

Before long, I was sweating profusely and detecting the scent of chicken roasting. *That smells good,* I thought, my stomach churning. I hadn't realized how hungry I was. And then it hit me. *That's not chicken. That's my skin burning.*

Choosing baby oil over Coppertone, I continued to bake in the sun. *The tan will be worth it,* I decided, *I just need to tough it out for a while.*

Although Donna and her friends used *Sun In* in their hair, my hair was already bleached blonde from several months of constant sun.

Although I didn't sleep, I did slip into a trance-like state—perhaps from heat exhaustion, quickly heading toward heat stroke.

Sting from The Police was halfway through their popular song, *Every Breath You Take*, when I finally tapped out. *I can't take it anymore*, I thought. My eyes were stinging from the continual flow of sweat, and my lips felt like cracked concrete stuck to my face. As I got to my feet, my head was swimming. *I need...need to find shade*, I realized, stumbling a few steps. I staggered toward the house like it was some mirage in the dessert. *I need water...bad.*

Upon returning the giant portable entertainment center, Cockroach conducted a final inspection, removing the D cell batteries from the back. "I don't want them exploding and corroding the rear compartment like Wally's did." He handed the used batteries back to me. "We're good," he said. "Just let me know when you're ready to play E.T.?"

"I will," I said, hoping to push it off for as long as possible.

For all of my time and effort, I suffered the worse sunburn. My abdomen resembled a candy cane, striped in different shades of red. The pain was excruciating every time I moved.

"Lather this on," Ma said, handing me a half-empty bottle of sticky green aloe. "It might be uncomfortable at first, but it'll cool your skin."

"Does it hurt?" Pop asked me, struggling not to smile.

I nodded, wincing from the cool touch of aloe.

"It could be worse," he said.

"How?" I asked, panting for breath.

"It could be me," he said, grinning.

Ma slapped his leg. "These boys are gonna grow up someday and be bigger than you," she said, teasing him, "and then you'll be sorry."

His grin disappeared. "No matter how big these boys get, they'll never raise a hand to me." He looked at me, his smile returning. "They've been raised better than that."

Still applying the cold aloe, I managed a nod. *He's right.*

Wally continued to stare at me, shaking his head. "You look like the Heat Miser."

"Thanks," I said, trying not to grimace in pain and add to his joy.

"Poor guy," Wally said, finally allowing himself to laugh, "I bet it hurts really, really bad."

Eat my shorts, Dirt Bag.

• • •

As I was getting ready for our first non-date, I imagined Donna doing the same—getting all dolled up, using every girl product I'd ever seen a commercial of: the Krimper, Lip Smacker lip gloss, Teen Spirit deodorant, a neon-colored scrunchy. The anticipation of seeing her made me feel giddy.

I stepped into the bathroom to discover that someone had used the last of the toothpaste. "Ma," I screamed, beside myself, "we're out of toothpaste!"

"I'll pick some up tomorrow," she yelled back.

A lot of good that does me now, I thought, rinsing out my mouth with Listerine, while giving my teeth a good toothbrush scrubbing between rinses.

Still upset at my thoughtless brothers, I nearly bathed in Wally's bottle of Halston cologne. *I should empty the damn thing*, I thought. From my stinging eyes, though, I sensed I'd already put on too much.

I peered into the mirror. *At least I'm lookin' deadly in this bodacious shirt.*

"Be the gentleman you were raised to be, Herbie," Ma told me, as Pop and I were getting ready to leave the apartment, "but don't be afraid."

"Huh?"

"Oh boy," my father said, walking out ahead of me. "I'll be out in the car where it's safe."

"Women…" Ma said, pausing. "All females are attracted to confidence, Herbie, remember that."

Although I nodded, I felt so uncomfortable with this talk.

"Most importantly, have fun." She placed her arm on my shoulder and rested it there. "A first date only happens once in your lifetime." She smiled. "So, make it a great one, okay?"

"I'll do my best, Ma."

My stomach was buzzing with moths and my head swirling with a million jumbled thoughts, as Pop turned the station wagon onto the road.

"You ready?" he asked, grinning.

I shrugged. "As ready as I'll ever be, I guess," I said, trying to breathe.

"Relax," he said, "I'm not driving you to the electric chair. Dates are supposed to be a good thing, right?"

I nodded, still concentrating on my breathing.

Out of nowhere, the giant mall sign appeared on the horizon. I wasn't ready for it.

"These friggin' malls are killing all the Mom and Pop shops!" my father complained, legitimately angry about it.

I robotically agreed, suggesting, "You can just drop me off outside of Sears, Pop."

The old man's forehead folded. "That don't make no sense. It's on the opposite side of the mall from the cinema."

Exactly!

My old man kept driving, while my body involuntarily shrunk in the passenger seat.

When I noticed that Donna wasn't waiting for me outside, I popped up like a Jack-in-the-Box. "Right here is good!" I told him, throwing open the car door before we'd even come to a complete stop. I had one leg out of the rusted wagon, when the old man yelled after me.

"Hey, what do you have for money on you?" he asked.

I stopped dead in my tracks. "What?"

"You're goin' on a date, aren't you?"

I nodded. "I saved a few bucks from my paper route. I think I'll have enough for..."

He extended a ten-dollar bill. "The first one's on me, kid," he said, adding a wink.

"Really, Pop?"

My father leaned in closer with the crisp bill.

Excited, I snatched the ten spot from his giant hand.

"Remember to be a gentleman," he said. "I'll be back in three hours, okay?"

I nodded. "I appreciate it," I said, lifting the ten-dollar bill.

The old man nodded. "I'll be at choir practice at the Vets Club, if you need me."

Walking into the mall, I couldn't believe my father's generosity. *Ten bucks!* I thought. *Where the hell did that come from?* It suddenly dawned on me. *Ma must have told him to give me the money.* I smiled, imagining all the snacks I could now spoil Donna with. *Thanks Ma.*

Beyond Radio Shack and Chess King, I picked up the pace. *I'm about to go on my first date,* I reminded myself, trying not to skip.

Passing the Sunglass Hut, I realized I would have stopped to fantasize about what the ten bucks in my pocket might buy me, if I wasn't going to spend the money on Donna. Walking past the Foot Locker, I slowed down to do a double-take at the leather Nike high tops that I could never afford.

At the top of the mall, I reached the restaurant, B.B. Binks, with its signature forest green awnings. I could only imagine how awesome it would be to take Donna there on a proper date. *It's too rich for my blood, though. Even with Pop's sawbuck.*

I was still chugging along, when I spotted Donna standing near the coin-operated gum and toy dispensers. Contrary to my father's belief, it felt like I'd just been electrocuted, freezing in place, and losing my breath—all at the same time. For a moment, I stood paralyzed and could only stare. *She's perfect,* I thought. *How did I get so lucky?*

With the help of Aquanet, her bangs stood tall—her hair completely pushed off of her beautiful eyes and face. She was dressed in a multi-colored, one-piece romper, with matching gel bracelets and jelly shoes—not much different from the baskets that Whimpy's Diner served burgers in.

All of a sudden, she looked up and spotted me standing there. The eye-to-eye collision caused my heart to race and my palms to sweat. *Not now*, I thought, immediately rubbing my hand on my pants.

As she approached, I could smell her. *She's wearing Love's Baby Soft!*

"So, you made it," I teased, cursing myself as soon as the lame comment left my mouth.

"Of course," she said, "what did you think?" Her lips were shining and smiling at me in the fluorescent light.

I paused to study her face. It would have been awkward had she not been doing the same. For a split second, I wanted to kiss her. *Don't you dare*, I told myself, *not yet.*

We turned and walked side by side toward the cinema.

Our first date is starting out exactly how I'd imagined, I thought, feeling as excited as I was nervous. I looked sideways to see her smiling at me. *This is unreal!*

"I don't know if you know this," she said, kicking off the small talk, "but my cousin's the one who put a frog in that water fountain last year." She gestured toward the small pond in the middle of the mall.

"That was your cousin?" I said. "I heard about that. Pretty rad!" The stupid prank had become legendary, spreading like wildfire.

She nodded, proudly.

We'd just passed Weathervane, Ground Round, and The Gap and were approaching Record Town, when I felt her hand bump into mine a few times before I caught it and folded my fingers into hers. *Thank God her palm's sweating, too,* I thought, feeling like I'd just entered heaven.

Hand in hand, we strolled past all the mall rats, kids from school who walked miles and miles of laps. Every one of them craned their necks to get a good look at us. *That's right*, I thought, never feeling more proud. One of the guys raised his shutter shades to get a better look.

Past Woolworths and Filene's—where folks sometimes got sprayed with perfume or cologne without their consent—we marched on toward the movie theatre. Right across from Kay Jewelers, we finally reached our destination. *Every kiss begins with Kay*, I thought, hoping it was a sign of things to come.

"What movie do you want to see?" Donna asked.

"Your pick, remember?" I said.

"Are you sure?" She giggled.

I nodded. *Please pick something good*, I begged her in my head.

"Good," she said, "because I really want to see Sixteen Candles."

Sixteen Candles? I thought, struggling to maintain my smile. *Ghostbusters is playing. Karate Kid's playing. Even Gremlins. And you want to watch Sixteen Candles?*

"I hope that's okay with you, Herbie?"

I nodded like some robotic bobblehead. "That's the one I would have picked."

We ordered a trough of buttered popcorn, two boxes of candy—Raisinettes for her and Malted Milk Balls for me—and one large Fanta Orange soda with two straws. I handed Pop's ten spot to the kid behind the counter like I was one of the Rockefellers.

As we stepped into the dim theatre, I also let Donna pick the row. She headed for the back. *Another great sign.*

We got settled into our seats, which were a lot like Chevy Camaro bucket seats.

As the cinema lights dimmed even more, the commercials kicked off—dancing hot dogs and popcorn buckets—but nothing from K-Tel or Ronco. *No free kitchen knife or cheese grater, if we act now?* I thought, as the funny ads finished playing and the place went dark.

I stole a peek at Donna to find that she was looking my way. I swallowed hard. *This must be heaven*, I thought, when we both took a drink at the same time.

From everyone's reaction, *Sixteen Candles* must have been a pretty good flick. I didn't care enough to pay attention. My mind was buzzing. I wiped my sweaty palms on my pants a few times before reaching for Donna's hand again. She was right there, waiting for me. Our fingers intermingled. We exchanged another smile.

This is too good to be true.

Throughout the movie, I kept stealing sideways looks at her, my heart racing faster every time I caught her doing the same. I was grateful we were sitting, because it made me feel lightheaded. *She smells like liquid baby powder.*

For the next hour and a half, I considered kissing her. But every time I came close to talking myself into it, I completely lost my nerve. *You big wuss,* I scolded myself.

Even still, just sitting beside her, I'd never felt such warmth. My whole body tingled. I instinctively tightened my grip. It was almost a hug. A swarm of butterflies fluttered in my guts. But even in the blackness, I couldn't bring himself to kiss her. I just couldn't do it. *Come on, Herbie,* I told myself, *you only get one first date.*

When the movie ended and the house lights came up, the giant popcorn bucket was half-empty, the candy was gone, and so was the soda. And we were still holding hands. I looked at her and shrugged. "Did you like the movie?"

She smiled. "I liked being here with you," she said, starting to stand.

As I sucked any popcorn kernel fragments from my teeth, I made sure we were the last to walk out of the theatre. It was only us and some teenage theatre employee who began cleaning up after everyone. *Who cares about him?*

My racing heart kept pace to an internal dialogue that could have helped commit me to any loony bin. *You got this, Ace. Stop sweating so much. Relax, this is gonna be awesome. It's only a kiss...I mean, how bad can you screw it up?* I felt dizzy from holding my breath.

Breathing past the terror to reach the payoff, I grabbed her by the waist and pulled her close to me. "Thanks for coming with me, Donna," I whispered.

"Thanks for asking me, Herbie," she said, leaning in closer to my face.

With dry lips and one eye shut, I closed the distance between us, kissing Donna Torres right on the mouth for the very first time. We stayed there for a second, our lips locked. Donna's lip gloss tasted like pineapple, the flavored lubricant slick enough for the both of us.

I fell hard. *I'm so in love with this girl!*

Hand in hand, I walked her back to where we'd first met up. As we passed the arcade, I considered trying to win her a stuffed animal to commemorate our first date. I quickly decided against it. I could picture the machine's jittery arm swaying back and forth, while I aimed for a stuffed animal that it grabbed, lifted, and then dropped before I could claim her prize.

I think she'll remember this date without a reminder, I thought. *I know I will.*

I looked over at her. She smiled like she was reading my mind.

"Well," I said, clearing my throat, "we should probably say…"

She leaned in toward me again and kissed me, this time flicking her tongue into my mouth, catching mine.

Oh. My. God.

"I had a blast, Herbie," she said, "Call me tomorrow." And with that, she was heading out the mall's side entrance to meet her mother—her intoxicating perfume lingering a moment or two longer.

I nearly skipped down the mall to meet up with Pop. Past Newport Creamery and Limited, I felt like I was gliding. I never paused at the Comic Book Store to peek in. I didn't even slow around the cookie kiosk to take in my favorite aroma. I just glided, feeling the smile on my face threaten to tear open my cheeks.

• • •

Ma was waiting for me at the kitchen table, wearing the same goofy smile as mine. "Tell me everything," she said, pulling out a chair for me.

I was too excited not to share every detail. "It was perfect, Ma," I told her, the smell of Love's Baby Soft lingering in my nose and the distinct taste of pineapple still on my lips. "Just perfect."

She nodded. "Good for you, Herbie."

"So, believe it or not, when we first got there, Pop gave me a ten-dollar bill."

"You don't say?" She smiled, confirming my suspicion.

"I don't even know where to start, Ma," I said, my head floating in a wondrous fog.

"Why don't you start at the beginning," she said, lighting a cigarette, "and talk slow."

CHAPTER 12

AUGUST 1984

CAMPING IN HELL'S KITCHEN

Seated at the kitchen table for one of our family feasts of chicken pot pies, Ma asked, "What do you guys think about having a fundraiser for the Jerry Lewis Telethon?"

My mind immediately flashed to those proud kids who donated money on TV, broadcast by the big Providence channels. I then considered the opportunity to help some sick kids. The second image sent a bolt of lightning through my entire body.

"That would be pretty righteous, Ma," Wally said.

"What were you thinking?" Cockroach asked, well beyond his years.

"I was thinking we could host a backyard carnival and maybe get the whole family in on it." Ma was brilliant, concocting an opportunity to teach my brothers and me the value of helping people who could never possibly return the favor—people who were hurting and needed a helping hand.

I jumped to my feet. "Yes!"

My mother and father laughed.

"But you guys are gonna do your fair share," Pop said. "Don't think your mother's gonna be doing everything on her own for this."

"We will, Pop," we promised—and meant it.

"That means you, too, Walt," Ma said.

"Of course."

My brothers and I looked away, so our father didn't see our smirks.

Too bad we have to wait a few weeks, I thought.

• • •

The month of August kicked off with a heat wave, my thread-bare bed sheets sticking to my sweaty skin like the fly strips that Memere strung all over her house.

I finally succumbed to my bet with Cockroach, honoring our deal and playing E.T. on Atari for an entire day.

I don't care if I never play video games again, I thought, my spirit nearly broken at the end of the torturous marathon.

"Wearing deodorant is now mandatory," Ma announced the next morning, while we ate pails of Trix cereal. "You boys are growing up, and when people go through puberty and start getting hair on their bodies…" She stopped in mid-sentence.

We stared at her.

Silly rabbit, I thought, *Trix are for kids.*

"Listen, you guys smell, okay?" She shook her head. "I've bought each one of you a Speed Stick and you need to use them."

"Speed Stick makes my armpits burn," Wally reported. "I think Right Guard might be…"

"Then buy your own, Wally," Ma interrupted. "You're making your own money now."

He shook his head.

I laughed, knowing that my older brother's armpits could

spontaneously combust before he'd spend a single penny of his own money on toiletries.

Making our surroundings even more foul, Pop was a classic crop duster. He moved from room to room, farting freely as he went—without any dog to blame.

But Ma never complains about the old man's nastiness, I thought. *Different rules for different people, I guess?* From where I stood, Pop's stink was so much worse, especially since there were only two window fans in our entire second-floor apartment.

At one point, to combat the rancidness in the hot house, Ma bought several cans of Lysol and began spraying everything in her path. She sprayed our sneakers. She sprayed our bedroom. At night, when I put my head on the pillow, the last thing I smelled was the vile disinfectant—and I knew my mother had visited.

Cockroach was convinced that Lysol could also be used as a mosquito repellent. "I'm telling you, it helps," he vowed. Even when he was covered in mosquito bites, scratching like a flea-bitten mutt, he never swayed from his belief.

Ma kept a can of Lysol in nearly every room. I think Pop even started using it as spray cologne. It was summer. It was hot. For a while, Lysol might have smelled better than our body odor—but only for a while.

A few days passed, and it got even hotter—muggier.

"Boys, make sure you stay good and hydrated," Ma warned, gesturing toward the garden hose hanging off the side of the house. "Drink enough water today."

Dressed in tank tops and cutoffs, we were never too far from the hose anyway.

"How do we know how much water is enough?" Wally asked, clearly setting her up.

"Your pee should be clear," she said.

"Oh no…" Wally said.

"What?" she asked, concerned.

"Mine looks like maple syrup," he said, causing our mother's face to cringe.

Holding back a laugh, I quickly jumped in. "You're lucky, Wally," I said. "Mine looks more like turkey gravy."

"That's it, I'm done," our mother said, walking away. "I'm just done."

• • •

I'd always wanted to go camping, but it just wasn't something our family did. I sometimes even daydreamed about sleeping under the stars, so as soon as Vic suggested that we borrow his brother Manny's tent, I was committed to making it happen.

"Can we, Ma," I pleaded, as she stood over the hot stove. "Please?"

"I…I don't know," she stammered, taking a break from her stirring spoon to look at me and Vic. "There are lot of bad people in the world and…"

"You can camp out in the backyard," Pop said, matter of factly, sitting at the kitchen table. He then looked at Vic, who was still working on growing a rattail. "Just stay together, okay Ponytail?" he said, poking fun at him.

Stifling a laugh, I looked at Cockroach. "You in?"

He shrugged. "I'm down for it, homeboy."

"Don't ever call me that again, you Fraggle Rock muppet."

Ma shook her frustrated head. "Fine, but you guys need to stay in this yard," she insisted. "Do you understand me?"

Nodding, the three of us hooted and hollered all the way out the front door.

Marching through Hell's Kitchen, we carried only the essentials: a Rubik's cube, two packs of Pop Rocks, my Magic 8 Ball, a pack and a half of Bubble Yum, three stale Scooter Pies, and a plastic baggie bulging with Chex Mix. Cockroach balanced a few Devil Dogs, the loud and obnoxious game, Simon—with fresh batteries—a new can of Potato sticks, probably purchased for Pop, and three cans of Mellow Yellow soda pop. *Everything we could ever need while camping.*

After setting up the tent—which took much longer than expected—we aligned Vic's Holly Hobby sleeping bag and our blankets. As much as I wanted to poke fun at Vic, there was no way I could. *Cockroach and I don't even have sleeping bags.* Although I was dying to know where he got it, I never asked.

Our lantern was nothing more than an inverted flashlight, with fresh batteries we'd snatched from Pop's emergency stash. "If we pile any more crap into that tent, we won't be able to fit in there ourselves," I told Fish Stick and Cockroach.

On appearance, it was the typical backyard campout. In reality, it was anything but.

After a hearty dinner of Devil Dogs and Mellow Yellows, which was both delicious and nutritious—or at least that's what we told ourselves—Cockroach handed me a wintergreen mint. It tasted as good as a fluoride treatment. "Of all the candy in R&S Variety..." I told him, shaking my head.

"Beggars can't be choosers," he told me.

"I'm hardly a beggar," I replied.

He grinned. "You just keep telling yourself that, Q-bert."

Vic extended his hand for a free candy, more than happy to play the role.

Dusk turned to twilight, purples and blues fading to black. As we roughed the great outdoors in the soft lap of luxury, the faint hum of streetlights played background music to a pair of dueling crickets. *So, this is what peace feels like?* I wondered.

Once the sun completely disappeared, I turned to Cockroach. "You should bring your Glo Worm out here so we can use it as a night light," I suggested, teasing him. The plush, pajamaed worm body contained a battery-powered device; when squeezed, the toy's vinyl head would light up from within, creating a soft glow.

"You have a Glo Worm?" Vic asked, starting to laugh.

"No!"

They both looked at me.

"Wait," I said, "I must have confused Cockroach for someone else."

"I don't own a Glo Worm!" my brother insisted, but the moment had already passed. We were already ignoring him again.

With the help of our flashlight, we took turns telling spooky stories. No matter how stupid or immature the tale, everything sounded scarier in the dark.

"If you say Bloody Mary three times," Vic said, "she'll appear in the mirror when you look into it."

Cockroach shook his head in disbelief. "That's not true."

"Bloody Mary...Bloody Mary..." Vic said it twice before stopping.

Cockroach stood.

He's going in the house, I figured. *There's no way he's going to take the risk.*

My brother smiled. "Unless you brought one with you, there are no mirrors out here, you dope."

While Vic gave it some thought, I laughed.

I started another story about one of the creepy houses in the neighborhood. "Some folks claim there's a haunted house on Oliver Street, at the end of my paper route."

"Nuh uh..." Cockroach murmured.

I nodded. "They say the house was built on an old Indian burial ground." I looked at them both. "Why don't we sneak down there on our bikes and see who has the guts to ring the doorbell?"

As Vic and Cockroach declined the generous offer, the smell of apple pipe tobacco wafted over from our next-door neighbor. The creaky sound of a rocking chair sang a constant tune; and swarms of flying insects, attracted to the fluorescent blue bug zappers, buzzed around until hypnosis took hold and they were led to their crackling demise.

"So, tell us about your big date with Donna," Vic said, changing the subject.

"Yeah," Cockroach said, excitedly. "What did you guys do?"

I stared at the two of them. "What do you think we did?"

"I'd like to think you..."

"Watch yourself," I warned Vic. "Don't you even think about disrespecting her."

"I wasn't going to dis her," he swore.

Cockroach shrugged. "I was."

Vic laughed.

"It's true," he admitted. "I want to hear all about it."

"It's not gonna happen, boys," I told them. "Gentlemen don't kiss and tell."

"So, you kissed her then!" Vic blurted, standing up.

Cockroach grinned. "At least you got a kiss."

"At least?" I repeated. "What do you think Donna is?" This time, I stood. "Forget I asked," I told him, "because if you answer the wrong way, Pop's gonna have to rush you to the dentist this time."

He opened his mouth but thought better of it.

Vic laughed.

"What are you laughing at, Monchhichi?" I asked him, calling him a stuffed monkey.

"Monchhichi, Monchhichi," Cockroach began to sing, "so soft and cuddly."

"You guys suck," Vic said.

We both nodded in agreement.

There was a great sense of serenity in the night's silence. For a while, we shut off the flashlight and gazed up at the black sky, twinkling with stars.

"Herbie, do you think…" Cockroach began to ask.

"Shhhh," I whispered, "just be quiet for a few minutes."

"Okay," he said.

When we grew tired of heaven, we made welfare S'mores. Although we couldn't light a fire, we improvised by using stale graham crackers, M&Ms—from a transparent candy cane tube Cockroach had found in his padlocked toy box—and globs of

Marshmallow Fluff from a giant plastic tub.

As we ate, we laughed at each other's silly stories.

Wearing his fake gold chain—what I dubbed "the Mr. T starter kit"—Fish Stick told a story that bordered on childlike.

"Once upon a time…" he began

"Once upon a time?" Cockroach repeated, laughing.

"Once upon a time," Vic continued, "I woke up around midnight, when I felt a ghost in my bedroom. I knew there was a bad spirit near my bed. Even though I really had to go to the bathroom, I didn't move. I was so scared that I…"

"That's enough," I said, interrupting him, "I can't hear any more of that."

"Me either," Cockroach agreed.

"Fine," Vic said, insulted. "If you can do better, then have at it."

"I can," I said, "and I will."

"Then let's hear it," he said.

"Let's not," Cockroach said, his voice pleading. Even in the darkness, I could see that his eyes had already gone wide.

"I'm waiting," Fish Stick said.

I realized it was a risk, as it had taken me months to get past the recurring nightmare of Clarence; but I was willing to gamble on the fact that the hideous creature was far enough behind me now.

"I remember the night when I spotted Roscoe lying still on the lawn," I began. "As you guys know, that's not just unusual for Roscoe, it's impossible."

"That's true," Vic said, "I've never seen Roscoe lying still outside of his coop."

I stopped to gawk at him. "Do you want me to tell the story?"

"Yeah, sorry," he said. "Go ahead."

"Anyway, I hurried over and almost threw my guts up when I saw that Roscoe had been killed…his legs ripped off his body."

Cockroach craned his neck to steal a peek at Roscoe's doghouse; he began breathing again when the four-legged silhouette moved.

"Poor Roscoe's jaws had been pulled apart, and his face looked like a huge hole. Worse of all, Roscoe's privates were missing. There was blood everywhere. For whatever reason, I looked around the field to see if I could find the dog's junk. But it was nowhere to be found. I choked a few times before I finally puked up a half-digested hamburger…a treat Roscoe would have really loved."

Both Fish Stick and Cockroach chuckled, nervously.

"That's when I took off running to go get Pop," I said, intentionally stopping.

"And?" Vic asked.

As though I was recounting an actual event, I shrugged. "The police asked a few questions and took some pictures, but they were never able to figure out what happened to poor, old Roscoe." I stopped again.

"That can't be it?" Vic said.

I shook my head. "That night, it was raining hard, when I saw that the shed doors were swinging in the wind. I walked out to close the doors, when I found some creepy guy named Clarence sitting in the corner. He was crying."

Glancing toward the shed, Cockroach shook his head.

"I squinted in the darkness. 'What's the matter?' I asked the scary-looking dude.

"'I've been thtarving for tho long now,' he said in a heavy lisp, sending goosebumps down my arms.

"Suddenly, a bolt of lightning lit up the sky, and that's when

I saw Clarence holding a large knife just inches from my face. His tongue was hanging outside of his sharp teeth, and he was drooling bad.

"I was so terrified, I felt like I was going to pass out. That's when Clarence started laughing. I'll never forget that awful sound," I added, shaking my head for effect.

Cockroach was now the one paralyzed in terror.

"I tried to run, but my legs wouldn't move. They felt like they were chained down." I took a deep breath and slowly exhaled.

"As the knife's blade sliced into my face, I thought about my Ma and Pop and how much they'd miss me."

"Oh God," Cockroach mumbled under his breath. Distracting himself, he got to his feet and stepped into the tent, scavenging for something he clearly didn't need at the moment.

I continued with the story. "What felt like a hornet's sting became a pain so bad that I can't even explain it. I screamed as loud as I could, but no one could have ever heard me."

"Why?" Vic asked, his voice a full octave higher than normal.

"The heavy rain and thunder were louder than I was," I explained.

As Cockroach's flashlight searched wildly in the tent's darkness, I couldn't help but smile. "What are you looking for, Mr. Magoo?" I called out to him.

He didn't answer.

Vic, however, was leaning forward, hypnotized by my gruesome tale.

"As the madman chewed off my ear, Vic, I did everything I could not to faint. I tried to scream again but couldn't. Clarence's knife had already made its way to my throat."

"Damn, that's crazy," Fish Stick said, engrossed in the story—

even though my ear was still intact and my neck didn't have a scratch on it.

"'Don't worry, my friend,' Clarence whispered. 'Wally will be joining you thoon. Maybe even tonight?'"

"Good," Vic muttered under his breath.

"Between chews, Clarence laughed and couldn't stop. That's when the wind slammed the shed doors closed and everything went black."

With impeccable timing, Cockroach returned to our circle, where all three of us huddled a little closer together—perhaps as some primitive defensive instinct.

As the night grew darker and quieter, I could still make out Vic's moustache.

"This campin' trip is really happening," he said.

Glad you're enjoying it, Teen Wolf, I thought.

"Campin' trip?" Cockroach repeated. "We live a couple houses apart." Vic bordered on being brain dead, and Cockroach enjoyed nothing more than to laugh at his stupidity.

"Oh yeah?" Vic said, wearing a demonic smile. "Lizzie Borden took an axe, gave her mother forty whacks…" For a while, Alphonse had feared that Lizzie Borden was hiding under our bunk bed, inspiring him to take a running leap onto his top bunk so that his feet never got near Ol' Lizzie.

"That's it," Cockroach said, standing, "I'm out." He grabbed his stuff, filling both arms and marching out of the tent.

"…when she saw what she had done," I yelled after him, getting in on the fun, "she gave her father forty-one." Wally and I loved tormenting Alphonse with the simple rhyme whenever we needed to set him straight—scared straight.

I heard the door slam to the house.

I looked at Vic. He shrugged. "Nice move, bowels," I told him.

"What are you talking about, Herbie?" he said. "You're the one who finished him off."

I shrugged, knowing we wouldn't see my little brother again for the rest of the night.

A few quiet moments passed.

"Wanna play man hunt?" he asked.

"Just the two of us? That's bogus."

"Flashlight tag?" he suggested, more hopeful.

I shook my head. "Because of you, Cockroach left and took the flashlight with him, numb nuts."

"Not just me," he said, "us."

"Whatever, dipstick."

"Well, this sucks," he said.

"Vic, if this sucks so bad, why don't you run home and play in your Snoopy and Woodstock water sprinkler?"

"Relax, Herbie," he said, shooting me a wink. "I'll stay the night and tough it out with you."

Lucky me, I thought, wondering, *Does this Cabbage Patch kid actually think he's doing me a favor?* When it came to Vic, you really needed to peel back the layers on the stinky onion to get to any type of truth.

We spent the next hour running around the yard like two fruit-cakes, trying to catch fireflies in one of Ma's empty Miracle Whip jars. Breathless and covered in sweat, we ended up catching three of them—enough for an incredibly pathetic nightlight.

For a while, we lay in silence. I had no idea what time it was. When Cockroach had left, he took his watch, his flashlight—anything we actually needed—with him.

I should have thought about that before pushing him too far, I thought. "What do you think, time to crash?" I asked Vic.

He shrugged. "I can always sleep," he said, rolling over in his Holly Hobby sleeping bag.

Tucked safely in our cotton cocoons, I tried to pick up where I'd left off on my spooky story. "Clarence waited in the shadows for hours," I whispered, "and just when…"

Something outside of the tent groaned, slapping up against the canvas.

"Eeeek!" Vic screamed.

I also tried to yell out, but fear caught the squeal in my throat and held it tight.

Wally stuck his head in and laughed. "Such lilies." He looked at me. "You should be scared, brother. Ma's so pissed at you right now," he happily reported.

"What else is new?" I commented, just starting to breathe again. "Why?"

"Because you scared the crap out of Alphonse." He laughed. "She'll probably have to be up late with him tonight, until he falls asleep."

I shook my head. *He loves dropping a dime on me.*

"I wouldn't sweat it until tomorrow, though," Wally said.

"Then why would you come out here and tell me?"

He grinned. "Sweet dreams, pillow biter," he said.

"You, too, lard ass."

As Wally's footsteps faded away, I wondered, *What the heck's a pillow biter?* I shrugged to myself. *I'll just ask him in the morning.*

As Vic and I lay in the pitch darkness, I whispered, "Goodnight, Fish Stick."

"Goodnight, Sherbet."

To the drift and drone of distant neighborhood voices and the occasional passing vehicle, we eventually giggled ourselves to sleep.

• • •

Every day that passed, we watched the mercury on the thermometer continue to rise, like it was aiming for some unattainable goal. It was hot and just kept getting hotter, with no letup. According to the meteorologists on all three major channels, "We're in for quite a heat wave, folks." The days seemed to slow to a crawl.

A window fan was placed in the living room, as well as our parents' bedroom, forcing voices to be raised when we talked. We were hardly jealous. The window fans seemed to do nothing but circulate hot air.

Our two bedroom windows were thrown wide open, with dirty screens protecting us from the outside world. At night from my bunk, I could hear the outside world much more distinctly: the draft of tires on gummy asphalt, crickets, and the giant willow tree whooshing in the breeze. There was an occasional dog's bark. Two cats screeched; I wondered whether they were fighting or doing something a bit more primitive. Ma always claimed to love the quiet of night, but I thought, *If you listen close enough, it's anything but quiet.* For me, each sound served as a lullaby that sang me to sleep—no matter how hot and sticky it was in my bunk.

One day sizzled into the next. The heat and humidity were relentless. While our cousins, who lived in the city, played in any open fire hydrant they could find—we had a garden hose.

Some kids used water balloons to cool down. My brothers and I considered the practice much too civilized. Instead, we filled water buckets from the long green garden hose. Although the pails were heavy, it was well worth the extra effort.

"No!" Cockroach screamed while being hunted—loving every minute of it.

Wally and I cornered him near the shed, where we simultaneously hit him with a wall of water.

He was bowled over, flattened to the ground.

I don't know who laughed more, us or him. But I do know that he felt cooler than we did, even if it only lasted a few minutes.

Although playing on our Slip 'n Slide was almost guaranteed to cause cuts and bruises, we also knew it promised just as many laughs. Our Slip 'n Slide was at the end of its life, so we decided we'd see it go out in style. Concealing rocks under the end of the plastic sheet, we told Vic, "You're up next, pal."

Our grandparents probably heard him scream two towns over.

I laughed so hard that I pushed cherry slush out of my nose, before dropping to my knees from the worst brain freeze ever.

The following day, we were laying beneath the willow tree in the grass, looking like three lizards perched on a flat rock, sunning ourselves—when we heard that magical circus tune.

Although Gus still couldn't manage to stock Screwballs, he double-stocked Ice Pops and Fudgesicles within his singing truck, each treat starting to melt before ever hitting our lips.

"I'm done cleanin' the toilet, Mama," I teased our mother, half the Fudgesicle smeared around my grin.

"I know that's a lie," she said, without giving my filthy face a second look. "You've never cleaned a toilet in your life, Herbie." She shook her head. "You just like dirtying them."

She didn't even yell at me, I thought, wiping my disappointed face. *This heat's starting to break her, too.*

Although we continued to play outside, the pace turned slower with the games played in the shade. We now wore thick dirt rings around our necks and in the creases between our forearms and biceps. Smelling funky was the curse of late summer, our armpits turning skunk-like.

"Are you boys using those Speed Sticks I bought you?" Ma asked. We all nodded.

"I'm gonna need a new one, Ma," Cockroach said, "mine's turned to liquid."

The thermometer continued to rise until the asphalt became gooey, sticking to our ratty sneakers. When they dried, we had new treads—although uncomfortably uneven.

I realized the entire situation was becoming scary, when Ma returned home from grocery shopping with three personal misting fans. Wally broke his right away, so he discreetly swapped it out for Cockroach's.

Within minutes, our little brother discovered the heinous crime. "Ma!" he screamed.

Wally quickly grabbed his broken fan back. "Big baby," he muttered.

At night, our parents began sitting outside, because it was too hot in the apartment. Thankfully, Pop stocked plenty of cold beer. When the temperature rose, so did the old man's thirst, doubling his order for Miller High Life.

"My tongue's starting to swell," he claimed; this was synonymous with him needing a beer.

"Not enough for you to stop talking, though," Ma fired back, teasing him.

I knew we'd reached a tipping point when Cockroach decided to spend some of his money. He'd had a snow cone machine on his wish list for the longest time. "But I don't know if I want to wait until Christmas," he admitted to me.

"But how can you get it now?" I asked him.

"Because I have the money."

I wasn't sure why I was surprised. My little brother still had his baptism money.

"I'll just ask Pop to take me to Toys 'R Us," he said, thinking aloud.

I felt jealous that he had that kind of money. *And I'm the one with the job.* Shrugging, I reminded him, "It'll probably just break the first time Wally plays with it. Remember my Evel Knievel chopper with real shocks?"

He nodded. "Wally broke it within five minutes, bending the front forks until they snapped clean off."

"Yup, thanks a lot, Wally."

"That's why I'm not telling him," Cockroach said.

"What?"

He nodded. "He'll never know because I'm gonna lock it in my toy box." He smiled. "We'll only use it when he's not around."

If anyone can pull it off, it's Cockroach, I thought. *He has the patience of a prison lifer.*

I followed him as he approached Pop in the living room.

"Pop, can you take me to Toys-R-Us?" he asked. "I want to buy something."

"I don't have money for toys," the old man said.

Cockroach nodded. "I know, but I do."

Pop studied him. "What are you looking to buy with all that money you have?"

"Either the Snoopy snow cone maker, or the Mr. Frosty slush master," Cockroach replied. "I need to check them both out before I make a final decision."

"Go ask your mother."

"I just did," Cockroach lied, "and she told me to come see you."

Fibber, I thought, concealing my smile.

"Well, she's not…"

"You might as well just take me, Pop," my little brother said. "That's what she's going to tell you to do, anyway."

Damn, I thought, *the old man's gonna lose his mind.*

He didn't. "Let's go then," he said, coming out of his worn recliner, "I'm pretty sure that Toys-R-Us has air conditioning." Stretching out his back, he looked at me. "You coming with us?"

"Hell, yeah! It's too damn hot to hang out here."

"Watch your mouth, Herbie," he said, kicking off his torn corduroy slippers and heading off to find his shoes.

Sure Pop, I'll watch my mouth…while your little boy plays you like his plastic recorder.

By the time we got home, I'd gladly traded in my Waterfuls Ring Toss game for a summer's worth of snow cones. They certainly weren't ICEE Polar Bear quality, but they were sweet enough—and cold. *Best deal ever!*

That night, as we sweated together in front of the fan in the living room, I looked at Wally. "Can I ask you a question?"

"What?"

"What would you do right now for a Klondike bar?"

Expecting him to laugh, he turned on me like a rabid pit bull. "I'd peel your face clean off, that's what I'd do."

Relax, Hong Kong Phooey!

"That's it!" Ma screamed. "I've had enough!"

She could have meant us, but I was pretty sure she was referring to the choking heat.

"Something's got to give around here," she said, looking at my father.

Stuck to his recliner, Pop looked over slowly—like a three-toed sloth—and shrugged. "This damned heat wave, I hope."

• • •

In the hope that *hell would freeze over,* Cockroach and I were sent to Aunt Phyllis' house to *cool our jets*—literally.

"It's just a sleepover," Ma told us, "one night, two max."

Panic welled inside me, threatening to burst every cell. "Two nights? But...but, Ma, I have my paper route to..."

"Wally can cover it."

"Oh, I don't think Wally will want to…"

"Wally's covering your paper route for you, Herbie," she said, matter-of-factly. "You boys need to get some rest, and it doesn't look like this heat wave's going to break any time soon."

It has been brutal, I thought, coming around to the idea. Aunt Phyllis was the only one in the family who had an air conditioner, and it was located in her bedroom window.

"But you need to be on your best behavior," she warned. "Your aunt doesn't have any kids, so she has no idea how difficult it can be."

"Gee, thanks Ma," I said.

"Wally's not coming with us?" Cockroach asked, as though he was hoping for a bit more backup.

Ma shook her head. "Besides covering Herbie's paper route, he has to work at the restaurant. And your father needs the car, so I won't be able to cart him back and forth." She half-shrugged. "He'll just have to suffer this heat with the rest of us."

I'm not sure who's luckier, I thought, *him or us?*

She looked at me. "This is exactly what you need."

I nodded in surrender.

No sooner were we dumped off, when Aunt Phyllis began cooking hot dogs and cheeseburgers outside on the grill, served with potato chips and creamy macaroni salad—one of our favorite summer feasts. *This is amazing!* It didn't take a trained detective to figure out that she was planning to treat us well. She cooked more than six people could have eaten. It only seemed respectful for Cockroach and me to give the visit our best shot.

With full bellies, it was still light out when we approached our aunt to say goodnight—and endure her infamous snail kiss. Even the skin tabs didn't seem so bad now. *They're obviously not her fault,* I decided, reminded of just how judgmental I could be.

The cold snails on our cheeks, the tiny penis on her neck—it didn't seem to matter at all. Cockroach and I were beyond exhausted, wanting nothing more than to enter our new cave for a long, chilly night of hibernation.

"Goodnight, Aunt Phyllis," we said, yawning.

"Goodnight, boys," she said, "sleep well."

Aunt Phyllis had a full-sized bed with more pillows than anyone could ever use. A chest of drawers, covered with a white lace doily, accommodated a matching jewelry box. I was tempted to take a peek inside but decided against it. *It's the same thing as a lady's pocketbook, and I've been raised better than that.* Our aunt's bedroom walls were covered in floral wallpaper, with several hanging oval frames of old people, presumably our ancestors. They were dressed from the last century, and every one of them looked mean—men and women alike.

There was a potpourri of smells that I couldn't identify, making me wonder whether she was trying to mask something. I hurried to change the subject in my head.

On Aunt Phyllis's nightstand, a small, colorful Tiffany lamp sat beside a wind up alarm clock and a paperback copy of *The Rockin' Chair;* the novel was worn, appearing as if it had been read several times. *She must really like this book*, I thought. There were two windows, both facing the back of the house. One was closed with the curtains drawn. The other housed a giant air conditioner that hummed and occasionally whistled. I knew right away, *That big baby's gonna sing us to sleep.* A braided, oval carpet covered the center of the wooden floor. In the corner, there was a doweled wooden rack with several blankets draped over it; it reminded me of the giant slide with its swags of carpet at Lincoln Park. There was no TV. There was no radio. Besides the tick of the clock and the hum of the air conditioner, there was only silence—perfect conditions to catch up on some lost sleep.

As I nuzzled into the bed, detecting the scent of Jean Nate, I realized that it was so cold that I needed one of Aunt Phyllis' moth-ball-scented afghans. Competing smells aside, lying there felt like heaven.

Side by side under the covers, I turned to Cockroach. "Aunt Phyllis is all right, isn't she?"

His brow creased. "Are you kidding me, Herbie? She's more than all right," he said, one-upping me. "That poor woman's gonna sleep on a hot couch, so we can have her room. I'd say that makes her awesome."

"I guess it does."

Within seconds, the world went black.

We slept nearly twelve hours, our aunt never once bothering us. When we finally emerged from our comas, she had breakfast waiting. No Frosted Flakes or Cookie Crisp cereal. There were bacon, eggs, and pancakes sitting on her kitchenette table.

Cockroach and I should move in here, I thought.

With full bellies, we played outside until it got too hot. When we came in, Aunt Phyllis offered us the remote control to her living room TV.

"What about your soap operas?" Cockroach said, stunned.

She grinned. "I won't miss anything, Alphonse, trust me.

Whatever happens on my stories today will happen again tomorrow and then the day after that."

My mouth hung open.

"Even if I missed a month of shows, I'd probably be able to catch up in an hour."

"So, we can watch MTV?" I asked, making sure I wasn't dreaming.

"Watch whatever you want," she said. "I'll be in the kitchen, making us lunch."

When she left the room, my brother and I looked at each other.

"Where the hell are we?" I asked Cockroach.

"Where we should have been all along," he answered, being serious.

For hours, we spent some real quality time with Alan Hunter, watching one music video after the next—from Billy Joel to Billy Ocean, from Michael Jackson to Michael McDonald—until our eyes and ears threatened to bleed. Even when the music of Bananarama filled our aunt's living room, there wasn't one complaint issued.

I decided not to push my luck and ask Aunt Phyllis to use her phone. *Donna knows I'm here for a couple of days. I'll just call her tomorrow night.*

Aunt Phyllis, however, still had her nightly chat with Ma. This time, I was able to eavesdrop on the other side of the conversation.

"No," Aunt Phyllis said, as Cockroach and I discreetly listened in, "they've both been very well behaved, Emma. Sometimes I think you make up half the stories you tell me. These boys are like angels, and they're welcome to stay here anytime."

Cockroach and I looked at each other—in stunned silence.

The world suddenly felt upside down when it dawned on me, *I really don't know who Aunt Phyllis is at all.* I'd made up my mind about her long ago and never allowed that judgment to change. *Time to rethink a few things.*

"No, I'm not pulling your leg, Em. They've been perfect gentlemen, the two of them."

With no distractions, no one around but her and us, perspectives were permitted to change. *Besides those cold snail kisses, Aunt Phyllis is actually good to us,* I thought, *really good.* I couldn't believe that one sleepover could change my mind so much.

After another great night's sleep and being spoiled with a few more delicious meals, Pop pulled the station wagon into the driveway and beeped the horn. It was time to say goodbye. I'd expected this to be the highlight of our visit. It was the opposite.

"You're welcome to come back here, boys, and sleep over any time," our kind aunt told us.

"Really?" Cockroach said in a surprised tone.

She grinned. "Of course, Alphonse."

I nodded, thinking, *We might just take you up on that.* For me, it felt like staying in a three-star hotel; we were able to order the food we wanted, we took over her TV without hearing a single word about it, and we slept like kings in the frigid air. *She never even made us get out of the house once.*

"Any time you want," she repeated.

"Thanks, Aunt Phyllis," I said, "that would be really cool."

"Cooler than our apartment anyway," Cockroach commented.

I couldn't believe it, but the heavyset woman actually laughed. *Maybe this heat wave is a sign that the world is coming to an end?* I thought. *I guess it's better than getting swarmed by killer bees.*

• • •

We weren't home an hour when Wally asked, "So how bad was it over at Aunt Phyllis' house?" He grinned. "Torture, right?"

"What do you think?" I asked him in response.

Wally looked to Cockroach, who simply shrugged.

Nodding contentedly, our big brother walked away laughing.

Cockroach and I exchanged smiles.

"The Mangler doesn't deserve Aunt Phyllis's kind of torture," Cockroach said.

"No, he does not," I said with a nod. "That'll be our little secret."

It was still so hot that we ended up descending into the cellar. Winter or summer—*we somehow always end up in the cellar where it's damp and cool.*

A wooden slatted door was unpadlocked and hanging on the steel latch. A narrow set of ancient stone stairs led down into the house's fieldstone foundation. Ducking my head, Cockroach and I descended into the throat of the beast. I wiped away the cobwebs that stuck to my face, hanging from the low ceiling's exposed beams and rusty nails. I was waiting to hear my little brother whine about how scary it was. He didn't make a peep. *It looks like this heat's helping to break some of his fears*, I thought.

The two small windows up near the basement's ceiling allowed enough natural light in to view the dank crypt. A pair of pull strings hung from two bare bulbs located on opposite sides of the dump: one above the washing machine, which made an awful ruckus because its drum was off kilter, and the other above our pathetic improvised gym.

In the center of the grungy space was a giant black, cast iron oil furnace, a behemoth that Cockroach had feared for years. He looked at it without complaint.

Wow, I thought.

Even with the strong smell of mildew permeating the air—generated from swags of old discarded carpets that were soaked year-round—the coolness of the place was a welcomed relief. The entire dungeon was blanketed in cobwebs, created by a community of daddy long leg spiders that begrudgingly shared the space with us.

A narrow weight bench, with enough plastic weights to hurt ourselves, was located beneath the bare bulb in the corner. The moldy walls surrounding the low-budget gym were decorated with a few rock-and-roll posters—Pink Floyd, Blue Oyster Cult, REO Speedwagon—and, of course, my favorite poster of them all, Heather Locklear in her crocheted bikini.

"Do you want to race Big Wheels?" I asked my little brother.

"I don't."

"Why?"

"Because I don't want to visit the Emergency Room again this summer."

"You're not going to…"

"It's not happening, Herbie," he said, making it clear that the idea wasn't even up for discussion. "Besides, it makes too much noise. The real estate people upstairs might call Ma and…"

"Then what do you want to do down here?" I asked, interrupting him.

"Cool down," he said.

I thought about it. "Fair enough," I said. "Let's just chill then."

He grinned at the pun, before reaching into his pocket and pulling out three packs of different flavored chewing gum: Juicy Fruit, Big Red, and a yellow box of Chiclets. "Which one do you want?" he asked.

I reached for the Chiclets. "There's a chance you're going to end up in prison someday, Alphonse," I told him. "You know that, right?"

He thought about it before shrugging. "It better not be for gum."

Laughing, we sat together in silence for a bit. "I wish we had some music down here."

As if on cue, Cockroach threw his left hand inside his stained Whacky Packy t-shirt, placed it under his right armpit, and began flapping his arm like a blue jay taking flight. One fart after the other escaped his shirt, creating a strange melody.

"Nice," I told him. "You ought to be very popular in prison."

He let a couple more rip, ending the impromptu tune.

"I'll be running shit in the joint, Herbie," he said, half-joking.

I stopped laughing. *I have no doubt.*

• • •

When the heat wave finally broke, an intimidating bank of storm clouds rolled in, darkening the summer sky. A jagged thread of electricity shot to the earth, followed by a distinct crack—like a baseball being launched from Jim Rice's Louisville slugger. A thunderous boom grabbed everyone's attention, reminding each of us that we were hardly in charge. Mother Nature had full control.

Within the hour, the heavy rains broke the heat wave like the

Karate Kid's indefensible crane kick. Downpours trickled into sun showers, allowing us to run around and dance in our driveway. Soon, a rainbow appeared in the sky. We all froze in place to gawk at it. *So cool,* I thought. I think we all did, though none of us would have ever admitted to it. *Sweet relief.*

CHAPTER 13

SEPTEMBER 1984

HECKLING CARNIES

"We're having company," Ma announced out of nowhere.

For whatever reason, those three words sent a bolt of exhilaration ripping through my body. *We're having company!*

"Who's coming over?" Cockroach asked.

"You'll see," she said, exchanging smiles with Pop.

Oh, this is gonna be good! I thought.

I couldn't decide which one I enjoyed more, the impromptu planning or the actual night that our "company" came over.

Our first stop was Lees Supermarket to buy a pound cake that my brothers and I would probably never taste.

"It's for company," Ma said. "You guys have enough junk to eat."

The next stop was the package store for beer and scratch tickets. "I can't tell you the last time I hit on one of these damn things," Pop said, tearing up another losing ticket.

The final stop was at Zayre's Department Store, so Ma could make a payment on her Christmas layaway.

We headed home to straighten up the house; this didn't actually mean cleaning. We put things away, even hid them—everything Ma yelled at us about when we cleaned our bedroom.

Feeling buzzed on the anticipation, I didn't even raise the hypocrisy.

Once Ma put out her spread and we were warned one last time to keep our "hands off," we were ready to accept company.

There was a knock on the kitchen door, causing a tiny squeal to escape my throat. In one sudden lunge, my brothers and I pushed each other out of the way to get to the door first. Over the years, we were easily able to identify who the knock belonged to. But not this time.

Wally swung the door open to find Aunt Phyllis standing there. *Aunt Phyllis?* I thought. *She's not company.*

"Hello, Wally," she said.

"Hi, Aunt Phyllis," he said, stepping up to take his punishment like a man.

Glad you got to the door first, brother, I thought. As I stood in line for my dreaded kiss, I looked to Pop for an explanation.

"We're playing pitch tonight," he explained. "Who did you think was coming over, the Queen of England?"

As if summoned, Memere stepped into the kitchen behind Aunt Phyllis.

"Come on, boys," she said, "come give the queen a smooch."

Once the greetings were complete, I thought about heading down to the clubhouse at the railroad tracks. *Ma can keep her pound cake.*

• • •

The light was fading fast when Wally, Cockroach, and I reached the old fort down at the tracks. *I can't believe this shack's still standing.* Even when it was new, the dump had been constructed from scraps of wood or other materials that some neighborhood kids—master carpenters—could scrounge; the rusty nails had been plucked from the backs of neighborhood sheds and hammered in with rocks or broken bricks.

"Why aren't you working at the Pearl tonight?" I asked Wally.

"Billy asked me to switch shifts," he said. "He's done it for me, so…" He shrugged.

"How come you're not cruising the Ave with Owen?" Cockroach asked.

"What is this, a hundred questions?"

No one answered.

"Owen's out with a girl tonight," Wally explained.

But you're not, I thought, keeping it to myself.

Helping each other, all three of us climbed up into the gut of the beast. Even in the dim light, I could make out the old, faded Boston Red Sox pennant, as well as a few curled posters of half-naked pinups, that papered the walls. Although the broken lava lamp remained, the two beanbag chairs—patched with silver duct tape—were gone. Wally and I both took a seat on the old Camaro's front seat, the leather ripped, the steel springs exposed and free floating.

Cockroach went straight for the old Playboy magazine, which was soaking wet under a square of carpet.

"You're going to go blind, if you keep looking at that," Wally teased him.

"I'm good with that," he said.

Wally and I laughed.

Cockroach squinted harder to get in a few final glimpses. "I knew

I should've brought a flashlight," he muttered under his breath.

"That's it," Wally announced, standing. "I'm bouncing."

"What?" I asked, surprised. "Why? We just got here."

"It was cool taking the walk down here with you dweebs, but I'm not hanging out." Taking one last look around, he shook his head. "There's nothing happenin' here."

Now the clubhouse isn't good enough for him, either, I thought, standing to join him. "Let's go, Cockroach," I said, "we're out of here, too."

•••

The family had just finished another potluck supper. With the same amount of fanfare that Pop delivered Ma's birthday gift—her beloved microwave oven—he muscled an even larger box onto the kitchen table, testing the strength of its legs in the process. "Happy anniversary," he panted.

Ma gawked at him. "I thought we weren't exchanging gifts this year, Walt?"

"Relax," he said. "It was on sale."

"Gee, thanks." She tore open the box. It was a behemoth air conditioner. She gawked at him again, not a hint of emotion betrayed in her face.

"What?" he asked. "You don't like it?"

"I'm sure I will next summer, Walt."

Pop's smile disappeared.

Wally looked at me and shrugged. "At least you guys won't get sent back to Aunt Phyllis's house."

I nodded. "Yeah, that was really rough," I fibbed.

Cockroach gagged on a laugh. "The worst."

. . .

Summer was quickly coming to an end. Our white tank tops had long ago yellowed and were bordering on brown—no fault of Clorox. Our white braided bracelets were nearly black and needed to be hacked off with Pop's wire cutters, leaving behind a white band of skin—highlighting just how tanned we'd gotten.

When the giant Country Time lemonade tub was down to its last few scoops, I knew that play time was nearly over. *Ma actually did it,* I thought, oddly impressed, *she made it last the whole summer.*

Throughout the hot months, Ma couldn't keep enough pitchers of lemonade in the fridge. *At the start of summer, it was dark and sweet, but as the weeks went by, she poured less and less of the yellow powder into the pitcher, diluting it—just as I'd predicted.* At this point, we couldn't even remember what Country Time lemonade tasted like. *For the last couple of weeks, we've basically been drinking colored tap water.*

"Looks like you really made that Country Time last, Ma," I teased her.

She nodded proudly, confusing my sarcasm for a compliment. "At least we got one thing right this summer, Herbie."

Huh? I thought. *We got everything right this summer.*

Whether my brothers and I wanted to or not, we needed to start thinking about returning to school.

Ugh…

Ma was already collecting brown paper grocery bags to fashion

into book covers. I couldn't wait to sketch graffiti all over them—
MTV, Van Halen, AC DC—before I even stepped foot into my new
school.

Although I hated shopping, I didn't trust my mother to buy my
school clothes. *Those days are long gone,* I decided.

We made our rounds in the station wagon, shopping at Liss for
Levi's jeans and different-colored corduroys. I'd saved for the perfect
pair of Levi's with the red tag, acid-washed jeans for the first day of
school. *And Ma had better keep her scissors to herself with these jeans.*

Bradlees was a great stop for concert shirts. I'd also saved for a
leather vest, which we grabbed at Wilson Leather at the mall—deciding against the matching chain wallet. I'd also managed to salt away
enough of my paper route tips for a pair of Colorado hiking boots
with the red laces. *No sneakers for high school,* I decided.

Cockroach opted for the jean jacket, dressing it up with *Quiet
Riot, Duran Duran,* and *Def Leppard.* button pins. Ma even made a
special stop at Kerr Mill for the popular swag.

There was no shopping at the Chess King. That store was better
suited for our cousins, who lived in the city. *They're the break dancers
in the family, not us.*

• • •

Middle School had been a cesspool of peer pressure and harsh judgment. Now I was entering high school as a freshman, and every day
that drew closer, I became more petrified of the unknown. *Will the
upperclassmen give me those toilet whirley birds I've heard about? Or the
nuclear wedgies that can draw blood?*

Sensing my nervousness, Pop asked me, "So are you ready for high school?"

I took a deep breath, trying to find the right words. My response took too long.

"Herbie, you're not gonna have to go through anything that thousands of other kids before you, including myself, haven't already experienced," Pop said. "It's going to be new for everyone in your class, so stop worrying so much. You'll be fine." He slapped my back. "You'll always be fine."

I exhaled, feeling a little better—though not much.

"Besides, I need your head in the game for the carnival. You know your mother and her fancy ideas…"

"It's a great idea, Pop. It's for charity," I told him, suppressing the excitement I'd felt for weeks over the event.

"Everything I do for this family is charity," he said, grinning.

As he walked away, I wasn't sure what he meant—and decided it was best I didn't ask.

• • •

It was nearly Labor Day weekend. Besides being the last hoorah for summer, it was also the annual MDA Telethon—with sweaty comedian Jerry Lewis calling out the totals. For years, my brothers and I watched the Muscular Dystrophy Telethon, psyched to see the tally rise again and again.

Although I'd never admit it, I loved variety shows—Carol Burnett, Donnie and Marie—but this one was the best. Between the different acts, there were heartfelt pleas for donations to help kids who couldn't walk.

I can't even imagine, I thought, feeling awful—almost guilty—that I was so much luckier than they were.

The MDA Telethon was a bittersweet event, announcing the end of summer as well as our dreaded return to school. *But this year's different*, I thought. *This year, we're hosting a backyard carnival for an incredible cause.*

I decided to make a list of everything my brothers and I needed to get done. "Let me borrow a pen," I told Cockroach.

He reluctantly handed me his favorite writing utensil, a thick pen with three different color inks to choose from—black, blue, and red. My hand couldn't write fast enough: *make signs, food list, games…*

"What are you doing?" Wally asked. "Ma's gonna take care of all that crap."

"But Pop wants us to pitch in," I said, "and we should…as much as we can, anyway."

He nodded.

"I'll grab the cereal toys from the blue cookie tin on top of the fridge, so we can donate them as prizes for the carnival games," Cockroach said, getting up to start his inventory.

It wasn't much, but it was important to contribute any way we could.

Cockroach and I made signs to be posted on telephone poles throughout the neighborhood. Besides spreading the word—and depending on word of mouth—it was the best marketing plan we could come up with. As the head of promotions, Cockroach burned through a box of his new markers. It was as generous as I'd ever seen him. Even Old Man Sedgeband allowed us to put up a flier in his cluttered store window—shocking us all.

We returned home to find Ma standing over the stove, stirring a large pan of chicken noodle soup.

Why Campbell's soup in the summer? I wondered.

But Pop was already seated at the kitchen table, waiting to lap it up like some big, goofy Saint Bernard.

The man considers spray cheese and Saltine crackers fine dining, I thought, *so I guess soup in the summer isn't that big of a deal.*

The weekend before the big event, the entire family had gone food shopping at a warehouse where Ma bought everything in bulk: popcorn, hot dogs, buns, Kool-Aid, Country Time lemonade.

If there's any left over, maybe Ma will start making lemonade that tastes like lemonade, I hoped.

From there, we were off to the Five & Dime, where Ma purchased two carts full of trinkets—stuffed animals, blow-up beach toys, posters, jump ropes, whiffle ball bats, hula hoops, Kewpie dolls, GI Joe action figures—everything she could find.

"We'll never raise any money with all of this overhead," Cockroach told her.

Ma grinned. "Your father and I are paying for this stuff, Alphonse."

Wow, I thought; it suddenly dawned on me just how generous they were. As Memere always said, "Those who have nothing are usually the ones who give away everything they have."

I was now convinced.

Grandma pieced together a clown costume, while Memere planned on dressing as a gypsy to tell fake fortunes for a small donation to Jerry's Kids.

While Uncle Skinny borrowed some pop-up tents from a friend

at his shop, Pop borrowed long wooden folding tables and two dozen chairs from the Vets Club where he attended choir practice.

The family's all in!

Over the smell of Ma's Sanka, we ate a real breakfast of waffles and blueberry muffins.

"Are you guys ready for today?" Pop asked.

"We are," Wally answered for all of us.

"We have a couple final hours to set up and then it's time to…"

"The boys have been wonderful helping me, Walt," Ma said, before turning her attention to us. "Just make sure you enjoy yourselves today…that you take it all in."

"We will," Wally said.

"I know I will," Cockroach added.

"Go easy, Punky Brewster!" Wally told him.

I nearly choked on my last bite of buttered waffle.

The elation of the final setup was overwhelming. After Pop prepared the yard—which meant gassing up his red tractor and cutting the lawn—the banner and streamers were hung. From there, the tables and chairs were arranged. Half were set up to create a food pavilion under our weeping willow tree; the long rectangular tables were covered with colorful plastic tablecloths, with rows of folding chairs tucked beneath them. The other tents were used to host the carnival games, arranged in a circular fashion around the dining area.

It's like a mini-Lincoln Park, I thought, the anticipation of the afternoon sending waves of adrenaline through my bloodstream.

"Oh no," Ma said.

"What?" I asked.

"I'm not sure we have enough charcoal for the grill. I'll need one of you guys to run to the corner store…and you need to hurry!"

"I'm on it, Ma!" I told her.

My little brother smiled, happy for the break.

I was panting when I swung open the heavy front door to R&S Variety. Old Man Sedgeband was lurking in the shadows like a poisonous snake, awaiting his next victim.

As I hustled toward the back aisle for a bag of charcoal briquettes, I noticed that Sedgeband had installed an arcade-sized Centipede.

Clever, I thought, knowing that this full-sized video game was guaranteed to drain the neighborhood kids of every quarter we owned.

I threw the heavy bag onto the counter. "And give me two packs of Carlton 100's, red pack." Ma hadn't asked for them, but I knew they wouldn't go to waste. "Put it on my mother's tab."

With a nod, he turned to grab his green spiral notebook. "Is the charcoal for the fundraiser?"

"Yes."

"Then it's on me," he said, making my bottom jaw hit my chest.

I stood there paralyzed, unable to reconcile the old thief's donation.

"But your mother still owes me on her tab," he added. "Tell her I'll need another payment soon."

Poor Ma, I thought, emerging from my trance, *we should probably be running this fundraiser for her.*

"If there's nothing else, then there's the door," he said, returning to his nasty self.

As I started out of the store, I looked over at the Centipede game.

Wally, the arcade God, already owned the top score at The Dream Machine at the mall. *He'll dominate this machine, too*, I predicted, realizing that the only real winner would be Old Man Sedgeband.

I returned home to discover that the family had already arrived to take their posts. Although hugs and kisses were exchanged, this time was different—we now shared a singular goal, like we were all soldiers in the same platoon, venturing out on a mission to help sick children.

"Did R&S have the...?" Ma asked.

I nodded, pointing toward the new bag of charcoal near the grill. "Sedgeband donated it," I told her.

She stared at me. "What did I tell you about lying, Herbie?"

The false accusation made my blood pump. Reluctantly, I handed her the two packs of Carlton 100s.

"Oh, good," she said, referring to the smokes, "I'm glad you remembered."

"By the way, Sedgeband says you owe some serious money on your tab, Ma, and that he needs a payment soon." I was happy to raise her blood pressure, too.

Her head snapped toward Cockroach. "Didn't we just give him a payment, Alphonse?"

Cockroach shrugged. "That was a while ago, Ma."

I couldn't tell whether our mother was showing the first signs of early onset dementia or my little con artist brother was simply playing with her head. *I hope it's just Cockroach being a dink.*

Ma scratched her head, scouring her memory.

"Well, that's what the zombie told me, anyway," I said.

She waved her hand, brushing it off for the time being.

I paused to look around. Besides the colorful balloons and

streamers fluttering in the late summer breeze, the yard was quiet.

I exchanged a nervous glance with Wally. *Did we put up enough signs?* I wondered. *Will people actually come and spend money in some rinky dink backyard carnival?*

"It's just the calm before the storm," Ma told us, trying to quell our fears.

Maybe I should twist animal balloons to help raise a few extra bucks for the cause? I thought, before admitting to myself that I didn't know how to make animal balloons. *Snakes and eels might not be the biggest hit.*

Ma assigned stations. Dressed in their costumes, the ladies worked concession, while the men handled the game tents. Ma had strung clotheslines within each game tent, hanging a variety of toys and trinkets by clothespins.

The first game—of all things—was the infamous lawn dart game. The sign read, *Hit the Bullseye and Win a Prize.* Remembering Cockroach being shish-kabobbed, I had to smile. *I thought Pop was supposed to take this medieval weapon to the dump.*

The second tent hosted a game that involved three softballs and an old, rusted milk can. *Except softballs can actually fit into this milk can.*

The third game tent simply hosted a dart board, three darts, and the adult who felt brave enough for the job. "I'm your man," Uncle Skinny said, happy to accept the dangerous duty for the day and lug his beer cooler into the shade.

The final tent had five of Pop's Miller High Life beer cans stacked in a pyramid, sitting atop a round plywood platform. Each player had three baseballs to knock all the gold cans off the platform and win a large prize.

If someone won—at any game—they won a large prize of their choice hanging from the clothesline. If they missed the mark, they still won a piece of candy or a smaller toy—once housed in the blue Danish cookie tin. *No one can lose,* I realized. *Ma made sure of it.*

Our first guests pulled into our horseshoe driveway and parked like they'd just arrived at Lincoln Park to spend the day.

Yes! I thought, excitedly, *this might actually work after all.*

Screaming kids ran from station to station, while their smiling parents paid for tickets. Right from the start, my mind raced with the same questions: *Is Donna coming? Are her parents coming? What if Pop and Uncle Skinny say something stupid…and act like themselves?*

Cockroach's boom box played music that echoed throughout the vast yard. Ma and Pop allowed rock music for the day—our music—betting it might attract more young people.

Pop used his red tractor to give trailer rides for twenty-five cents, driving happy kids two full laps around the yard. I couldn't believe when their parents paid for it. At one point, there was even a line of kids waiting to ride.

Before long, the old man allowed Wally to take over. "Go slow, Wally," Pop warned him. "I mean it."

My big brother nodded once, loaded the trailer with a few of the neighborhood kids and then took off like a bat out of hell. The hooting and hollering lasted the length of the yard, until Wally took a sharp left, jackknifing the trailer and tossing each of his riders onto their heads.

"You've gotta be shittin' me," Pop yelled, hustling toward the accident scene.

I laughed hard. I couldn't help it. *Good thing it's only the kids from across the street*, I thought. *Besides, no one looks hurt.*

"The gas pedal must have gotten stuck," Wally yelled out for anyone who would listen.

Pop aggressively removed him from the tractor, while the accident victims' parents merely waved off the incident. "It got stuck, all right," our father hissed, righting the trailer. "Go find another job."

Watching this, the line of future riders dispersed, heading for a safer thrill.

My brothers and I were in and out of the house, checking on Jerry and his latest tally. We announced this to the entire yard. "It's up to $74,123 so far!" It was rare to be able to deliver such valuable news and each one of us embraced the opportunity to make the important announcement.

When my brothers, Vic and I manned the game tents, we took it very seriously.

"Step right up and try your luck!" Vic screamed out, luring two boys to his softball toss game.

Not to be outdone by Fish Stick, I began screaming out, "Knock down the cans and win a prize. There's nothing to it, folks. Twenty-five cents for three baseballs."

A small girl stepped up and handed me her quarter.

Just like taking candy from a baby, I thought, explaining, "Okay, you have three baseballs to knock all the cans off the platform. Just make sure you stay behind the line." I pointed to a red string that Pop had strung along the ground from one tent pole to the next.

While she chewed on her bottom lip, the girl tossed the first ball, knocking half the cans off the platform. I clapped loudly, knowing this would draw more attention to my tent. It worked. As a few others stepped up behind the player to watch, she let the second baseball fly, wiping the wooden platform clean.

"Yes!" I screamed out. "We have a winner here!"

Loud applause echoed over Mr. Mister's music.

The proud girl hurried off to show her parents, as three more kids each handed me a quarter.

After restacking the pyramid of cans, I reminded the next player, "Just make sure you show some respect for the red line."

At the concession stand, Ma and Aunt Phyllis grilled hot dogs, smothered in mustard, onions, and Memere's secret Coney Island sauce. There were brown paper bags filled with popcorn.

I wish they were Ma's fries, I thought. *I'd buy a couple bags.*

Rows of pre-filled plastic cups—Country Time lemonade and cherry Kool-Aid—were also sold in volume beneath the hot sun.

"The telethon's tally is now at $165,000!" Cockroach screamed, as he ran out of the house to return to one of the game tents.

The entire yard was filled with magic. One kid walked by, hugging a stuffed bear. Another little girl had won an inflatable beach ball which Ma had purchased at the Five and Dime. My chest felt warm. I was overjoyed.

I wish Donna was here, I thought, *so I could win her a prize.*

When my brothers and I played the games, we paid—just like everyone else, except Vic. Knowing Fish Stick was penniless, Ma and Pop allowed him the run of the yard for free. As our parents watched me and my brothers work the crowd, I'd never seen either of them look more proud.

In the end, our family carnival raised a grand total of $114.65.

I can't believe it, I thought. *I really can't.* It was more money than I'd ever seen in my life. *And we're going to give it all away.* I smiled. *It's only a drop in the bucket, but at least our family cares enough to pitch in.* The pride I felt for our whole clan was inexplicable. Giving felt so much better than receiving; the experience was life inspiring, and I knew it.

• • •

"I'm so sorry, Herbie," Donna said on the other end of the telephone, "I really wanted to go today, but my mother wouldn't take me. I'm so mad at her."

"It's fine," I said, trying to conceal my disappointment.

"So?" she asked.

"So?" I repeated.

"How did it go?" she asked. "How much money did you guys raise for the telethon?"

"One hundred fourteen dollars and sixty-five cents," I said, unable to hide my pride.

"Oh, my God," she said, "that's so amazing, babe!"

Babe? I repeated, swallowing hard. "I know," I finally managed.

"You and your family just did an amazing thing for people who really need it."

"I know," I repeated, before offering her a detailed recap of the day's events.

"That's so great, Herbie," she said after listening patiently, "I'm so proud of you."

"Thank you," I whispered, looking up to see Ma waiting for the phone. This time, however, she wasn't pushing for me to get off.

"Are you ready to go back to school?" Donna asked, sighing heavily.

"I'm excited to go back," I answered.

"Really?"

"Yes, to see you."

"Me, too," Donna whispered.

I looked up to see Ma grinning at me.

"Listen, Donna," I said, "I should go for now. My mother's been waiting to use the phone, and it's already been a long day."

"No problem," Donna said, "we'll talk tomorrow."

"I'm looking forward to it. Goodnight."

"Goodnight," she said, hanging up.

I turned and handed my mother the phone.

"Thank you, sweetheart," she said. "Now go get a good night's sleep. You earned it."

It was late when Ma talked to Aunt Phyllis on the telephone. She stepped into the living room where she could add more cigarette butts to her overflowing ashtray.

They were with each other all day, I thought. *What could they possibly have to talk about?* While I sneaked a few sips from the milk jug, I listened in.

"I know," Ma said, "I've never been so proud of the boys in my life."

The comment made my chest swell. I took another sip, happy it wasn't lemonade.

"Of course, I'm happy they're returning to school. I won't have to feed them every couple of hours like parking meters." She paused; I could actually hear her taking a long drag on her cigarette. "I'm looking forward to getting back into a routine. Sunday dinners at Ma's again and…" She took another drag and laughed. "That's right and returning to my soaps without all of the interruptions will be great."

Interruptions? I thought. *What interruptions? We weren't in the house all summer.*

"Jeopardy's good," Ma said, "but it's not Wheel of Fortune. What I wouldn't do to get on that show and win a trip." She listened for a second. "By myself," she said, laughing again. "It wouldn't be a vacation if anyone else went with me, would it, Phyllis?"

Maybe Cockroach and I should move in with Aunt Phyllis? We'd be treated better. As I tiptoed back to my bedroom, I gave it a bit more thought. *Nah, I'm sure that would get old, too.*

● ● ●

The night before returning to school, Ma served chicken mozzarella over ziti. It was her best dish—and everyone's favorite. "And we're having Funfetti cake for dessert," she announced.

Something must be up, I thought, already looking forward to the cake. *Dessert is as rare as a full roll of toilet paper around here.*

"What's the big occasion?" Pop asked.

"Does there have to be a big occasion for me to treat my family?" she responded.

We all waited, knowing full well that she was celebrating our return to school; we knew that the dinner was more for her than anyone else at the kitchen table.

She shrugged. "I wanted to celebrate our success with the fund-raiser."

"So, it's not because summer's over and we're going back to school?" Wally asked.

She looked him straight in the eye and smiled. "That, too."

Pop laughed all by himself. "I don't care why we're celebrating. All I know is that I could eat this dish every night."

Ma glared at him across the table. "Then ask for a raise, Walt, and maybe we will."

This time, my brothers and I laughed.

The rest of the meal was a symphony of gnashing teeth and joyful moans.

* * *

Ma took photos of the three of us—lined up in our annual pose—with her Polaroid instant camera. The flash was so bright that it took a few minutes for my sight to return to normal.

"I'm so happy," she said, shaking the picture a few times to help it develop, avoiding a stop at One-Hour photo.

"We know, Ma," I said.

"So happy," she repeated.

"This is like Christmas morning for you, huh, Ma?" Wally asked, perturbed.

She looked up from the photo and grinned. "I love Christmas morning," she said, "but today…" She shrugged off the rest of the comment, while her grin mutated into a full-blown smile.

Damn, I thought, *we're not that bad, are we?*

"Have a great first day, boys," she said, before walking back into the house wearing that giant smile.

I dragged my new boots to the bus stop like I was heading to the gas chamber. I looked at Cockroach, and the fear in his face announced that he felt the same.

"You'll be fine," I told him. "All your friends are starting Middle School for the first time, too, so you're all in the same boat together." They weren't the exact words my father used, but they were close enough.

"Thanks, Herbie," he mumbled, his words betraying his high level of stress.

"I'm the one who needs to worry," I muttered under my breath.

Wally's head snapped my way. "Relax," he said, "you'll be fine, too."

Bus 6 suddenly appeared on the horizon, making my heart rate pick up. "Is it as bad as they say?" I blurted to my older brother, the nervousness evident in my voice.

"What, high school?"

I nodded.

"Well, the food is better but the classes are longer and..."

"That's not what I mean," I said, obsessing over the dreaded hazing—which was a real threat for high school freshmen. *Not to mention the power noogies.*

Both Wally and Cockroach looked at me, as the yellow dot in the distance grew larger.

My stomach flopped sideways, making me burp. "I'm talking about all the bullying," I clarified, suppressing the sensation to ralph all over my new hiking boots.

Grinning, Wally put on his best Pop impression. "Even when you're afraid, really scared, and it's hard to stand up," he said, sounding a lot like our father, "that's exactly when you have to stand up and be a man. You'll regret it, if you don't. Trust me, it'll haunt you your whole life. Do you understand me?"

Realizing that it was Pop's classic speech—verbatim—I nodded.

"You make sure of it," Wally concluded. "Fear or no fear, just make sure you stand up."

Cockroach shook his head confidently, as though he needed to hear the same message.

I laughed. "I will," I said, knowing full well that I would. It was hard coded in my DNA.

"Just handle it the way you did with Steve Pimental at the mall this summer," Wally concluded. "All you have to do is stand up for yourself once and you won't have to worry about it for the rest of the year."

"I will," I repeated.

As the bus squealed to a stop before us and the folding door swung open, I pictured Donna's beautiful face. *It won't all be bad*, I thought, taking my first step toward the unknown.

CHAPTER 14

PRESENT DAY

SAYING GOODBYE

Emerging from Memory Lane, I opened my eyes and sat up straight in my recliner. *What a great summer*, I thought, smiling. *What a great childhood!*

The 1980s were a magical time. But little did we know, the Atari 2600, cable TV—all the new and amazing technology—would be the beginning of the end for a certain era of innocence, replacing babysitters, as well as normal healthy exercise.

I sat still, giving myself a few minutes to process the old film that had just played in my head.

My brothers and I had been born to a mom who smoked when she carried us and may have even enjoyed a drink or two while pregnant. Our crib—which we each used—was painted in light green lead-based paint. Our father was about as crazy and unorthodox as any dad could be. Together, they were the best parents any kid could hope for. *If people got paid for raising children,* I thought, *they would have been millionaires.* Just as I'd learned during our backyard carnival, I was still amazed at how people, who had essentially nothing, gave away everything they had. *And because of that, Wally, Cockroach, and I were blessed.*

Being in a family sometimes felt like serving time in prison—at least how I'd imagined prison might be. There was a definite pecking order, with each step defended to the death. *But I wouldn't have traded it for anything.* My family was the solid foundation on which I now stood.

Picturing my father's face, I felt nothing but gratitude. Through lessons like, "Look after others, especially when they can't look after themselves" and "It's better to be kind than right," he'd taught my brothers and me to become good men and our younger sisters to become wonderful women. Pop's death was a confirmation of everything I believed in. *Being successful, or winning in life, is not about dying with the most toys. The real winners are those who give away the most.*

Stretching out in the recliner, my bones ached and creaked. *That never happened back in the day*, I thought, preparing to stand on sore feet. We were facing the second day of redneck shiva, and there were many preparations to be made.

Smelling coffee, I hobbled into the kitchen to find Donna standing over the stove, flipping a fresh pancake onto the stack.

"Well, good morning," she said.

"Good morning." I kissed the back of her neck. "What time is it?"

"Almost nine o'clock."

"Wow, I really got swept away this morning."

She turned to face me. "Where did you go?" she asked, pulling me in for a hug.

"Back to where it all began…to when we met."

She gave me a kiss; it was soft and tender. "A simpler time, for sure," she whispered.

"It was." I shrugged. "But as my mother used to tell us, 'It's fun to visit the past, but make sure you don't stay there too long. If you linger, you'll miss the present—moments in your life that you won't want to miss.'" I kissed my beautiful wife more deeply. "And this is exactly where I'm supposed to be right now."

"I thank God for that every day."

I released her from the hug. As she turned to continue cooking, I asked, "Are the boys up yet?"

She snickered, playfully. "Are you kidding? They'd sleep until afternoon, if we let them."

I remember those days, I thought.

"If you want to go grab them, that would be great. Breakfast is almost ready."

I nodded. "I'm on it."

I was walking out of the room when I heard, "Herbie…"

I turned.

"Are you okay?" she asked.

I managed a smile. "I'm not going to lie; it's going to be rough saying goodbye to Pop, but we'll get through it."

She nodded. "We will," she repeated. "Hon, remember that I'm here for you." From across the room, I could see a deep love in her eyes. "You're never alone," she said; these were the same faith-filled words my mother had repeated throughout my childhood.

"I know, babe," I said, a wave of goosebumps rolling over both of my arms. "I'm blessed."

I stepped into the dark crypt that served as my sons' bedroom. Lifting one of the shades, I watched as Dylan shrunk away—vampire-like—from the light.

"Let's go, you bums," I said, "it's time to get up. Ma will have breakfast on the table in a few minutes."

Alex stirred in his bed before sitting straight up.

"Good morning," I told him.

"Good morning," he yawned.

"We have a tough day ahead of us, but…"

"We'll get through it together," Dylan said, finishing my sentence.

"That's right." I was happy they'd been listening to me.

They were both sitting up now, preparing to launch into another difficult day.

I sat beside Alex, needing to share the gratitude I felt for my life. "Our family will be together over the next few days. Although we'd obviously prefer it to be under better circumstances, make sure that you appreciate the time we have together."

Eyes blank, they nodded robotically.

"When I was twelve," I said, hoping to get them to relate, "I used to think that to be family, you had to share a last name—blood. What I didn't realize until I got older is that my family is better defined by the love that we share with people. You'll be around lots of folks over the next few days who don't have our last name, boys, but they're still family. Remember that, okay?"

This time, there was something behind their nods.

"Lots of people will want to pay their respects to your grandfather."

"Because he was such a good man," Alex said.

I nodded, deciding to deliver the same spiel to my grieving boys that Pop had offered me and my brothers. "Your grandpa died a wealthy man, guys," I explained. "He gave away everything he had, even his last nickel." I searched their eyes. "Remember that it's not how much you accumulate in this world; it's how much you give away." I nodded. "That's the only real way to measure a man's success." I remembered that after hearing the respect in Pop's voice, I wanted to be generous and kind too. *I hope Dylan and Alex get the message.*

"Grampa sure was successful," Dylan said.

I nodded. "The greatest I've ever known."

Just then, Donna stuck her head in the door. "Breakfast is done. Are you guys…" She stopped.

"We'll be along in a few minutes," I told her, "we're just finishing up."

She nodded. "Take all the time you need. I'll keep it warm."

"Thanks, babe."

She winked at me before leaving the room.

"You guys have a great mom," I told my boys.

"We know," Alex said.

"I hope you also know how much I love you both?"

They nodded.

"And that I only ask three things of you."

They waited.

"The first is to have the courage to be who God made you to be. Second," I said, counting on my fingers, "is to take responsibility for your life. Whether it's happiness or misery, it's your choice." I paused.

"And the third?" Alex asked.

"The third is to never forget that if you work hard enough and never lose faith, your dreams really can come true." I shot them a wink. "Because we don't get what we wish for…"

"We get what we work for," Dylan said, finishing my thought.

I smiled, confirming, *So, they have been listening.*

They returned my smile.

"Always remember that," I told them.

"We will," Alex promised.

"And also remember that whenever life seems crazy," I smiled again. "that's usually the good stuff."

My boys nodded, the same way Wally, Alphonse, and I used to all those years ago.

"Your grandpa loved you so much," I told them. "You know that, right?"

They nodded.

"Good," I said, "and don't you ever forget it, either!"

"We won't, Pop," Dylan said, making my skin turn to sandpaper.

"Yeah, Pop," Alex said, mimicking his older brother.

Every hair on my arms stood on end. *They've never called me Pop,* I thought, *until now.* Somehow, it now made sense; the timing was perfect. *My father was Pop, and he's gone.* As my eyes filled, I nodded. *I'm Pop now.* Suddenly, I realized that a sacred torch had been passed; I was now the cornerstone. I'd never felt so honored or aware of my place in the world.

I stood to hug both my boys. We faced a long day ahead: sitting for another round of redneck shiva, followed by Pop's graveside memorial, and then dinner at his favorite restaurant.

As I started out of the room, I said, "Have a nice weekend."

"What?" Dylan asked.

I turned around at the door. "Nothing," I said, smiling, "it's just a funny phrase your grandpa used to say."

• • •

My mother was the first to arrive, and I was grateful for a few moments alone with her. As a kid, she'd been my rock. In many ways, the years hadn't changed a thing. "Did I really beat your sisters here this morning?" she asked, grinning mischievously.

"Of course you did," I said, escorting her to the kitchen. "I'm not sure Louann and Lynn have ever been on time for anything in their lives."

As she took a seat at the table, she half-shrugged.

"After surviving me and my brothers, it couldn't have been easy starting over twenty years later with two girls," I said, pouring her a cup of coffee.

She finished her shrug. "Nothing worth having is easy. You must know that by now." Her eyes drifted off. "God, how your father adored his girls."

"I know. He was different with them." I searched for the right words. "Easier, I think."

"Of course he was," she quickly countered. "He was much older and completely worn out."

We both laughed.

"It's a strange thing, the bond between a father and his daughter. One of life's great mysteries, I suppose." She took her first sip of the hot coffee.

I held her gaze. "They were lucky to have you both," I told her. "We all were."

Grabbing my forearm, she gave it a loving squeeze. "Go easy on your sisters when they get here, Herbie," she said. "Remember, it's not easy getting little kids ready."

I nodded.

"So how are you holding up?" she asked.

I shrugged. "As well as can be expected, I suppose."

"Have you been praying?"

I nodded, confirming that I had.

"Faith is what sustains us during our difficult times," she said.

My mind immediately raced back to when I was a kid.

"It's so important to have a relationship with God through prayer," Ma told me and my brothers. "You're never alone. None of us are. But there will be times in your life—trust me—when you're going to need God. And it's a lot easier to reach out and ask for help from someone you've been talking to every day and not someone you've been ignoring."

I returned to the present to find her staring at me.

"Ma, can I share Pop's eulogy with you?" I asked her. "It's not very eloquent, but I think…"

"Of course," she interrupted, taking a seat at my kitchen table.

I cleared my throat. "To be loved so much by so many people, now that's what I call a life worth living."

She grinned wide, while I hurried to compose myself. *This is going to be harder than I thought.*

"Go on," she said, smiling at me with her soft brown eyes.

"I believe we were all connected long before we came into this world, have been blessed to share our journeys together, and will remain connected long after we all leave this place. None of us is ever…" I stopped, a wave of grief threatening to shatter my shaky voice. "…alone."

Nodding once, she smiled.

I tried to go on but struggled to utter a single word.

My mother waited patiently, allowing me the time I needed.

"When I was a kid," I continued, "my father swore that death is nothing more than a temporary separation. I believe that as much today as I did the day he told me. 'We'll all be together again some-day,' he said. 'Don't you ever doubt it.'"

I began to weep, unable to manage another word through the childlike convulsions.

My mother stood. "It's okay, sweetheart," she said, pulling me in for a strong hug—the same way she did when I was a boy. "Your father knows your heart. He always has." She squeezed me tighter. "Words are nice, but they're really not necessary."

I nodded, soaking her shoulder with my tears.

"Your father knows," she whispered. "He knows."

The End

MOM
BY STEVEN MANCHESTER

Out of love, I was given life
and it was that love
which nurtured and protected me.
You took my tiny hand
and carefully guided me.
As I grew, by example, I learned
honesty, compassion, and simple goodness.
Through the years,
the soft echo of a wise voice soothed my worries,
the gentle touch of labored hands mended my wounds,
and the searching gaze of knowing eyes healed my soul.
Although you often had less than others,
with joy, you generously gave it all away.
You always put my needs before your own
and taught me to do the same for others.
I have laughed with you, cried with you,
celebrated, grieved, and prayed with you.
Because you were never selfish with your time,
my memories are cherished,
and my dreams within reach.
Everything that I am,
everything that I achieve,
is because the Lord
blessed me with your love.

New England's Storyteller Steven Manchester is the author of the soul-awakening novel, *The Menu,* as well as the '80s nostalgia-fest, *Lawn Darts & Lemonade.* His other works include #1 bestsellers *Twelve Months, The Rockin' Chair, Pressed Pennies* and *Gooseberry Island*; the national bestsellers, *Ashes, The Changing Season* and *Three Shoeboxes*; the multi-award winning novel, *Goodnight Brian*; and the beloved holiday podcast drama, *The Thursday Night Club.* His work has appeared on NBC's Today Show, CBS's The Early Show and BET's Nightly News. Three of Steven's short stories were selected "101 Best" for Chicken Soup for the Soul series. He is a multi-produced playwright, as well as the winner of the 2017 & 2021 Los Angeles Book Festival, 2018 New York Book Festival and 2020 New England Book Festival. When not spending time with his beautiful wife, Paula, or their children, this Massachusetts author is promoting his works or writing.

Visit:
www.StevenManchester.com
facebook.com/AuthorStevenManchester
twitter.com/authorSteveM

Be sure to visit www.StevenManchester.com and sign up for his mailing list.